The Unhappiest Place on Earth

JADE GONZALEZ

The Unhappiest Place on Earth

Copyright © 2025 by Jade Gonzalez

First edition 2025

Trade paperback ISBN: 978-1-7372546-3-8
Hardcover ISBN: 978-1-7372546-4-5

To my friends who unknowingly gave me the inspiration to write this story on a cold winter night during the pandemic.

Content Warning

This novel contains themes of anxiety, panic attacks, and mentions of parental physical abuse. Reader discretion is advised, as these topics may be distressing to some. Please take care while reading.

Contents

1. Senior Trip — 1
2. Meet Me at the Castle — 9
3. Dole Whip Girl — 27
4. Laugh Out Loud — 35
5. Noon — 51
6. Teacups — 65
7. Ghosted — 73
8. Distraction — 87
9. The Castle — 95
10. Speechless — 103
11. Seeing Red — 123
12. Apologies — 147
13. In Theory — 161
14. Hit Send — 171
15. Fro-Yo — 181
16. Awkward — 191
17. Graduation — 201
18. The Yearbook Message — 211
Epilogue — 221

Acknowledgments — 231
About the Author — 233
Also by Jade Gonzalez — 235

CHAPTER 1
Senior Trip

Weston

The alarm goes off at 6:00 am sharp, and my first thought is: I hate Disneyland. I've been awake for hours. I couldn't shut my mind off. It's probably because I've been dreading this day since it was announced last semester. Part of me still can't believe it was my idea to go. How I let that happen, I'll never know. I digress. Best get a move on so this day can be over already.

I hop out of bed and head straight to the restroom. I set a timer for five minutes. There's no need to waste water if I can help it. Once I'm done showering, I set another timer to brush my teeth. Ma walks by the door, yelling to hurry up. I groan with a mouth full of toothpaste. Why does she insist on speaking Korean at this hour? Sometimes it can get under my skin, since I prefer English, but I try to be accommodating.

I hear a light pounding at the door. "In-Su, it's been over six minutes. You need to go wake up your brother." My jaw tenses after I place my toothbrush back in the medicine cabinet.

I rinse my mouth. "It's Weston, Ma," I say after wiping the excess water from my chin. Normally I don't insist on her calling me by my American name, but it sort of slipped out. Quickly, I open the door to apologize. She's not there. I yell out, "Sorry, Ma." I wait for her to reply, but I'm met with silence. I rush out of the bathroom and go back to my room to get changed.

As I'm buttoning my gray shirt, I hear her say through the door, "I have an early showing in San Clemente today. So I'm no able to drive you. Min-Su will take you to school."

"It's '*Not*,' Ma," I say, correcting her while walking over to my door. I open it to see her glaring up at me, arms crossed. "It's 'I'm *not* able to drive you.'" I don't understand why she looks annoyed when she is the one who asked me to do that. Her English is pretty good, but she tends to misspeak here and there. At first, I felt disrespectful correcting her, but ever since she got her real estate license, she has become determined to speak English flawlessly. She assured me I would never be berated for helping her.

She huffs, still standing in my doorway. "Wake him up now." She turns to walk down the hall.

My shoulders slump. I realize my correcting her is not why she's exasperated. I linger in my doorway for a minute longer than intended. I mumble to myself, "Do I really have to wake him up?" I hate this chore. He's definitely not the most cheerful person in the mornings. Maybe I can get a ride from Trey or better yet, I'll just ask Ma to take me now. So what if I show up an hour before the doors open? That's better than riding in a car with Brenden, who always shows up late. That's one of my biggest pet peeves and causes my anxiety to shoot through the roof. My pulse is higher than normal as it is. Today, of all days, I do not need to feel more anxious.

I slap the door post and walk down the hall towards the kitchen. I find her filling up a glass water bottle from the fridge.

"I'm almost ready, Ma," I say. "Can you take me right now? Just give me two minutes."

"I am sorry, but I must go now," she says, walking over to the desk in the living room. She collects a handful of papers and places them in her briefcase.

"Ok," I groan, turning my back to her. Walking back into the kitchen, I decide to fill up a cup of water in case Brenden refuses to get up and I need to throw it in his face. Rude, I know, but today I do not want to take any chances. He must get up and take me to school. On time.

Ma calls out from the living room where her office desk is. "Hold on." I can hear her fingers tapping on the computer keyboard. "Weston, what's this meaning?"

Startled at her disapproving tone, I set down the now full cup and approach her. "What are you talking about?" I ask, racking my brain as to what I could have possibly done incorrectly.

She clicks her mouse and points to the computer screen. It is an email from the administrative assistant from my uncle's office. It reveals I did not sign the employment papers to work again at his law firm. I gulp. She was not supposed to find out. She places her hands on both hips.

"In-Su, you were supposed to sign these months ago. Do you know how hard your uncle worked to get you a paying job at his law firm this summer?" Her voice is higher in Korean and more judgmental. "A lot of interns at your age with hardly any experience ever get chances like this."

My eyes grow wide. My lips part, but no words come out. I can't tell her the truth, but there's no point in lying either. She knows me too well.

She glowers at me, demanding an explanation. "You tell me right now, why you have not signed these?"

I lower my gaze, sighing. All the excuses in my head shoot off like fireworks. I could tell her I didn't have time because of my final exams. Then there was basketball practice every day after school, plus games. On top of that, there was also prom. I don't even want to mention my breakup with Hannah because she would say, "How did you even have time for girls this semester?" I could remind her of my tutoring schedule with the freshmen on Tuesdays and Thursdays, but then she would say I am a bad example. I frown. None of these legitimate excuses will be good enough for her, and the truth is, none of these reasons are why I didn't sign them. Simply put, I didn't want to. I shudder at the thought of her knowing the truth. She will kill me. She will say how disrespectful I am to her and my uncle. How ungrateful I am for this opportunity. Worst of all, she will say I am behaving like my brother. He is the last person I want to be compared to.

Lifting up my chin, my eyes meet hers. Her dark eyes bore into mine. "I don't like this." She shakes her head. "This was not part of the plan. No. This is not good." Her face suddenly changes, going from angry to fearful in a matter of seconds. I can already tell what she's thinking.

Quickly, I try to say something to ease the tension. "Ma, it's going to be ok," I reassure her. "I'll just move to Boston a little later this summer. I'm still going to Harvard. I'll graduate top of my class and become a successful lawyer with my own firm just as we planned." She looks up at me and searches my eyes for the truth. I know she is afraid I'm going to end up like my brother, but she's wrong. I've been trying to show her that for what feels like my entire life. I grab her right hand. "I can always start work once classes begin in the fall. I'm sure Uncle Henry will need help anyway." I try sounding enthusiastic. "Everything is still going according to plan. I'll just have a little break after graduation." Smiling to myself, I realize this is why I didn't want to sign the employment papers. I want one summer for myself before I have to officially grow up. Is that too much to ask?

She scrunches her eyebrows. "One summer off? No, I will not accept this." She pulls her hand back. "I cannot allow you to fall behind in your life plan when you have worked so hard to get ahead. All that work will go to waste." She shakes her head. "No. I will not accept this. " She clicks the mouse and the computer screen goes black.

I'm slightly irritated, but I bite my tongue to keep the annoyance concealed. I watch her grab a few more papers from the desk, then follow her to the garage door. I clench my eyes shut for a moment, attempting to simmer down the bubbling thoughts about to leak out of my mouth. She can't do this to me.

Every summer for the last 15 years, I put dedication to my studies above anything else and I worked part-time. Not once have I had a summer for myself. All I want is to take a break, before I dedicate the next phase of my life to college and a career. I open my eyes at the sound of the garage door lifting. I wave at her to remain parked. She rolls down the window, and I inhale a deep breath. This is my chance to tell her how I really feel, even if it's contrary to her opinion. It is time for me to take a stand for what I want.

"We will take care of this when I get back," she explains, looking down at her phone. "I need to leave now."

My hand is lightly pressed onto the window's edge. I want to protest, but the courage I felt a second ago has faded. So, I lower my head in defeat.

She places her hand on top of mine. "I can see you are upset. I know because you are like me when you feel busy." she says sympathetically. My eyes light up. Perhaps she sees a break is just what I need? I know she could use one. "You must listen to me, In-Su. You are not a…uh…how you say, fail-failure, yes, because you forgot this important task. It happens to me sometimes too," she explains softly. The hope that my mother finally understands me quickly dissipates. She pats my hand. "But what must we do when we make a mistake?"

Sighing, I reply solemnly, "We work harder to not make them again."

"Yes." She grins. "But don't worry, In-Su, I know how terrible you must feel now so I will fix this one for you."

My eyes flicker. "What do you mean?"

Ma places her hand on the steering wheel and shifts the car into reverse. "Don't worry, In-Su, I will make things right." She grins lightly. "I'll call your uncle today to tell him what happened." She backs out of the garage and drives off.

Blinking, I can't believe this. She's going to call my uncle. My uncle who is a very smart businessman and just so happens to be partners at one of the most prestigious immigration law firms on the east coast. If Ma has anything to do with it, I'm sure she will sign what she has to on my behalf. She's like a Korean Karen on steroids. I tighten my fists. There's nothing I can do to stop her.

Completely gutted, I return inside to wake Brenden. Better to wake him now than wait until later when the probability of him delivering me to school on time is drastically lowered. Plus, I'm irritated and won't mind taking out my frustrations on him. I grab the full cup of water and head to his room. I open his door and find him sprawled out across his bed with the blankets on the floor, twisted and lumped together, like some sort of ball. His heavy breathing is one octave away from a snore. His room is a disaster, like always. There are at least three different video game consoles and a bunch of cords tangled up in each other beneath his TV, which is on the ground because he sold his dresser. There are clothes everywhere and random stuff like old cameras and iPhones displayed in piles on the floor. The only organization seems to be in his stacks of CDs and vinyls, which are laying alphabetized near his acoustic guitar. He has a vintage stereo on the windowsill, along with multiple guitar picks. What seems to be the only non-dusty items in his room are the surfboard that hangs above his bed and the guitar. I shake my head. This is too much. It's making me claustrophobic. I don't know how he can live like such a slob.

Ma raised us both the same, yet Brenden chose to rebel. She taught us to be neat and organized, to never waste time. I do that. My room is simple and clean. It's practically an IKEA display. It's put together, as is my life. There is no disorganization. Everything has its place.

My brother, on the other hand, has a completely dysfunctional space he calls a room and spends his days surfing, not even bothering to find a job even though he's 21 years old. On top of that, he's constantly in and out of trouble with the law. It's clear he has a real problem with authority. I suppose he can't help himself. Ma says it's in his DNA. He can't help but act like our father. Still, witnessing how his behavior seems to upset our mother really motivates me more to follow her instructions perfectly. She adores me for it. I'm sure it's the reason why Brenden and I don't get along anymore. I'm the golden child, and he hates me for it. After all, he's supposed to be the mature one. He's older and therefore should be the more successful, more responsible brother, but he's not. Brenden is my opposite in every way.

Now I stand at the foot of his bed, cup in hand, ready to splash. I stare at him for a second and notice how deep he's sleeping. My grip tightens. How can he be sleeping so peacefully when I couldn't sleep the entire night? He knows I'm going to Disneyland today. So, how could he be ok right now? The more I stare at him, the angrier I become. My thoughts begin spiraling out of control. It's not fair, I think to myself. I'm under so much pressure from Ma and school. What kind of pressure is he under? None. It's not fair. While he's out goofing off everyday, I'm doing homework or playing basketball, because Mom said it looks good on a college application. Well, she was right since I got accepted, but that's neither here nor there. Brenden dropped out of high school, got sent to juvie at 16 and yet she still doesn't kick him out. I don't get it. He's a lost cause, and because he's a lost cause, I have to be the overachiever. My hand shakes a little from getting so worked up.

"It's just not fair," I say out loud. My hand accidentally jolts. Water spills onto my brother, and the cup slams into his head board. My jaw drops, stunned.

Brenden thrashes around, yelling groggily, "What the-"

"Oh shoot…my bad." Of course, he ignores me while stumbling out of bed. That's my cue to run back to my room.

"I'm going to kill you!" he shouts. I spin around and bolt out of his room.

I fly down the hallway and make it to my room, just before he slams into the door. Locking it, I say, "Get dressed, Bren, you're driving me to school."

"You're dead, Weston!" he screams before retreating. I hear him go back to his room and slam his door from down the hall. He is pissed.

My heart is beating so fast. For a second, I really thought he might pummel me. I wince at the notion. I'm not exactly afraid of my brother. We used to wrestle all the time when we were younger. It sort of used to be fun. Brenden used to be fun, until one day he stopped. I can't remember why. Maybe it was puberty. I don't know. Nevertheless, I know if given the chance, he wouldn't actually do damage. If anything, I would be the one to cause harm with how much I've been benching these days. I may be the little brother, but I am definitely not the weaker one. Not anymore.

Throwing on a black hoodie, I grab my backpack and unplug my phone from its charger. Why am I thinking about having a physical altercation with my brother, anyway? This is the last thing I want to be thinking about right now, today of all days.

CHAPTER 2
Meet Me at the Castle

They call Disneyland "the happiest place on earth," but when I hear that supposedly benevolent name, my body instinctively shudders because, plainly, I hate Disneyland. It is a simple statement but accurately describes the intensity of my feelings when I think of that awful place. There must be others who feel this way. Others who may dislike the theme park just as much as I do, just none in my graduating class. Good thing is, no one knows the true nature of my feelings, and I plan to keep it that way. From what my fellow classmates can tell, I'm as neutral in my opinion of the park as the next teenage guy who lives in Los Angeles. No one is the wiser, especially since it was my idea to go there for our senior trip.

Of all the places within a two hour drive of school, it had to be there. Why did I do this to myself? I hate that place. I hate it. I hate it. I hate it. It's juvenile to think this way, yes, but using a simple word such as dislike does not remotely begin to cover the many reasons I have for never wanting to step foot in that terrible place again. I could try to narrow it down to its cheesy characters or the silly rides, but it's much more than that. For one, they are liars. They sell the idea of happily ever afters. Well, I bought into those lies as a child and learned a very hard lesson, one I never intend to learn again.

The possibility of happily ever after and fairy tales is a complete farce. You cannot simply wish upon a star and expect all your problems to disappear. Reality doesn't work like that. I know this because I tried. As a brightly spirited child, those lies were all I ever believed in. I was wrong. There are no happy endings in life. That belief is a magic trick, a mirage.

In addition to the false claims of fairy tale endings, the entire theme park exudes commercialism. Do not get me started on the preposterous ticket prices they charge to get in there. Who has the money to waste on that these days? I certainly do not. If it wasn't for Ma's generosity, I wouldn't be going today. Normally, my lack of funds would be the perfect excuse to bow out of this trip. Only problem is, Trey will kill me if I don't go, not to mention my entire graduating class will be beyond disappointed if I do not attend. I'm rendered with no choice. I'm going whether I want to or not.

No matter. I can fake a smile or two for one day, just one day. I've been doing it my whole life. Besides, I have graduation to look forward to. It is the light at the end of the tunnel. The sweet reward after taking all those Advanced Placement classes Ma suggested. One more week of carrying the weight of the entire student body. Then I'll finally be free. Spending one day in the unhappiest place on earth is not going to change anything.

Brenden pulls into the school entrance as late as I predicted. Normally, he drives like a street racer, as if he was in a gang from LA, but today he drives slow. I can only assume it is a form of payback for the water incident. I breathe in and out slowly and try to not let it bother me. To distract myself, I press my head against the passenger side window to peer outs at everyone who is lined up for the bus. From what I can see, not everyone is here yet. That makes me feel a bit better. Yet, my stomach is still in knots. Deep down, I know it's not because I'm running behind.

Ignoring the strained feeling inside me, I stare at my classmates on the sidewalk. I spot Kaite and Hannah quite easily. I grind my teeth. They are hard to miss with their matching pink miniskirts and those notoriously obnoxious mouse ears. I take note of where they are standing in hopes of avoiding them. The last thing I want to deal with is the aftermath of my breakup with Hannah. Ever since our breakup, interactions with her have been exceptionally awkward. I do not have the mental fortitude to sit next to her on the bus today. I thought I let her down easy. Maybe I did, a little too much.

"Drop me off here," I tell him, pointing to the yellow yield sign. I pull my hood over my head in hopes of looking more discreet.

"I still can't believe you're going back there," Brenden scoffs, shifting the car into park. He pushes away some of his shaggy black hair out of his eyes and answers a call just as I hop out of his dented Ford sedan. "Speak…" he says to the person on the phone.

Leave it to my older brother to take a jab at me without giving me a chance to defend myself.

He grins into the phone. "The pier? Pshhh, yeah, bro, let's goooo!" He hangs up with who I think is his piece-of-work best friend, Anton. Looks like they are blowing off work again for another day of surfing. I conceal an eye roll. Wait, did he say he's going to the pier? That's about two and a half hours in the opposite direction.

I lean on the door before closing it. "You're still picking me up right?" I ask, attempting to confirm my ride home tonight.

He scoffs. "Uh, no. I've got plans."

I bite down on the inside of my cheek. "But I need a ride."

"You should have thought of that before you threw water in my face," he retorts angrily. "And it's not my fault you decided not to buy a car."

I knew he'd get revenge for this morning. I just didn't predict it would entail ditching me in the school parking lot after a whole day at Disneyland. He knows Ma asked him to pick me up tonight. That's the problem right there. I should have known if she asked him, he wouldn't do it.

I huff. "I told you already, I could have bought a car, but it's not part of the plan." I adjust my arm on the car door. "Plus, it doesn't make sense for me to get a car when I'm literally moving to Boston in a week."

"Enough lecturing." He raises his hand. "If I'm not mistaken, you are mister Prom King, right?" He revs the engine. "So finding a ride should be easy for someone like you."

Now, he's just being a jerk. "What is with you?" I blurt.

"Nothing." He sighs, turning his head. He places one hand on the steering wheel. Even in profile, I can tell his eyes are a bit sunken in, like he hasn't slept in days. That's odd. He seemed to be sleeping just fine earlier this morning. Should I be concerned?

I bring myself to ask, "Are you ok?"

"What do you care?" he says as he shifts the car into drive.

I lean my head down. "I'm just asking, Bren." I pause, unsure of my choice of words, but I admit anyways, "You don't look so good."

"Thanks for that astute observation," he shares sarcastically. "I'm actually doing great. You wanna know why?" He looks at me with a twisted expression. "I'm not the one who's going to Disneyland."

My eyes narrow. I bite back a retort, understanding the reasons for his disdain of the amusement park. I'm pretty sure it was him who started calling it "the unhappiest place on earth." Knowing why he did restrains me from lashing out in defense. Still, he has no idea what kind of pressure I have to deal with on a daily basis. If I did not show up today, I'd be shattering an image I've worked so hard to maintain over the course of eight years.

With nothing to say in rebuttal, I slam his car door shut. Brenden wastes no time in peeling out of the parking lot, faster than I can walk over to the sidewalk. The heat in my face is rising. I frown disapprovingly, but I watch my brother drive away in envy. For the first time, I wish we could trade places. Although we lead very different lives, he's right about one thing. At least he doesn't have to go to Disneyland, the place we swore to never return.

I see Trey out of the corner of my eye, bopping to some tunes with bright red Dr. Dre headphones. He must have a new mix ready. He's very proud of his mixes. Although I don't know much about music, he's going to be the next Zed, I swear. I admit his beats are good, but I doubt he can handle that late night work flow. The dude falls asleep at the drop of a hat. He might even be narcoleptic, undiagnosed of course.

"Sup," I nod, sliding next to him in line. "Hey guys." I wave behind me to Gabe and Jeb. Drew is with them too.

"Hey, Wes," Hannah calls from the front of the line. Shoot, she spotted me. Her grin is wide, hopeful.

I give her a slight wave, hoping she won't walk over here. She smiles happily back at me but doesn't come to where I'm standing. I feel myself start to relax a little. That's a good sign.

"Bro, listen to this. I think I really nailed the drop this time," Trey says, handing me his headphones, stealing my attention off of her. "Hey, why are you late though?" he adds curiously. He knows I am never late.

I put one headphone over my ear. "Brenden," I say, shrugging. "Hey, actually, can you give me a ride home later?"

Trey frowns dejectedly. "Bruh, you know I would, but I got my license taken away."

"What? When?"

"You know Dorthea." He rolls his eyes. "She's a control freak! I forgot to say *yes ma'am* one time, and she freaking took away my license. That should be illegal, right?" Trey complains, rubbing the top of his upper lip where there is a thin black line that he considers more than stubble. "She said I can get it back on good behavior. Whatever that means."

"Ah, that sucks." I hand him back his red headphones. "Hey, that's a sick beat, though."

"Thanks." He pats me on the back. "Aye, why don't you have Hannah take you?" he suggests, looking over at her and waving. Great, now she will definitely come over here.

My chest tightens. I pivot towards Trey slightly, and while hiding my face from her view, I remind him, "We broke up, remember?"

He bites down on his lip. "Oh that's right." He looks off to the side. "Well, what about Kaite?" He stifles a chuckle, knowing how much that girl disturbs me.

"She's psychotic, bro, and she probably hates me right now cause of the break up with her bestie," I comment, pulling the strings on my hoodie. "Hey, shouldn't we be on the road by now?" I check the time on my phone. The buses are late.

Trey scoffs. "Chill, I'm sure we'll be leaving soon. You're right about Kaite, though. I feel like she's someone's evil twin."

I turn my head back. We both give a sidelong glance at Kaite. She's fidgeting with something that looks like a butterfly hair clip in her hand and gets so mad she breaks it and tosses it onto the concrete. A shiver runs down my spine. I have no doubt she could do something like that to me even if I'm more than twice her size. The girl is scary.

"Just the sooner we leave, the sooner we get back." I cross my arms, dreading when the buses do pull up.

"Wes, this whole senior trip 'bout to be lit. You better enjoy it," Trey states enthusiastically as he places his headphones into his backpack. "Oh, I almost forgot. Here." He takes out a blue yearbook and hands it to me. It completely slipped my mind he had it.

"Sweet, thanks." I start rifling through the pages. "So how was it?" I ask, still completely embarrassed by the fact that our school made a bunch of 17 year olds sign each other's yearbooks, like we are back in the third grade. I'm so glad I had a dentist appointment yesterday.

"It was chill. We just hung out in the gym for a while. It was actually kind of nice," Trey answers. "But you missed it. Carrie Thomas passed out during the third period, and they had to call an ambulance and everything. It was freaky, bro."

"Nice," I say, shaking my head in acknowledgement. "Is she ok though?"

He waves his hand. "Oh she's fine. Drew found out she was anemic or something. She must have skipped lunch yesterday. You know how those cheerleaders do."

My eyes flicker over to him. Hopefully he doesn't notice I wasn't listening. I completely tuned out. I just keep thinking about how I probably won't get to enjoy the summer. Ma has my whole life planned out and anything not approved by her is immediately dismissed. Trey didn't catch my disassociation because he's already in another conversation with the guys about the last game we played against Irvine. I have no interest in chiming in as the season is over. Basketball is the least of my concerns. All I care about now is graduation.

Finally, the line starts to move. I look up to see the buses have arrived. I swallow. My fingers stiffen on my yearbook. Here we go. I continue flipping through the pages as we inch closer to the nearest bus. I raise my eyebrows. Something catches my eye. On the last page, in between all the "stay in touch" and "here's my number" messages, is a note that says,

"Meet me at the castle just as the fireworks start. I'll be waiting." I stare at those words till I reach the bus door. What could these words possibly mean? I follow Trey mechanically up the steps, and when we sit, I show him the message.

"Who wrote this?" I ask eagerly.

He takes the yearbook out of my hands and stares at the message, eyes widening with intrigue. "No idea, but that's sexy, bro." Trey grins.

I point to the message. "You seriously didn't see who signed this?" My voice cracks. That sounded way more desperate than intended.

"No chance," he says. "Books were being passed around and around— no one was keeping track of theirs. For all I know, this isn't even yours."

I pinch the bridge of my nose. "Great. Money well spent."

Trey places his gray backpack onto his lap and pulls out his headphones. He puts them on. "Relax. It's just a dumb yearbook." He leans over again to take a look at the message. "But this trip just got a whole lot more interesting," he jeers, rubbing his hands together excitedly. He zips up his backpack then sets it on his lap.

Leaning back, I close the book. What a random note. Who knows if it was even meant for me? I won't waste any more energy trying to process something so unnecessary. I put the book away and prop my backpack neatly against the side of the bus. With one elbow on it, I gaze casually out the window until the driver starts the bus. When we start moving, I glance over at Trey, who's completely dead asleep. I shake my head, smirking. Took him less than five minutes to pass out. I look at my phone and calculate how much longer I have to endure this trip. Only 12 more hours. I can manage that.

Two hours later, we begin pulling into the park's entrance. Mrs. Anderson, one of the class chaperones assigned to our bus along with the vice principal, replaced our tickets with wrist bands. We are then told to exit the bus and wait in another line so security can search our bags. I stand behind Trey and Gabe who are excitedly chatting with Jeb and Drew about the game plan once we are inside. I do not want to be a part of whatever they are planning. As much as I want to spend time with my boys, I want this day to be over even more. Being with them all day would only make it worse. One hundred percent they would want me to go on rides and when I refuse, they will inevitably find out about my distaste for the park, then ask questions. Not interested. If I'm lucky, I can quietly sneak away from the group and not get on any rides at all, especially the tea cups. "We gotta do Space Mountain," Gabe says excitedly. "That's the best ride in Disneyland."

"Woah." Jeb raises his hands in protest. "Thunder Mountain is clearly the best ride."

Drew speaks up. "Nah, it's Space Mountain for sure."

Trey and Gabe agree in unison.

Jeb smacks his lips. "Fine. But save the best for last, bro. So where should we go first?"

"Um, Galaxy's Edge, obviously," Gabe replies, pointing at his baby Yoda hat. "Wait, are the girls coming with us?"

Drew and Jeb both check their phones. I also look at mine, hoping he doesn't ask me to message Hannah. Then I hear Trey lifting his arms, yawning. He approaches us from behind. "We need a strategy, my guys," he adds while he places his arms on my shoulder and Gabe's.

I put on my sunglasses, hoping to dissuade them from involving me in this nonsense.

Gabe snaps his fingers. "Wes, you're the strategic one. How can we hit up every single ride before closing?"

I blow out a heavy sigh. "Oh, you know what, I have a thing,

I forgot. I have to do this thing for the school newspaper. Yeah, so...I'll just catch up with you guys later," I bold face lie.

Gabe scoffs, "Are you serious?" He sees right through it, but I get the feeling he won't care if I'm actually bowing out or not. Of all my friends, he's the one I butt heads with the most. He is exceptionally opinionated. Guy throws the best parties though.

"Haters gonna hate," Drew mocks, slapping his hand around Trey's.

The four of them separate, and Trey heads forward through security first.

Once he's through, he turns around grinning. "My guys, don't give him such a hard time. Our boy got his own mission to complete."

There's intrigue in his tone. My eyes dart sharply over him. Why did he say that in front of the guys?

I mouth, "Shut it," bringing a palm to my face.

Trey laughs. "Bro's got some mystery girl that he's supposed to meet tonight."

Both Gabe and Jeb share a glance as Drew walks through security next. They all burst into laughter at my expense.

"Oh, what?" Gabe snickers, slapping Jeb on the back.

I can already feel the color in my face changing, betraying me. Those two in particular enjoy giving me a hard time a little too much. Even when I was going out with Hannah, one of the prettiest girls in school, they managed to haze me. It makes sense they are cousins.

After I pass through the metal detectors, Gabe elbows me lightly. "So what happened to you and Hannah? Things not work out so well? What's Kaite think?"

"I don't wanna talk about it," I say, grabbing my backpack off the security table. "And who cares what Kaite thinks," is what I don't say out loud.

"So, look, in all seriousness," Trey starts. "I know you got this whole secret admirer thing going on, but this is our senior trip. Let's make the most of it."

"Trey's right," Drew adds. "Come on, Wes, we need a strategy."

I grit my teeth. None of them know how much I don't want to be here. Hitting up every single ride is literally the last thing I want to do. My stomach quivers.

"I know. I just need to…"

"Ohhh, wait, is that what you were messaging me about?" Gabe asks Trey, putting on his checkered backpack.

I lightly punch Trey in the shoulder. "Bro, not cool! You were messaging him on the bus? I thought you were asleep?"

"I knew you were wondering about who wrote that message, and Gabe knows everybody. I knew Mr. Serious was curious." He laughs. "Oh shoot-What if it's Hannah?"

My jaw clenches. I grind my teeth. The possibility had crossed my mind. I really hope it's not her. It'll make this whole breakup thing even more complicated.

"Looks like you can ask her now cuz she's coming over here." Trey slaps my back, retreating with the guys.

The two girls enter the park as I spin around. They are making their way through security. Now is my chance to hide. I run to the big tree in front of the grand stone wall, with the name of the theme park etched in bright colors. Valedictorian, Harvard-bound and this is the best hiding spot I could come up with. There is no time. It will have to do.

I lean against the tree, arms crossed, hoping to look very content. It takes Hannah less than two seconds to see me. Some pathetic hiding spot.

"Hey," she says, approaching with a little caution in her step.

I greet her dryly, "Hey."

"Everything ok?"

"You look like a creep," Kaite spits out judgingly. She's never been one to hold back her opinions. "How did they even let you through security?"

I give her a blank stare as I'm sure she's referring to the hoodie over my head and sunglasses, which undoubtedly make me look a bit suspicious, but I don't want to give her the satisfaction of knowing she ever gets to me. I say nothing. She crosses her arms disapprovingly and raises a brow and pops her gum. I open my mouth to attempt a rebuttal, but Hannah interjects.

"I thought you'd be with the boys?"

I shake my head casually. "Oh I am, I just have to do this thing for Mr. Herman, you know with the school newspaper, so…" My voice wavers like I'm nervous to be talking to her.

She starts grinning. "Right."

Oh no. I wave my hands. "Don't worry, it's just a solo project." How could I forget she also works on the school newspaper? No doubt she caught my lie. "The project doesn't concern you," I quip coldly.

"Okay, sus," Kaite blurts.

My hand hits my forehead. "No, that's not-" I object, but Hannah says, frowning, "Sorry for assuming, it's not like I'm the assistant editor or anything."

I admit I messed up by lying to her. To compensate, I ask to speak with her privately. Kaite gives me a dirty look but obliges us by stepping a few paces away. Hannah stands near me, arms at her sides.

Placing a hand on my chest, I say, "Look, Hannah, I didn't mean to lie to you." I pause, looking down at her. Despite this being an awkward exchange, I can still admire how beautiful she is, even with all that Disney propaganda on her body. Her face is glowing. Squinting at her from afar, I think she could pass as Sabrina Carpenter. Her hair is the same shade of blond and her eyes are just as blue. God, she's gorgeous. She stares at the ground then back up, looking like a wounded kitten, ears and all.

"Why did you lie then?" she asks.

I shove my hands into the pockets of my hoodie. "I don't know, but I'm sorry, ok? Are we cool?"

She lowers her head. "You're seeing someone else, aren't you?"

And just like that, we are back to the reason for our break up, well, one of the reasons. She could not let go of the fact that I've dated some of the other girls in her cheer squad. Hannah is extremely jealous. Besides that, she and her mom were already making plans to come visit me in Boston. I didn't even invite them. It freaked me out.

I sigh. "Do we have to go over this again? Hannah, you know there's no one else." I meet her eyes. "Can you please let that go and enjoy today? You deserve it."

She purses her lips and looks down. "I was supposed to enjoy this day with you."

The pit in my stomach drops lower. I already feel guilty enough as it is, but I had no choice. Once my acceptance letter came in the mail, I began to think about the future. The more I thought about where I'd be in five years, the less I saw Hannah there. Besides, I was already planning on starting college as a single guy because I'll need to focus. My studies always have and always will come first.

Even if I had wanted to continue our relationship, I knew it wouldn't be fair to her. We would be long-distance and, quite honestly, I just don't want the hassle. As painful as it is to let someone down, I knew it had to be done. I truly wanted to hold off until after our senior trip. However, once she and her mom got to planning, I knew I couldn't wait. Had I held off, I knew it would have given her the wrong idea.

I open my mouth then close it after exhaling. There's nothing I can say at this moment to rectify the situation. We are broken up. I can't change that. Least I can do is say two words I know she'd love to hear.

"I'm sorry," I profess, quietly. Realizing I won't be saying anything else, Hannah juts out her lip. That did not work like I wanted it to. She huffs then spins on her heel, leaving me alone by the tree. She walks over to Kaite, linking arms with her. The girls enter the park, leaving me to stew. I should run after her and apologize again, because once I walk through those gates, the madness is bound to start. I am not ready to fall down that rabbit hole again.

"And what are you waiting for, Mr. Hill-Cho?" Mrs. Anderson approaches me. She rolls up a paper copy of the park map and places it under her arm.

Stepping away from the tree, I say indubitably, "Just making sure everyone is accounted for, Mrs. Anderson." I give her the most genuine smile I can conjure.

"Oh, Weston." She grins at me approvingly. "Of course you were. Such a good boy. Alright, well, come on then. Everybody's inside," she adds chipperly, pointing to the entrance with her map. "Let's have a magical day." I cringe.

She escorts me through the gate while mindlessly chatting about the last time she was here with her grandchildren as, of course, she too is a fan of Disneyland. In the main courtyard, she leaves me momentarily to use the restroom. Now is my chance to ditch.

Once I am officially in the central plaza, I look around for Trey and the guys so I can avoid them. I have to walk all the way down Main Street until I notice them standing near the castle. Alright, they are just trying to taunt me. I slowly back away, hoping they don't spot me. I search the area for the quickest getaway, ready to trudge off on my own. As the best rides are to the east, I'll just head in the opposite direction. That leaves me to wander off toward Adventureland. I fall into the crowd and disappear without them seeing me. Excellent.

Walking aimlessly, all I can think about is that yearbook message. It's highly illogical, but curiosity is getting the best of me. I see an empty bench and drag my feet over to it. While I sit, I seriously think about what would happen if I do show up in front of the castle at exactly 9:30 pm when the fireworks go off. Yet, what could I possibly gain from meeting this mysterious person in such an irrational and albeit, slightly intriguing, type of way, in front of a fictional Disney Princess castle that serves as a business tactic to trick children and their ignorant parents into buying Disney's lie about this park being the happiest place on earth? When, in fact, all they are doing is getting robbed blind while the mouse dangles before them shiny and interesting characters of nostalgia; its only purpose is to serve as an intentional distraction.

"Do you have 50 cents?"

No. I will not be a part of this scam and encourage someone else who has already bought into Disney's lies. I refuse.

"Hello?"

"Huh?" I stammer, ending my ridiculously long mental rant.

There is some red headed chick in overall shorts bent down with her hand held out.

"Do you have 50 cents?" she asks again, head cocked to one side.

"Yeah, sure." I reach into my pocket and hand her a dollar because why on earth would I carry change.

"Thanks, Wes." Her cropped hair flows from side to side as she walks away. My face feels a bit flushed. That's strange.

She knew my name? That girl does seem familiar. I get up to follow her.

"Wait, are you from school?" I ask, standing behind her at the food cart across from the bench.

"Typical," she mumbles, refusing to turn around. She orders a Dole Whip ice cream at The Enchanted Tiki Bar. I resist an eye roll and shove my hands into my pockets. No wonder she needed money.

"This is why I packed a lunch," I mutter under my breath.

"Not that it's any of your business, but I also packed a lunch," she says, spinning around. "I just had to get a Dole Whip because it's a Disney tradition."

Now I really can't stop the eye roll. "Good for you."

She grabs her ice cream and tries to hand me some change.

"No, it's fine. Keep it."

She shrugs and throws it into the tip jar at the Tiki stand. She treks off, ignoring the fact we just had an altercation. Odd girl.

My gaze shifts back over to the bench. A family approaches it with a large stroller and decides to sit, taking up the whole thing. I groan. Why did I move? Finding another empty bench is going to be next to impossible. Just beyond the bench, a familiar group of teens appears to be heading in my direction. Crap. It's my friends being trailed by Hannah and Kaite. I thought for sure they would go straight to TomorrowLand. Great. I gotta act now before they spot me.

I turn my head back in the direction of the girl who asked me for change and call out after her. "Hey wait!"

She acts as if she doesn't hear me and continues waltzing deeper into Adventureland. I wish I could stay put, but my feet start trudging off after her like they have a mind of their own. I know it's because my ex is within 20 yards of me. So I go with it. Anything to keep me from bumping into them.

"Hey, I didn't get your name?" I state, catching up to the Dole Whip Girl.

"Are you serious, Weston Hill-Cho?" she says with a hand on her hip.

My brow arches, taken aback. "What?"

She eats a spoonful of Dole Whip and exclaims sourly, "I can't believe I voted for you."

"What are you talking about?" I ask genuinely. "I just gave you a dollar."

"Ooooh, lucky me," she mutters sarcastically. "Thanks for the dollar."

"Look, I know who you are," I start to say, then it dawns on me that every girl from my graduating class could be the one who wrote the yearbook message, including her. "Hey, were you at school yesterday?" I ask, changing the subject.

"Woah, what's with the interrogation?" she mentions between bites.

"Just answer the question," I state bluntly.

She stares at me blankly and replies with a deliberate, "No," then resumes downing her Dole Whip.

I pinch the bridge of my nose. "Look, someone wrote yesterday…" I pause, stopping myself.

She tilts her head. "Huh?"

"Never mind," I say, turning around. She doesn't seem to notice my sudden change of subject, again.

Walking past her, I notice another bench right by the entrance to Indiana Jones. Yes, perfect. A sense of relief settles over my shoulders. Now I can sit back down and wait out the next, I glance at my watch, nine hours I have left in this forsaken theme park.

"What are you doing?" Dole Whip Girl asks, following me over to the bench.

I place my backpack in the empty space next to me, leaving no room for anyone else to sit down. My eyes slowly look up to meet hers. "Sitting."

She lets out a light chuckle. "Oh really? I didn't know." She turns around, walking toward the ride.

What a sarcastic reply. I stare blankly at her half in amusement and half wondering if she really is the one who wrote the yearbook message. Yet, if she wasn't at school yesterday, then it couldn't be her. So then who was it? I shudder.

This is all starting to sound like Cinderella and her missing shoe. How ironic.

I don't know why I even care about it. The mystery of it is not even that intriguing. For all I know, that message wasn't even for me. Best thing to do now is probably forget about it.

My eyes shift to my backpack sprawled across the bench. Suddenly, my knee starts bouncing. I make a conscious effort to sit still. Really, though, I should check to make sure the book is even mine. Quickly, I pull my backpack onto my lap and start unzipping. My name should be inscribed somewhere. Ma paid good money for this. I know she plans on keeping it when I leave for Harvard. I flip to the front page and read "Weston Hill-Cho. Class of 2024." I knew it.

Contemplating, I realize maybe this mystery does have my attention. Yet, I have my work cut out for me. There are over 300 girls in my graduating class. This is going to be like finding a needle in a haystack. I suck in a deep breath. My hand instinctively finds its way to my brow. A truth sets in.

I'm Weston Hill-Cho, class Valedictorian and voted most likely to succeed. If anyone can find this needle in a haystack, it'll be me. Honestly, I can't think of a better way to spend my time in "misery-land" than to look for a mystery girl who wants to meet me at the castle.

CHAPTER 3
Dole Whip Girl

Are you following me?"

I glance up to see Dole Whip Girl, surprisingly without her Dole Whip. Has she been standing there this whole time?

"What, no!" I say defensively.

Quickly, I try to close the yearbook and put it away, but she snatches it from my hands.

She rapidly flips through the pages. The more she looks, the more I fear this girl is the one who wrote the message. Not that it would be a bad thing, but this girl is not exactly my type. For one, she has on a Lilo and Stitch t-shirt underneath overall shorts. I think I can reasonably conclude she is more than just a Disney fan. Besides, her socks have pokéballs on them. Reminds me of something Brenden would wear.

"Look what we have here," Dole Whip Girl starts. "Class President Weston Hill-Cho, named Valedictorian, voted most likely to succeed." She turns to another page. There's a hint of rage in her fingertips. Is she mad at me? What did I do? She continues, "And there's Weston again, head of the Spanish club, and head of the cooking club." She smirks, pointing to a picture of me standing next to Hannah at the prom. "What a shock, you were also Prom King. Oh and you're in the drama club for some reason even though you get stage fright." She shoves the book back at me, upset. "You are the king of the school. You know everybody. So what's my name?"

Now I understand. My eyes cautiously shift to hers. I admit her face is so familiar, but any recollection of her name escapes me. "I'm sorry," I say, ashamed. "I don't know." I sigh, disappointed in myself. Although part of me feels relieved that she did not mention the message.

Dole Whip Girl crosses her arms. "So disappointing." She shakes her head.

My head tilts. I peer at her with a quizzical expression. She sounds like my mother.

"So why are you over here in Adventureland all by yourself, Mr. President?" she asks, changing the subject.

I sneer. "Don't call me that."

"I just assumed you'd be with your posse, getting the most out of your 'epic senior trip' at Disneyland. Woah!" she exclaims with false enthusiasm.

"Well, you know what they say about those who assume," I quip, smirking. Her expression remains unfazed. My charm does not seem to be doing me any favors today. "Besides, I hate Disneyland," I add with a straight face. Oops. I didn't mean to admit that to this random girl.

She covers her mouth in a melodramatic fashion. "Whaaaat?"

I squint at her. "And?" Not like it's any of her business. Shouldn't she be with her friends right now instead of bothering me? Well, I guess I'm the one bothering her. I run a hand over the back of my neck. What is with me today?

She smiles maniacally. "But, Mr. President, this trip was your idea."

All the muscles in my entire face turn into a solid mass. The memory of making that decision during study hall with Hannah returns to haunt me. I blurt, "It wasn't like it was entirely my idea, ok? I was just trying to be a good boyfriend." I look away. This is such a strange altercation. Why on earth am I even telling this girl? I don't know her and have nothing to prove. But Dole Whip Girl is quiet and looks at me with a raised brow of suspicion. Against my better judgment, I tell her, "It was a spontaneous decision, one I'd never make on my own because like I said, I hate Disneyland."

What was supposed to be a romantic gesture turned into an ironic charade to celebrate our graduation. A celebration that marks our inevitable emergence into adulthood, and thus signifies the end of an era. I, on the other hand, could not think of a better place in which to mourn the loss of our dwindling innocence from the past four years, namely our childhood, than in the very place that inspires eternal youth. I regret the idea completely.

"Interesting," Dole Whip Girl mutters, jarring my thoughts.

"Huh?" If she was talking, I think I missed it.

Dole Whip Girl stares at me for a moment. There's a whimsical gleam in her expression that alarms me.

"What?" I ask, afraid of the answer. She is starting to freak me out.

"I'm gonna make you like Disneyland."

My mouth drops open. What an idiotic and most ridiculous notion. "There's no way on this entire planet anyone could ever make me like Disneyland." I fold my arms. The idea is just absurd. Who even is this girl? "Ever," I add.

"Challenge accepted." She grins wide, displaying an almost perfect row of white teeth. Her smile is actually quite exceptional.

I clear my throat, shaking my head. "Excuse me?" My brow arches.

"Hey, do you still wanna know my name?" she asks coyly, like she's holding an ace.

I'm unsure of how to answer the question without sounding like a jerk. "Yeah, sure," I say with uncertainty.

"How badly do you wanna know?"

What? I steel myself.

"Ooh, I've got it." She snaps her fingers. "For every ride you come on with me, I'll give you a letter to spell out my name. It won't be in order, but in the end, you will guess it, easy," she proposes.

"No way. Not happening," I respond immediately, backing away with my hands up as if I am in imminent danger.

"Why not? It'll be fun. And what else have you got to do besides sitting here, hating Disneyland? Besides"—she looks at me sideways—"you owe me."

Every muscle in my face goes stiff again. What does she mean by that? I bite the inside of my lip. Part of me is intrigued. "For what?" I ask, gingerly.

She scoffs. "Fine. I figured as much." She takes a spiral tie off her wrist, wrapping up the pieces of her short, cherry red hair, leaving her wispy bangs to dangle in her face. "You don't care and why would you? You're Weston Hill-Cho, one of the most popular guys in school. Why would you spend your senior trip with some random girl from your class, whose name you'll learn quickly but just as easily forget by tomorrow?" She purses her lips, pausing for a moment. "For what, Mr. President? Well….there is no reason, but I'm bored and seeing that you're trying to avoid your friends, the challenge would help you do that, wouldn't it? Wouldn't you rather have fun for 12 hours with someone than just sit here alone in the sun with your thoughts?"

Frantically, I debate the situation in my head. How did she know I am avoiding my friends? I guess this girl is observant. But the reason why I'm avoiding them is the same reason why I don't want to tag along with her. Unfortunately, it looks like there is no straightforward solution to this problem. This isn't calculus, I have to remind myself. Maybe getting on rides is inevitable?

Dole Whip Girl begins walking away.

"Wait," I say, extending my hand, heart pounding.

She stops to turn her head. What a strange girl. Her challenge is preposterous, but tagging along with her might be better than the alternative. Me stewing alone just waiting for this day to end or catching up with Trey and the guys who will inevitably run into Hannah and Kaite. I shake my head. That is a hard pass for me. My eyes shift. I can't believe I'm about to do this. I'm just hoping this will make the time go by fast, and honestly, I'd like to see this girl try and change my mind about a place I loathe so much. She won't.

"Alright, I'm coming," I state clearly. "But there's no way I'm getting on any rides."

She claps, jumping up and down. "Yes!" Her tiny ponytail bounces with her. "Let's go!" she screams, heading into Indiana Jones.

I plant my feet and state in all seriousness, "I said no rides."

"Rides are part of the deal. You don't go, you don't get a letter," she yells from inside the big rock-like structure.

"Ugh," I groan, wrangling a hand through my gelled hair. Crap, I think I messed it up. "What if I decide to ditch you?" I add, smoothing back the unraveled parts of my hair.

"I really don't care," she shouts plainly from the cave. "I'll have fun either way, Mr. President."

I contemplate walking away, but my feet are already moving forward. I knew getting on a ride was going to be inevitable. I just need to set some ground rules.

"Ok, wait, there's one condition," I express, catching up to her.

She pauses, annoyance written in her expression. "What is it now?"

"I will not under any circumstances get on those teacups. You understand me?" I declare, a little harsher than intended.

"Aww, no. Those are my favorite. We have to go on those. It's a Disney tradition."

"I'm beginning to think you have a lot of those." One corner of my mouth curls upward.

"You're catching on, Mr. President," she reels. "We are getting on those teacups."

Grabbing her gently by the elbow, I look her dead in the eye and say, "No."

She pouts, "Why not?"

"They are off limits, ok?" I retort, letting her go. "I'll get on any other ride, just not those."

She mutters under her breath, "Killjoy," then darts further down the cave-like hallway.

"I must be out of my mind," I mumble as I proceed to follow her.

It's so dark I can hardly see where she is anymore. "Dole Whip Girl?" I yell, my voice echoing down the hall. It's not like we rope-dropped this ride, but it's still pretty early so there aren't that many people here. I can practically run down this entire lane until I reach the end of the line. There she is.

"Dole Whip Girl?" She raises an eyebrow as I catch up to her.

Behind us, the empty lane quickly floods with eager riders. I hold back a laugh. "Well, you refuse to tell me your name. So that's the best I could come up with."

"You're not very creative, are you, Mr. President?" She shakes her head and moves up a space in line.

"Anything besides calculus and basketball, I'm lost," I admit. "Well, I guess I'm pretty good at English, oh and history too."

She crosses her arms. "You're so modest for our class

valedictorian." Her mouth forms into a half smile. "I know you're good at everything, Harvard boy."

"Man, we should have opted in for the Genie+ pass." I point at the lightning lane, ignoring her comment. She obviously reads the school newspaper. If that didn't tell her I was accepted into Harvard, I'm sure the entire student body was talking about it. News really travels fast in high school.

"Oh come on, the wait isn't that bad."

"It is though." I recognize I may be exaggerating a little now, but later, the wait times are going to be astronomical.

"What, you don't want to spend the extra time with me?" She puts a hand over her chest.

I start shaking my head in a frantic objection. Maybe too much. "No, I mean, it's just that I didn't want to spend the extra money." Panic strikes my eyes. I hope I didn't give her the wrong impression by following her here.

"Don't worry, Wes. I get it," she retorts. "I know this isn't like a date or anything." She crosses her arms. "This is a mission, should you choose to accept it, about finding your heart because honestly who in the world hates Disneyland?" She uncrosses her arms to poke me so lightly I barely feel it through the thick fabric of my hoodie.

"Mission Impossible, really?" I tease, smiling. This girl is sort of amusing.

"Shut up, I couldn't think of anything else." She playfully slaps my arm. Her fingers linger a little longer than I think she anticipated. We share an awkward glance. "Ehm, what I mean is," she adds, nervously clasping her hands together, "you took almost every class offered in school, but we aren't in school anymore, are we, Weston? This is a lesson in life."

I suppress a laugh, pulling back my lips.

"This is a class on how to enjoy Disneyland. I'm your teacher. Lesson one: if you cannot afford a Genie+ pass for the lightning lanes, then always get on the popular rides first. That way the wait time is lower. That or use the single rider lanes, if the ride has it."

"Bet," I say in agreement, looking down at my shoes. She must have a season pass to know all these tips. That's probably why she doesn't have the add-on service, because it wouldn't make sense. She wouldn't need the lightning lane because waiting would never be a problem if she can come here whenever she wants. It makes me think back to the last time I came to this park. I cross my arms. That was so long ago.

Dole Whip Girl turns to face the ride. "You know, even with single rider lanes, they do keep riders in pairs, so odds are we are going to sit next to each other for quite a few rides." She winks at me. "Hope your girlfriend doesn't mind."

I almost say, "We aren't together anymore." But why would I tell her that? My eyes fall to her little ponytail, bouncing about. I feel the urge to touch it. Why would I do that when I don't even know her name? That is assuredly an intrusive thought I will not be seeing out.

CHAPTER 4
Laugh Out Loud

The ride at Indian Jones finally stops after what feels like hours. I practically trample over a few people, rushing down the exit lane as fast as my legs can take me. Why the exit is so far away, I'll never know. My eyes frantically look for a trash can. "I could puke right now." Oh, there's one. "Thank god," I exclaim, hovering over one. Holding onto the rims, I dry heave.

Dole Whip Girl arrives right behind me and shouts, "Don't!"

The dizziness is starting to subside when I realize nothing is coming out. I suck in a deep breath, feeling better already. Must have been a false alarm. I manage to compose myself, stomach contents intact. "See, this is why rides are not a good idea," I struggle to say, letting go of the trash bin.

She laughs. "You are so dramatic." She rests her hand on my back. Her touch is as light as a feather. "Indiana Jones is one of the best rides in this place." Dole Whip Girl pulls her hand back to take out her paper map. "Ok, it's this way to Jungle Cruise." She points, walking away.

"Slow down," I groan, stumbling after her. I swing my

backpack around and dig into the front pocket. "You're supposed to tell me a letter, remember? Also, who uses paper maps? You don't have the electronic version?" I take out my mini hand sanitizer and squeeze a drop into my hand before putting the bottle back.

"Fine, A." She pauses. "You know, some people like having something physical to hold. It reminds me of simpler times."

"A, huh?" I repeat while appreciating her comment. There really is something about having actual paper in your hand. That is probably why I wrote down my valedictory speech instead of typing it into my phone. Why does it remind me so much of the old CDs and vinyls on my brother's bedroom floor? Maybe we have more in common than I thought? "Abbey, uh, Aubrey, Aimee?" I bring myself to guess.

"I'm not giving them in order, genius, and no, it's none of those."

She darts again down the path without a moment to lose. A long drawn out sigh escapes me. This is probably such a huge waste of my time. It is honestly a miracle I was able to keep down my breakfast. I should text Trey to see where they're at, but I know the type of rides they like; my stomach will not be able to handle them. Plus, Hannah and Kaite will probably be trailing closely behind. My gaze settles on the girl with cherry red hair. Perhaps sticking with her is the path of least resistance. I pull out my phone. Only 10 hours to go.

"Woah, hold up," I shout.

We're standing at the entrance of the Jungle Cruise ride fairly quickly as it is not far from Indiana Jones. Alarms go off in my head.

I plant my feet. "I cannot do boats. Nope. No way," I state, shaking my head.

Dole Whip Girl puts a hand on her hip. "Why are you being so difficult?"

"I'm not being difficult, DW, I just-"

"Wait, wait, wait," she says, holding up a hand. "Did you just call me DW?"

"Short for Dole Whip Girl?" I flash her a smile with all the charm I can manage. It usually works on teachers and not to brag, but most girls swoon over it.

"Not bad, Mr. President." She returns a smile filled with as much charm as mine. It catches me off guard. "Clearly, the creative bone in your body is just suppressed," she teases.

I bite the inside of my cheek, which oddly is beginning to feel very warm. I shake my head. "No. I'm serious. Boats are off limits. Pick another ride."

DW raises a brow. She huffs, then grabs one of my backpack straps and pulls me into the line anyways. I should stop her. I need to stop her. Once I get on that boat, I know for a fact I will get sick, but I let her drag me away. Call it the science of basic attraction, I don't know. The way she is pulling me makes my head feel dizzy in an exhilarating way. That's it. There must be something in the air. Disney must have sprayed some kind of secret illegal drug that causes teenagers to act crazy. How else could it explain why a highly intelligent person like myself is acting so irrational? We enter the line, and I log the thought away for a later time.

"There you go again." DW elbows me.

"I don't know what you're talking about."

The boat slightly turns and I cling to my seat for dear life. My head is whirling in a frantic daze. Everything is starting to spin. I don't think this ride is supposed to do that.

DW places her hand over mine. "Try to focus on my voice." How does she know I'm spiraling?

I look over at her. She's taken out her little ponytail, leaving her short cherry hair to fall in a perfect angle exactly at her jawline. She says something again, but the only thing that's stopping the spinning is focusing on her lips. Weird. She really does look familiar.

"Theater class?" I say, accidentally moving my hand.

She pulls her hand away and sticks it under her leg. "Um, what?" she asks nonchalantly.

"Were you in my theater class freshman year?"

"I've been in a lot of classes with you, Wes," she answers disappointedly. Well, now I feel like a complete— "Don't beat yourself up, Mr. President. I'm sure half your posse doesn't know I exist," she states. "I'm nobody," she says, using air quotes in a monotone voice.

Now I feel even worse for not knowing her name. I lick my lips. "You're not a nobody."

"Oh, I know I'm not a nobody," she quips, flipping her hair. "Just according to the popular kids; you guys only pay attention to people who worship you."

Sighing, I realize I want to redeem myself. I want to tell her that what she is saying is absolutely ridiculous. When I start to think about it, though, she may be on to something. The people around me at school don't exactly speak their mind. Practically everyone I hang out with agrees with everything I say and I'm constantly surrounded by people. It's exhausting.

"Relax, Wes." DW nudges me with her arm.

I turn my head slowly and meet her eyes, wanting to apologize, but the words do not come. Suddenly, I begin to notice things about her I shouldn't, like the color of her irises. They are just brown. Why should I care what shade? I conclude I'm simply logging information. Why am I staring at her nose? It's quite perfectly proportioned to her oval-shaped face. Then there's that red hair. Clearly, it's dyed. It's not natural, but anyone can see how great a complement her red hair is against her pale complexion. Other people would notice this, right? So, it makes sense why I am realizing it.

The boat lightly hits the side of the dock, signaling the ride is over. That went fast. She looks away from me at the same time I tilt my head down. We exit the ride in silence, but I can't ignore the fact that I stopped feeling queasy.

"I'm impressed you haven't made a run for it," DW says.

"Me too." I grin.

We continue to walk, but my knees start shaking. I ultimately end up emptying out this morning's breakfast into a nearby bush. Disgusting.

DW hands me a napkin from a nearby restaurant. "Here."

"Thanks." I wipe my mouth then take a swig of water from my backpack. "So, where are you going to drag me off to next?" As I put my water bottle away, I decide to take off my hoodie. It is ten in the morning on a Friday in May. It really shouldn't be this hot already, but this is California so the temperature is nearing 80 degrees. Mixing the heat with my motion sickness is sure to wreck me today. Another reason I can confidently say why I hate Disneyland.

"I'm really sorry, ok. I didn't actually think you were gonna get sick," DW admits. "I honestly just thought you were being a wuss." She unzips her backpack and hands me a small pink bottle of hand sanitizer. There are sparkles inside the liquid. Even though I have my own, I use hers regardless. She's a very thoughtful packer; I will give her that.

"You're probably right," I start to say, "but a deal is a deal, and I have nothing better to do for the next 9 hours or so."

DW ponders. I kind of like that she doesn't object to me sticking it out even though she just saw me blow chunks. I'll just add it to the tab of reasons why I hate Disneyland. Taking out the map, she frantically searches for the next perfect ride to torture me, or so I assume. I know from the way she smiles it's going to be bad.

"Follow me."

I gently grab onto her arm. "Wait, I need another letter." I am uncomfortably aware of her skin temperature. A shiver runs down my spine. That's an odd sensation.

She shoves her hands in her overall shorts pocket, making me lose my grip. "A."

"You already gave me an A."

"It is possible there might be two of the same letters in my name," she quips sarcastically.

"You're not going to make this easy for me, are you?" I furrow my brow.

She smirks. "Where's the fun in that?"

We trailblaze further into Adventureland until it quickly becomes New Orleans Square.

"Oh no. Not this one. Any ride but this one."

She says snarkily, "And what is wrong with this one?"

"Well, nothing is wrong with it, but-"

"Then we're going," she orders, pulling me by my backpack strap again, which causes my feet to drag a little. I don't know why this amuses me. Yet, I let her. She turns around and flashes me an amusing look of irritation. Her bright brown eyes seem to tear down my will to object so I move along.

We get into line, and I'm flabbergasted by how many people are here. So many children. So many brainwashed victims. I look down at my phone. This will probably be the longest wait so far and for what? Another boat ride in a weird smelling man-made canal with an incredibly tacky theme. It's not like the pirates even do anything. What a pointless ride. I still can't believe they created a candle that captured the scent of this ride. Do people actually like that smell? I sure don't.

"What do you think about so much?" DW asks.

"You really wanna know?" I ask, tilting my head towards her.

She nods delightfully, making the freckles on her cheeks dance. I can't believe I don't know her name.

"Nothing good," I dispute, looking down. "Let's just put it that way."

"Ew, sicko."

"No, ugh," I groan, slamming my face into my palm. "Not what I meant."

"Elaborate." She unfolds one arm, tucking her fingers into her right pocket.

Shrugging, I reply, "I don't know. I guess I think about how useless everything is."

She raises an eyebrow as if to encourage me to continue.

"I'm a very intellectual person," I say in a very poor attempt at explaining what I actually mean. I hear myself. It sounds super arrogant.

"Ha," she scoffs sarcastically. "Ok, Harvard boy, we all know you're smart." She rolls her eyes. "But what are you really thinking about, like right now?"

"Right now?" I say, debating whether or not to tell her about the yearbook message. Yet, something I mentioned earlier comes to mind. I snap my fingers. "You were in my theater class. Tell me I'm right." This time I'm sure. Mostly.

She unfolds her arms and leans against the metal railing. "Ok, yeah. I was there. So what's my name?"

I bite my lip. "Avery? No. Au-Audrey? I-I don't know."

"It doesn't start with an A for the love of god." She closes her eyes in a dramatic fashion.

"Well, that narrows it down." I lean against the metal railing beside her. The tips of our fingers accidentally graze each other. I pull my hand away a little too quickly, making DW slide over. I hold my breath. It was nothing. Just an accident.

"Not to change the subject," she says, tucking some hair behind her ear, "but-uh-why did you and Hannah break up? Is that why you aren't with your friends today?" I wonder if she asks this because she too is alone. Well, at least she was before I joined her.

"They have their own agenda." I give a very unconcerned wave. "I'm not really into it."

"You still didn't answer the break-up question."

The nerve of this girl. "You're nosy," I state bluntly.

"And?" she questions, nearly raising her eyebrow into her hairline.

"I don't even know your name and you expect me to talk to you about my break up?"

She wraps her arms around herself. "I was just curious."

I sigh, unsure why I am even about to talk about this with some girl I barely know. "Hannah is a great girl, you know. There was just no point in keeping the relationship going."

"No point?" DW unfolds her arms. "Don't you-didn't you love her?"

"What does love have to do with anything?" I exclaim, barely suppressing an eye roll.

DW's mouth opens, appalled. "Love has everything to do with it."

"Love doesn't exist," I say defensively as I feel a rant bubbling forth. "Oh wait, I forgot. We are at Disneyland, the happiest place on earth, right? Well, it's a lie." I stare at DW. Her eyes are telling me to stop, but I keep going. "It's all just a facade," I tell her, hands outstretched wide. "But you probably grew up wishing on a star, hoping one day your Prince Charming will come and save you, right? I'm sorry to be the one to tell you that he's not coming. He never will. Stop waiting for him." My eyes shift to the floor. When I get the confidence to look up, Dole Whip Girl is staring at me intensely, eyes wide, and her face wears an expression of dismay.

She crosses her arms. "You really are heartless, aren't you?"

We move up a couple spaces in line. She's the quietest she's been since I met her this morning. I work up the nerve to break the silence in attempts to explain further, lying straight through my teeth. "I kinda got carried away back there. I didn't-I didn't mean any of it."

DW looks at me, grimly. "Now I understand why you keep your thoughts to yourself." She is right. I would rather keep thoughts like that to myself. It does no good saying them out loud. Learned my lesson, I think.

The line is starting to move a bit faster now as we near the front. I tap DW on the shoulder, but she doesn't turn around. No doubt she will probably want to ditch me after this. I don't blame her. However, there's no point getting on this ride if we aren't on good terms. What's the point of me even staying here with her when I keep letting people down? I shake my head. Something is wrong with me today. I blame Disneyland.

Gritting my teeth, I tap her on the shoulder again. "You're right. I'm sorry. This place just brings out the worst in me," I say emphatically.

DW spins around. "Why?"

I swallow. "What do you mean?"

"Why do you hate Disneyland so much? There has to be a valid reason. I mean it's obvious you've been here many times since you know the rides, your way around." She squints at me. "I even have a feeling you used to love, no, you were obsessed with Disneyland before, am I wrong?"

My eyes shift to the ground, breaking her glare.

She clasps her hands together and exclaims excitedly, pointing, "Ha, I knew it."

"You don't know what you're talking about." I fold my arms. There's no way she could ever understand. No one would.

"Oh, I can prove it because you act like such a know-it-all." She rises on her tiptoes to poke my chest. "If you can name who the castle belongs to, then you know Disney."

My eyes flicker to hers. Why did she mention the castle? Did she write me the message? Now I really need to know her name.

"Weston Hill-Cho. Answer me right now or the deal is off," she demands.

My jaw tenses, as I am about done talking about Disneyland. "If I answer, will you drop this conversation?"

She purses her lips, giving me a long stare. "Alright, fine."

She bobs her chin. "Now tell me, which princess does the castle belong to?"

I close my eyes and say through clenched teeth, "Sleeping Beauty." If only I grew up on something else, anything else but Disney. I pry open my eyes.

She raises a brow, placing a hand on her hip. "Her actual name?"

"Are you serious?" Biting my tongue, I mutter through a groan, "Aurora." I seriously hate how much I know about Disney. What a frivolous thing to have in my head. It's probably because growing up, Brenden and I would play this Disney trivia game until we practically memorized the questions. We played it over and over again, year after year, until my parents split up, then we stopped.

"Ah, I just love to torment you." DW laughs, playfully slapping me on the shoulder. It jolts me out of my own head.

"I'm so glad I could be of some amusement to you." I roll my eyes, smirking.

I roll my neck, letting the frustration out with it. DW turns and faces the front, dropping the conversation. Although I'm glad she did, I still want to talk to her— about anything else.

We move up a couple spaces in line. The boats are in view by now. Fear creeps into my stomach. I want to get out of here already. This ride better be over fast and I better not get sick. Honestly, I might dip out on this girl. Hanging out by myself is starting to look like a vacation compared to all the motion sickness I've been having to deal with this morning.

"That poor girl. You probably broke her heart," DW states, changing the subject matter in my head unknowingly.

"Huh?" I say after a long second.

"I guess it doesn't surprise me." DW sighs. "You guys are all the same."

I keep my lips pressed, afraid of what I might say.

She puts her hands back on the rail. "You know the story."

"I do?"

She turns her head slightly and stares at nothing in particular. "Yeah, you know the cliché premise: Girl falls for guy, guy dumps her, guy moves on, leaving the girl to wonder what she did wrong and if they will ever get back together...." She doesn't quite finish the sentence.

I lean back on the railing. I place my hand deliberately next to hers. I don't care if our fingers touch. She doesn't adjust them, so neither do I.

"That's messed up. Sorry," I say solemnly, though it doesn't change the way of the world. Breakups happen. They just do.

She shrugs. "Whatever. It's ancient history. I'm over it." The line starts moving again. She pushes herself off the railing. Her words echo in my ear. "Leaving the girl to wonder what she did wrong." It reminds me of Hannah. Although I believe in our breakup, I at least hope she doesn't feel that way. That was never my intention. Maybe I should find her and set the record straight.

"Ok, let's change the subject, for real this time," DW insists. "So you're going to Harvard after graduation, that's exciting, Mr. President."

"Stop calling me that, Dole Whip Girl," I grumble. "And yes, it's all very exciting. I'm going to be a lawyer, yadda yadda. What about you? What are your plans?" My curious glance falls on her small frame. She twists a lock of hair. Her story must be a mystery worth unraveling.

"I don't know. I don't really have any plans."

I slap my chest, a little melodramatically but enough to prove a point. "What do you mean you don't have any plans?"

"I'm more of the seize-the-day type of girl, and no offense, but life's not going to happen behind the walls of some university."

I raise a brow. She did not just say that. How does anyone not have a plan for the future? Ma practically created mine before I was born. I literally could not imagine my life without some sort of life plan. The thought of not having one makes me dizzy. Dole Whip Girl taps on her phone and puts it away. This girl is really something else.

"To be honest," she shifts her feet and says softly, "I got a full ride from UCLA in theater-tech, but I got invited to live with my cousin who lives in Bali in a camper van."

I shake my head. That's exactly like something Brenden would say. I clasp my hands together while trying to maintain a straight face. "That sounds cool," I spit out. Not exactly a lie, but not exactly the truth. I'm not huge on travel, but it's nice for most people without a proper life plan.

"So, I might do that and forget about the scholarship, but who really knows?" she adds, chuckling.

I swallow, "Ok, wait a second," and pinch my nose. "You mean to tell me you got a scholarship to UCLA but you're actually thinking about giving it up to go live in some van, like a homeless person?" I stare down at her with a very concerned expression. "I can't." My tone suggests I'm being very judgmental, but that's only because I think I am actually judging her choices. What is wrong with me?

She laughs at me like my reaction is so amusing. "You take life too seriously. I swear, you're practically an old man."

"Life is serious," I state. If her laugh wasn't so adorable I'd probably have more to say, like how important it is to make a plan because the economy is unsteady, and it's only going to get worse. She needs to be smart and invest in her future now, or else she will find herself living in her parents basement with no job or any financial stability whatsoever, like my brother. A shiver runs through me. I think just like Ma.

"Ok, we need two single riders over here," a ride operator yells.

DW shoots up her hand. I guess we are going now. Yes, finally.

We approach the boat. My stomach is beginning to feel uneasy already. "Oh god."

She grabs my hand, pulling me into the boat. "Will you relax?" She keeps telling me that. How can I relax when her hand is so soft?

We pile into the back of the unsteady boat. DW lets go as she sits down in the left back corner. I sit beside her and look to my right where a little girl in an Elsa costume, sucking on a lollipop, is being seated. I bring my arms close to my chest, but they add another three kids so touching is inevitable. They should not be allowing this many people on the ride. My shoulder is practically jabbing into DW's chest. I casually lift up my arm and see no other logical place to lay it other than around her shoulders.

"I see what you're doing," she states coyly.

"No, that's not-I'm not trying to make a move," I reply, lifting my arm back up. Her cheeks grow a little more pink.

I look over to my right, where two rambunctious children sit. The lollipop girl stares at me with full curious eyes. It really wouldn't be the full Disney experience if I didn't have to sit next to some children, now would it? I turn my head back to DW and let my arm fall naturally around her shoulder since the alternative is extremely uncomfortable on so many levels. She merely clings to the side of the ride, completely unfazed by my touch, and starts tapping the side of the boat, ever so eager to get moving.

"It'd be ok, you know?" DW shares delicately.

"What would be ok?" I shut my eyes as the boat is starting to float down the stream. The nausea is already hitting me. I open my eyes and try fixing my gaze on the man's head in front of me. Perhaps focusing on a stationary object might stabilize the spinning.

"If you made a move."

I shoot her a surprised look but her attention is on the water.

She has her hand outstretched, hovering above it. How am I supposed to respond to that when all I can think about is how much I want to feel the softness of her hands again?

Just after passing the first mechanical pirate that looks like Johnny Depp, the boat turns a corner. The inertia forces me to lean closer to DW. She turns her head slowly, meeting my hesitant gaze. When our eyes meet, I can see the uncertainty in her expression. My lips part, but I don't know what to say. My fingers twitch against her arm, making me question why my breathing has quickened. I press my lips together, looking away. I hardly know this girl, and yet, I can't ignore the strange connection between us. It makes no sense. It's illogical. But the science doesn't lie and that I can trust. I glance back over at her. She is looking out into the water. The desire to touch her hand is not there anymore. I missed it. The moment is gone. It vanished, as if it were never there.

The ride takes a turn through another canal. The young girl in the Elsa costume is now standing. Should she be doing that? Where are her parents? Of course, she loses her balance on another swift turn, making the lollipop slip out of her hand. She catches herself on my knee, sticky fingers and all. Gross. When she sits back down, we share an uncomfortable glance. I reach down to grab the lollipop off my shoe. I hand it to her in disgust. "You still want this?"

She snatches it out of my hand, then shoves it in her mouth without so much as a word. I could throw up from that alone. I hear DW trying to stifle her laugh.

"It's not funny," I say, turning to her.

"It kinda is though." She grins, giving in to her laugh. The sound is contagious. Naturally, I break out into a laughing fit with her. Alright, as much as this girl is not my usual type, I have to admit she is fun. That counts for something.

DW exhales. She forms her lips into a soft smile. "Now,

where would you be right now if I had not forced you to come on this ride?"

I wouldn't be having fun is what I don't tell her. "Probably on a bench somewhere."

"You are such a party pooper," she teases, nudging me.

"Shut up," I say, nudging her back.

"That's so sad. If you were on a bench somewhere, you'd miss out on meeting the queen."

My brow raises. "Queen?"

DW bites her lip, holding back a laugh. "Queen Elsa of course." She tilts her head in the direction of the lollipop girl.

I glance at the girl. She's almost done with that dirty candy. Oh, shoot. She's looking right at me, smiling with missing teeth. I return a polite smile, but then she sticks out her tongue at me. Kids are such strange creatures. Guess that means she doesn't like me. That is kind of refreshing. I turn my head so the girl is out of my peripheral vision. DW bursts out laughing. It's ridiculous and completely infectious. It's not that funny. Yet I laugh with her to the point of tears. When the ride is over, the scene replays in my head. I have to cover my mouth from laughing out loud again.

CHAPTER 5
Noon

After leaving the Pirates of the Caribbean ride, we shortly find ourselves in the middle of New Orleans Square. The strong whiff of french fries makes my stomach rumble. Now, I'm wishing I hadn't packed lunch for myself. I could go for a giant turkey leg. Although these food prices are pretty high. Yeah, never mind.

"Hey, are you hungry?" I blurt.

DW shrugs. "I could eat."

We venture over to Harbor Galley and sit at a small round table in their courtyard. DW takes out a brown bag from her backpack. I whip out my glorious PB&J that is both very cost effective and filling, along with a container of kimchi that my mother makes by the bucket full. I pause for a moment to look down at my food. It somehow encompasses the exact cliché of who I am, being half Asian and Caucasian. DW doesn't say a word about it.

"Oh, yeah," she moans joyously as she takes a bite out of a relatively large sandwich. I can't help but grin as she digs in. From what I can tell, its contents are simple; white bread, tomatoes, lettuce and sliced ham. I'd say her choice also seems to reflect who she is. At first glance, you may pass it up, but after looking at it more closely, you come to realize the seemingly basic choice is actually quite classic and completely underrated. Watching her devour it makes me crave a bite.

"Oh, we have to get beignets before we go back home."

"What is that?" I ask, biting into my PB&J.

"Are you joking? I thought you've been here a million times?"

I arch my brows. "I never said that."

She sets down her sandwich. "Look me in the eye and tell me you haven't been here at least ten times."

We stare at each other for a solid five seconds. I squint, trying not to break eye contact, but my eyes start watering. I blink. "Alright, fine," I admit. "We had a pass when I was a kid, but I still don't know what a bin-what? What did you call it?" I wipe my eyes. Staring contests are not one of my strengths.

She smirks at me, pointing. "I knew it! You do love Disneyland."

"No, no. Not anymore," I state plainly. I start picking at the crust on what's left of my PB&J. "End of discussion." I really hope she drops it because I am not in the mood for a free therapy session.

"And it's pronounced like bin-yay." DW chews quietly for a moment and then adds, "It's like a donut."

"A donut?"

"The best one you will ever have in your life." Her eyes light up.

"I doubt that," I say plainly.

She continues to nibble on her sandwich. Not eating very fast, I see, unlike the way she downed that Dole Whip from earlier. I give in to a laugh. Oops.

"What?" she exclaims with a mouthful.

"Nothing." I look away, embarrassed for staring at her. I sip on my Capri Sun and try to ignore the random reminder of how my arm felt wrapped around her shoulders. It means nothing. If anything, it could just be making me reminiscent of what it feels like to have a girlfriend. There is something so nice about having one.

"So, any guesses for my name?"

"What was the last letter again?" I stammer, my thoughts embarrassing me.

She looks up at me annoyed. "H."

"Oh right, right." I visualize the letters together. There's too many variables for me to guess. How could I possibly narrow it down? "Oh no," I exclaim, eyes widening with dread. "Your name is not Hannah, is it?"

DW's jaw drops. "Are you kidding me?"

"Two As and a H, it sort of makes sense."

"Oh, I get it now." She wipes her mouth. "You're still in love with her, aren't you?"

I wave my hands. "No. No, no."

"Ohh," she squeals. "Now, we are getting somewhere. What does she really mean to you, Wes? Is she your first love? Did she actually break up with you?" She gasps. "No way!"

With a mouthful of kimchi, I scrunch my eyes and groan. "Ugh, no, can we just leave her out of this? It was just a guess." I swallow.

"Fine." She doesn't argue. Thank god.

The girl does not cease to amaze me. That or it's just pure annoyance. When I'm done with my lunch, I sit with my hands folded, waiting for her to finish eating. I look at my phone and see that it's noon. No wonder the park is so full now.

Many interesting people walk around us, but I can only seem to focus on one thing: Dole Whip Girl. She has to be from theater class, and I know just how to prove it. After wiping my mouth, I snap my fingers. I grab my backpack and start unzipping.

"What are you doing?" DW asks, concerned.

Oh, gum. I forgot I had packed that. I toss a piece in my mouth before pulling out my yearbook. "I don't know why I didn't do this earlier," I say, flipping through it.

Remnants of DW's sandwich drops. "That's cheating." She points. "Give that to me."

She practically sprints around the table to try and nab it. I stand up and hold it over my head. Even on her tiptoes it's out of reach. This does not deter her, though, which is quite adorable. I try to block her with my free hand, but she grabs it, pulling my arm down.

DW stops for a moment. Our fingers naturally start to interlace. She points, saying, "Weston Hill-Cho, you have to earn my name," as her hand tightens around mine.

It must be from the way she's holding my hand or the color of her eyes reflecting back into mine, but I get the impulsive urge to kiss her. That is not what I should do right now. I swallow, restraining myself from doing something so irrational.

She looks up at the yearbook above my head, reaching for it again, then jumps. I take a step back and move it out of the way, causing her to almost fall. I panic and instinctively grab onto her, not thinking about how my actions might be interpreted. She wraps her hands around my neck, and now, I'm all too aware of how close we are to each other. Her touch seems to light fireworks under my skin. My eyes peer into hers and suddenly, I feel hotter than the sun.

"Wes?"

Hannah's familiar voice stuns me. I turn around, immediately letting go of DW. She stumbles a bit to find her balance, but my eyes are glued to Hannah's. Her and Kaite approach us with very perplexed expressions.

"Cheater!" Kaite accuses blatantly. She blows up a pink bubble, then sharply pops it with her teeth. I shudder, then let go of DW. She wastes no time in retreating to the table with her head held down, her confidence seemingly gone.

I wave my hands. "This is not what it looks like."

"I knew it," Hannah interrupts. "You're seeing someone else." Her lip quivers. "I loved you, Wes." Her eyes start to pool with tears. Turning to Kaite, she says, "Let's go." They leave without giving me a chance to explain my actions.

Kaite sticks out her tongue at me, revealing it's very pink. "Not ok."

"Wait, it's not what you think-" I say, shouting after her. I hesitantly start after them, but Kaite pushes me back. "Don't follow us, perv," she orders.

My jaw flexes. I turn around, debating what to do. I think DW knows I don't want to leave, but she gives a wave. "It's ok, Weston. Go." Her brown eyes glisten at me with sweet understanding.

I nod assuredly and state, "I'll be right back." I spin around and take two steps, then pause. The girls moved quickly and are already out of sight. My chest tightens. If I go after Hannah now, the probability of me returning is quite low. I look back at DW. She resumes eating her lunch, unfazed. I realize, watching her, I don't want to leave. I'll deal with Hannah later, if at all.

"You're back," she says with a hint of disbelief in her voice as I sit back down across from her.

I lay a hand on the table. "Yeah, sorry about that." I scratch the side of my head. "Those two are nothing but drama."

"I'm guessing that's one of the reasons why you wanted to avoid them today."

I nod. "Is that pathetic of me?"

The right corner of her lips curls up subtly. "Nope." She takes a swig of her chocolate milk. "I think, if you're broken up, then it's not your problem anymore."

This reassures me that I'm not the jerk Hannah and Kaite probably think I am. Even though I can't stand the thought of them, or anyone for that matter, hating me, it felt good to let it go. My eyes shift to the ground, then back up to her. "You're probably right."

She shuffles in her seat. "Oh, I know I'm right."

"Your confidence amazes me," I compliment, wishing other girls our age were similar.

Her mouth partly opens like I caught her off guard. Her shoulders slump a little before saying, "I'm not-well, I…" She trails off, looking at the ground. Her gaze quickly shifts back to me. "I try to be," she states plainly.

I put a hand in my jeans pocket. "Well, you're doing a good job."

She sits a bit straighter. "It's not something that comes natural to me, and I'll never be as cocky as you, Mr. President," she chuckles. That is one adjective I've not used to describe myself. Interesting. I smirk.

She adds, "But one day I was talking to Monica. She's my best friend by the way, and we just decided to stop caring about what anyone thinks of us. So that helps."

"I wish I didn't care what people thought," I say without thinking. Why would I admit that to someone I hardly know? Yet, as I sit here across from her, dare I say it feels so comfortable. I know how illogical it sounds, but it's like I've known this girl my whole life. Maybe I have?

DW tilts her head. "You really care what people think of you?"

"How do you not?" I huff, running a hand through my hair lightly so as to not mess it up.

She stares at me concernedly. "But-but you're the student body president," she stammers. "You were the Prom King."

I prop my elbows on the table and bury my face in my hands. "I know," I say, exhaling. I remove my hands, uncovering my face and state, "And let's not forget how I was captain of the basketball team, also the valedictorian. Oh, what else…." I count on my fingers all the clubs I've been a part of throughout the course of four years. "Spanish club, golf, French, cooking, foreign language club, debate team and the list goes on." I'm out of breath. DW looks at me horrified. Her brows furrowed, face frozen.

After a moment of silence, she breaks it by saying, "Wow, Wes, that seems like a lot."

"Facts, and imagine if I didn't care what people thought of me, being a part of all those clubs?" I shake my head. "It's a luxury I can't afford. I envy you."

DW slowly turns her head from side to side. "I don't understand. If you didn't want to be in all those clubs, why did you enroll?"

"I didn't really have a choice." What I don't say is this was all my mother's plan. All those clubs and extracurriculars look good on college applications. I had nothing to do with picking them out. Admittedly, if I were to do it all again, I probably wouldn't change a thing. It was a lot of work, but it definitely paid off.

"Everyone has a choice," she states profoundly.

That's where she's wrong. I look away and at the same time hear a couple of kids from our school say, "Hey, it's Wes." I see Kim Krestruder right away. She was a girl from my AP history class I took last year. She walks up to our table with two guys, Aaron Daniels and Kip Reagen. There's another girl with them who looks familiar, but I can't place her name. See, DW shouldn't be offended. It's not just her name I can't remember. It was too much of a challenge to successfully memorize all 500 of our graduating class. Truthfully, I am good at many things, but I do have my limitations.

I stand to fist bump them one by one. "Hey."

"Sup," they each say in greeting me.

"Where are you headed?" I ask Kim who seems to be the leader of the group. I stifle a smile, realizing they must have also ditched their prospective chaperones. Classic.

"We got the lightning lane for that new ride where Splash Mountain used to be. So, we were heading over there," Kim answers, attempting to hurry her group. "Let's go, guys."

"Sick. Have fun," I tell them.

"See ya, Weston," the group says in unison before heading off.

It was a brief interaction, but I am painfully aware of how none of them acknowledged DW's existence. I hardly know those kids, and yet, this type of thing happens to me all the time at school. I gulp. For the first time I feel a little embarrassed by my popularity. I turn around slowly, not wanting to see DWs reaction, but she's gone. Where did she go? I look at the table and see that the brown bag that held her lunch has disappeared.

"DW?" I yell, looking around the courtyard. "Dole Whip Girl?" She has to be nearby. I walk around the restaurant, looking high and low. There is no sign of her. I take my chair and drag it into the middle of the New Orleans district courtyard with the intent of standing on it. I bring one knee up, resting my foot against the seat. People around me are starting to stare. Grimacing, I set my foot down. Nope. I am not doing this. I return the chair promptly back to the table because I refuse to act so impulsively about a girl I barely know.

"Weston?"

My heart thuds.

DW laughs. "What are you doing?"

Nonchalantly, I place the yearbook back into my bag, then take the plastic baggy and empty juice box to the trash. "What am I doing? Nothing. Just cleaning up. You?" I sound like an idiot. And-oh my gosh, her backpack was still in her chair this entire time. How did I not see that?

She quiets her laugh. "Aww, did you think I ditched you?" she goads, grabbing her small blue backpack with Stitch ears popping out on either side.

"No." I throw on my own backpack and stand ready to go.

My face feels a bit flushed. That's embarrassing. "So what's next?" I say, desperately trying to make her forget what transpired. She kindly obliges me by taking out her map again to pick the next torture devise, I mean, ride. She points to one, which I think for the first time I will not object to.

We hop into the monorail, following a large group that I think are visiting from France because I cannot understand a word they are saying. I only took one French class freshman year. Yes, I was in the club but I only learned how to say, "Où se trouve la bibliothèque?" Not very helpful in this instance.

Sitting towards the back of the first train car, the large French group jumps into the seats in front of us. I try to ignore the feel of DW's leg grazing against mine. The monorail starts to move. This time, I feel no anxiety about it. In fact, I'm relieved. Maybe she will only pick out calming rides like this for the rest of the trip? I know that makes me delusional, but I'm pretending right now. The wind feels great on my face. We could use the shade too. The heat is getting unbearable.

"Are you going to stop whining and just follow me onto the next ride?" DW asks, smirking. The monorail is coming to another stop. I hear the conductor tell us where we are, and my insides twist. Why does this not surprise me?

I groan, "Ugh, Star Wars Land?" following her off the monorail.

"It's actually called Galaxy's Edge," she corrects me. I think she's a little too excited. I recall from this morning how Gabe said he wanted to come here. My fingers instinctively start tapping on the side of my leg. Great, now I feel all jittery. I really don't want to run into them because I know I won't hear the end of it. "Why did you ditch us? You're our strategy guy. What happened to Hannah?" I close my eyes, then open them. I just can't.

"Something wrong?" DW asks, folding her paper map and

putting it in her pocket. She frowns. "Don't tell me you're not a Star Wars fan?"

I fold my arms. "Well, actually, no I'm not. In fact, I've never seen the movies, but that's not why-"

DW's jaw drops. "Wait, you've never seen any of the movies?" she interjects.

"I mean, I may have seen clips at friends' houses," I state, thinking of the times I've spent over at Gabe's house and had one of those movies playing in the background. "But no, I can't say I ever have. They aren't my cup of tea."

"Why not? And you can't say it's because you hate Disney because the director didn't sell his movies to Disney until 2012," she says with all seriousness. This girl knows her stuff.

I try not to laugh. Actually, I do find her passion for sci-fi fantasy films to be very cute.

"Look, I get the hype, and I'm not dissing anyone for liking Star Wars. I just personally don't have any interest in it."

DW ponders that then adds, "Ok, I can respect that, even if I think you're wrong." She smirks, her fingers pulling on the straps of her backpack. "I'm curious, what are you interested in?" Her face reddens. "Like movie-wise, of course."

The corners of my mouth curl. "Of course," I repeat to her. Taking in a breath, I release it and say, "To be honest, I don't remember the last time I went to a movie and actually paid attention. I don't have a lot of interest in films. That and I don't have a lot of spare time to actually watch them."

DW looks down. "Oh, I see, but if you did have the time," she asks, looking up, "what would you put on Netflix, for instance?"

"I don't have Netflix."

She gasps. "You don't have Netflix?"

"No, but my brother does," I answer, concealing a smile. She looks so bothered. I'm way too into it. "What I do have is Discovery+ and when I get around to watching anything, it's usually documentaries on the universe or DNA." She glances up at me. "Pretty boring, right?"

She shakes her head. "I'm going to have to circle back to the you-having-a-brother thing, but," she pauses.

Shoot. The last thing I want to talk about is my family right now. I hope she forgets I said that.

"Ok. No, that completely makes sense." DW smiles. "It should surprise me but it doesn't. You really love learning, don't you?"

"Yeah, I really do." I peer at her and she looks at me with understanding. At this moment, I can deduce how well she seems to know me. I feel a ripple in my chest. If only I could remember her name.

Breaking my gaze, DW pauses in front of a coffee shop where there are a couple of signs telling us where to go. I suck in a breath. Better draw her attention away from anything related to my family. The last thing I want to do is divulge dull information about how we are completely dysfunctional, much like most American families. This reassures me that maybe she would understand, if I decided to share it.

"Hey, how about I wait here and you go on whatever rides you want? I'll buy you a coffee or smoothie, whatever you want." I point at the coffee shop with the overpriced menu. The alternative would be to buy her a souvenir. I'm hoping getting a drink is cheaper. God, I wish tutoring math on the weekends paid more. I hope she lets me buy my way out of this one. I just don't want to be here. The people in this part of the park are very intense fans. I wonder if they can sense my disdain just by glancing at me.

True, they didn't make this area of the park until after I swore to never return. By that fact alone I should not have a problem being here. Yet, from what I've seen on the internet and heard from Gabe, these rides are bound to make me more motion sick than any of the other rides at Disneyland. Especially after we just ate. I'd rather not repeat the same retching episode from this morning. I shudder. Throwing up is the worst, but dizziness is even more horrendous. Perhaps I should hunt down some Dramamine. Right now I feel fine enough, though.

DW places her hands on her hips. "I thought we were past this? Now did you or did you not agree to this game?"

"I mean, not really."

She stares at me, one brow raised. "You're joking?"

I acquiesce, "Ok, ok, you're right. I agreed." I throw up my arms in defense. "But if I get sick again, I'm out."

DW brings her hand to her chin, making a reflective face. "Fair enough." She grins, rocking on her heels. "Since I'm pretty sure it's all in your head." She grabs my backpack strap again and pulls me along. Silly girl. I suppress a grin as I drag my feet behind her.

At least, this part of the amusement park wasn't here back then, and as long as I don't run into my friends or Hannah, I actually think there is a slight chance I won't completely hate it. Maybe I'll even have a little fun? I frown, kidding myself. This is still Disneyland. How could any of it be fun?

DW leads me to the ride with the longest line yet. We stand at the entrance of Rise of the Resistance, another ride bound to leave me feeling dizzy and debate whether or not it's worth the two hour wait. I try very hard to convince her that it will be as a lightbulb turns on in my head. The longer we wait in this line, the less rides I'll be dragged onto, but she sees right through my poor attempt to trick her into staying here. It was worth a shot.

"We can always come back to this one during the fireworks," she says, pulling me out of line. I shoot her a cryptic look that she doesn't catch.

Fireworks? Why would she say anything about the fireworks?

Logically, she must not have anything to do with the yearbook message if she's talking about coming back here to miss them. So, it's not her. I make a mental note in my head to rule her out. Although, maybe she's trying to throw me off? Maybe she doesn't want me to know it's her yet. I scratch my head. That makes no sense. I groan silently. This is getting complicated.

"What are you thinking about now?" she inquires playfully, acknowledging the silence on my end.

"Oh, nothing. I just assumed you would want to watch the fireworks," I challenge her.

We stand in line at the Millennium Falcon ride. There are a ton of people ahead of us. DW stands in front of me, waiting ever so patiently to move forward.

She glances back at me, smirking. "You know what happens when you assume…"

I roll my eyes very slowly. "Well, I *assumed* it was Disney tradition." I mimic her emphasis on "ass" in the word assume.

"Not everything has to be a Disney tradition." She chuckles, turning back around. "Plus, I make my own traditions."

She said that very ambiguously. If she really is the girl who wrote in my yearbook, then maybe this will trigger her to confess. Feeling flirtatious, I bend down and say close to her ear, "You want to know a secret?" My pulse quickens. Her breath stifles. She doesn't move an inch. I lean a little closer as I whisper a true fact about myself, "I love the fireworks."

CHAPTER 6
Teacups

O k, that wasn't so bad," I admit to Dole Whip Girl, exiting the ride. She looks all too pleased that I did not get nauseous. There was a moment when I thought I was done for, but watching DW laugh and squeal with the other riders seemed to have tricked my mind into being fine.

She gives me a light shove. "See, I told you it was all in your head."

Suppressing a grin, I roll my eyes. Yet she calls me the know-it-all.

We walk down a set of stairs and find ourselves in the shadow of the giant ship called the Millennium Falcon. Unfortunately, Disney built it extremely well, and I admit, it is impressive to look at. I still can't believe I just experienced a ride like that without it ending up with me spilling more contents of my stomach. I give DW a side glance and contemplate what she said about it being all in my head. Maybe she is onto something? Nah. I may not have gotten sick, but there were moments during the ride I truly felt a bit dizzy. Nonetheless, I'm sticking with her.

She is fumbling through the map and looking at her phone, going back and forth, like a mad woman. "Ugh, we won't have time to go all the way down to Tomorrowland without us missing out on the rides in Fantasyland," she mutters. "But maybe we can cut through the castle before the-" Her voice is low. I don't hear the end of that sentence.

I raise a brow. "You know, you owe me another letter."

"Yes, yes, hold on Mr. President." She looks a bit flustered.

I step beside her to see if I can help. "Want me to take a look? I am very good at making strategies, or so my friends tell me."

DW laughs, "What, are you suddenly fine with going on the rides now?"

I give her a light nudge. "I've gone through the five stages of grief and am now at acceptance," I quip, grabbing the right side of the map. She keeps hold of the left side. "We should go this way first to maximize our trajectory of hitting all the rides before sundown," I say, pointing at Fantasyland.

"All of the rides?"

"Shut up." Even I am in disbelief of what I just said.

After begging DW to use the Disney app to optimize wait times, we practically run to Peter Pan's flight. The approximate wait time is about 35 minutes. DW said it's normally an hour wait to get on this ride, since it's one of the popular ones. The last time I rode this was with Ma and Brenden. Actually, thinking back on it, it was Ma's favorite. I can easily recall running through the line and all three of us hopping on the ride. I don't know what it was, but something about flying through the air really made me feel like Peter Pan, the boy who refuses to grow up. Whatever that means. For once, since joining DW on this adventure, she does not have to drag me on. I must have underestimated the power of nostalgia.

At the end of the ride, we start in the direction of It's a Small World. DW had to practically beg me to agree to that one, but it's one of her favorites. Regrettably, I go along with it. At least it is not the heinous teacups.

"It's not the ride I have a problem with. I just can't stand that song." I clench my eyes, shaking my head. "It gets stuck in your head." So annoying.

"You are such a hater, you know that, right?" she says, chuckling.

"I know," I reply smugly.

Passing the flying Dumbo ride, I hear DW make a muffling noise, like a quiet gasp. I don't think she meant for me to hear that. I peer over at her and notice she's looking at the teacup ride with such longing. The pit in my stomach I thought was gone returns. Under no circumstances will I get on that ride. I remain silent as we walk right past it. DW's peppy energy seems to be muted. Our pace slows. Why do I feel guilty? I've been going on every other ride and even came up with a plan to get on the rest of them before the park closes. My only stipulation was saying that this ride is off limits. I think that's pretty reasonable.

DW slows her steps to an altogether stop next to a food cart. "Oh," she utters with a breathy tone. "I forgot to give you another letter."

I sigh. "You really want to ride the teacups, don't you?" My stomach is in knots.

She flashes a shy grin. "Was it that obvious?"

I return a grin. "Yeah."

"Well, look, I know you said it was off limits. You don't have to go with me." She bites her lip, looking around, then meets my gaze. "But would you mind waiting for me? The line doesn't look too long." The hopeful gleam in her brown eyes is back. She is completely hopeless.

"Yeah, of course." I nod. "Here, let me hold your backpack." My hand is already outstretched.

She takes off her tiny Stitch-eared backpack. Smiling, she hands it to me and says, "I'll tell you my name when I get back."

She winks at me. A chill enters my body. Finally, she will be more than Dole Whip Girl. She will have a name and I will remember it.

I hang onto the blue leather straps of her backpack and watch her saunter over to the ride. Without realizing it, my feet begin trotting off after her. I suck in a deep breath. It doesn't make sense for me to wait for her all the way down here. There's really no harm in getting closer. I gulp, not believing how close I am to the ride I vowed to never set foot on again. Maybe she will want a picture? No. That's dumb.

I stand off to the side and out of view of DW. She practically walks right onto the ride, since there are not many people in line. She hops into a blue tea cup with flowers painted on the outside, looking all too happy. The ride starts, and everyone begins to spin. My brow furrows. I touch my chest, which is starting to feel a little tight. No. No, I can't do this. Why am I here? I should go, but I can't just ditch DW.

My eyes frantically look for her. Oh, no. I lost her. There are so many teacups spinning round and round. Which one is her? Searching the tea cups has my vision in a blur. The more I watch them spin, the more dizzy I feel. I bring a hand to my chest. It feels so hot. Am I sweating? Of course I am sweating. The sun is beaming right down on me. This is not good. I'm about to take off when bright red hair catches my eye. There she is, spinning away in a giant teacup, having the time of her life. She is smiling so big. I think I love her smile. One corner of my mouth curls upward. She is Alice in her own Wonderland. I stare at her in amusement. As I watch her, a vague memory comes to mind. Yes. It's coming back to me. Wait, I do know her. I know Dole Whip Girl.

At the same time I have this realization, the ride comes to a stop. Breathing in and out, I get the overwhelming urge to run to her. I do just that. Throwing her backpack over my shoulder, it lands on top of mine as I rush over to the line.

"Excuse me, sorry," I say, cutting the people that have been waiting. They are muttering insults, but I don't hear them. My eyes are fixed on Dole Whip Girl. She is standing in the teacup, ready to exit the ride. I wave my hands to get her attention. She doesn't see me.

At the front of the line, I close my eyes, dreading what I'm about to do. "Sarah!" I shout, opening them. She steps out of the teacup and freezes at the sound of her name.

"Hey, you can't do that," the ride operator yells.

Ignoring him, I dash into the ride. This is probably the most impulsive thing I have ever done. I run to her like some lovesick teenager, very unlike me. She grins at the sight of me. As I approach her, my lips part and I say, "Sarah. Your name is Sarah."

Her eyes grow wide. She stares at me, slack-jawed.

"Alright, fine," I hear the operator say. "What do I care if you cut everyone, just get in a teacup and sit down."

My eyes flicker over to the operator. "Wait, no." I spin around. Almost all the teacups are filled with eager riders.

"Here, this one is open," I hear DW-I mean, Sarah say. I turn around to see her climbing into a pink one.

I close my eyes, trying to stabilize my already spinning head. No. No, I need to get off now. I pry my eyes open, but the music is starting, and so is the ride. The operator commands me for the last time to sit down. Lamentably, I'm forced to climb in, next to Sarah. I set both our backpacks down in the empty space next to us.

Sarah looks at me concernedly. "Are you ok, Weston?"

The cup begins to spin. My stomach quivers. I will undoubtedly throw up by the end of this ride. Clenching to the sides of the cup, she says something else, but I can't hear her. The sound of her voice is stifled. That's strange. The music is also fading. I reel in pain over the steering wheel. My insides feel like a boxed puzzle being tossed around violently. The ride spins faster and faster, making the tightness in my chest increase. I inhale deeply. What is happening to me? I take another deep breath, but it's cut short. I breathe in again and again. Faster and faster. It's not enough air. I sit up, grabbing my throat. I can't breathe. My heart is racing out of control. Why can't I get enough oxygen? I fear I may be suffocating.

Gasping for air, I look over at Sarah, but she is not there. She's gone. I turn my head around to look at the people in the other teacups; all their faces are blurred. Frantic, my eyes search beyond the ride. My heart rate slows a little at the sight of the other people still in line. Yet, everything starts to spin in slow motion.

I look down at my hands, shaking. I glance up at the crowd and recognize a face I haven't seen in years. Is that him? Tears fill my eyes which should impair my vision, but what I see, I see clearly. He's there. I can't believe it. He's actually there, like he promised.

The sound of my brother's laughter fills my ears with delight like an old song I haven't heard in years. I look over at him. He's spinning the tea cup wheel as fast as he can. I join in the laughter, then point out at the crowd. I say, "Look. Appa. He's here." We both wave, but he doesn't wave back at us.

"Dad, look over here!" my young voice shouts. Father isn't looking at us. Instead, he's focused on my mother who's pointing at him, then back at us. She is frowning, yelling. Her demeanor is intense, angry even. Why is she so angry? Dad finally meets my gaze. He stares at me, only at me, with swollen eyes. He mouths something, but I can't make it out.

I try calling out, "Dad!" waving wildly. I yell again, "Appa!" He remains there for a moment. Hope flutters through my chest. My eyes shift to my mom who's now turned her back. Why is she doing this to me, to us? My teary eyes shift to my father, but he isn't there anymore. Brenden laughs, unfazed. Optimistically, I help him spin the teacup, round and around. We smile like there's nothing to be upset about because we are at the happiest place on earth. Nothing bad ever happens here.

Next thing I know, everything fades to black. I close my eyes and open them again, only to find myself in my third grade classroom. It's morning. I had just been dropped off at school. I am sitting at my desk, next to my friends who are silent. In fact, everyone is silent because they all know what happened and no one knows what to say. The entire day flashes before my eyes. No one speaks to me, aside from my teachers who are trying to distract me by giving me the most envied job of the third grade, erasing the white board. I, being naturally good at games, always get to do it as a reward for winning, but that day we didn't play any games.

After erasing half of the board, one of the girls in my class comes up to me. Her hair is tied up in uneven pigtails. She grabs the other eraser to help me reach the higher spots. She is taller than me. I can hear the kids at their desks snickering to each other because her socks don't match. I erase faster. Right as I finish, she hands me a piece of paper folded over like a card. She smiles at me, wide, revealing two missing front teeth. The card has a heart on it with the word "sorry" misspelled. I take it, but the sound of my friends' laughter makes my cheeks redden. I crumple it up and throw it in the trash. She frowns and walks away, shoulders slumped. At the end of the day, I am the last one to leave. Huffing, I run to the trash can and take out the card, shoving it into my pocket before anyone notices. When I get home, I take it out and read what's on the inside. "I don't have a daddy either. Let's be friends." I cry myself to sleep.

When I wake up, something is still not right. It's like I'm stuck inside this hazy dream that I almost remember. Dole Whip Girl is there. She's 14 years old like me. Her pretty smile has me in a trance. My eyes flicker as a switch turns on in my head. Her name is Sarah Lackey. She is the same girl who gave me the purple card. I remember now because I had seen her freshman year.

Our entire grade had to participate in a school play, Beauty and the Beast. I was cast as Cogsworth the Clock of all characters. I remember being so nervous, I succumbed to my first panic attack. Not knowing what to do or how to breathe, I found myself locked away in the props closet. I didn't know I was having a panic attack at the time until I started sobbing profusely. I snuck into the closet so as to not embarrass myself, but Sarah was there. At first, I was horrified that a kid from class saw me in such a vulnerable state. Despite feeling mortified, I couldn't get a hold of myself. I don't recall much else, except she stayed with me until I calmed down. When it was over, I simply said thank you and begged her not to tell a soul. Instead, I should have asked for her name.

CHAPTER 7
Ghosted

"Can you hear me?"

I try opening my eyes. "Huh?" My pupils adjust to the dim light of the twilight sky. It's still so bright, I blink multiple times.

An EMT medic is hovering two fingers above my face. "How many fingers am I holding up?" he asks.

"Sir, is he going to be ok? I'm calling his mother," I hear Mrs. Anderson's frantic voice.

I force myself to sit up. "What-what happened-"

"Whoa, hey, slow down, son. You had a severe anxiety attack that rendered you unconscious."

"Really?" I ask the medic in disbelief, blinking sporadically. My face does feel covered in sweat.

"Yes, but it could have been worse. If it wasn't for your girlfriend there, you would have suffered a concussion."

"Wes!" Sarah calls out, kneeling at my side. "Are you ok?" Her eyes are panic stricken.

"Back up. Give him some space." The medic lifts an arm. "Now, tell me, how many fingers am I holding up?" He follows up with some other questions about my name, birthdate, and the location. I answer each one to his satisfaction. He then reaches out a hand to promptly help me to my feet. "Here. Get hydrated." He hands me a water bottle.

"Thanks," I say, taking a long swig.

"Ok, see you soon." Mrs. Anderson hangs up with who I can only assume to be my mother. She turns to me and says hysterically, "Oh, good gracious, Weston." She offers me a consoling glance. "First, you kids disappear from my group, and now I find you unconscious?" Her eyes flutter frantically as she scowls. "Sir, should he go sit down somewhere and wait until his mother arrives?" She rubs her hands together.

The medic shakes his head up and down. "Yes, I'd advise it. Now, tell me how are you feeling, son?"

Mrs. Anderson's face is riddled with concern. She keeps rubbing her hands together. "Alright, let me go tell the other chaperones."

I let the corners of my mouth curl into the biggest smile I can manage. "Hold up, I'm good, completely fine." I touch my chest, assuring her and the medic. "Honestly, you don't need to worry about me, and if it's alright with you, I'd like to go on a few more rides." I don't really want to ride anything else, but I definitely don't want to hang out with Mrs. Anderson for the rest of the trip.

"As long as you drink that entire bottle and give it about ten minutes, I don't see a problem with that." The medic fist bumps me. "Just make sure you take it easy. No big rides or spinning ones, like that teacup ride where we found you."

"Oh, you won't have to worry about that. I will not be riding those again," I exclaim assuringly to the medic and Mrs. Anderson, giving them a half hearted laugh. Mrs. Anderson is not paying attention. She is too busy telling the others over the phone about my situation. I slump. Great. Soon, everyone is going to know what happened. That means it's a matter of time before Trey and the guys show up. Good Lord. I bet everyone on this trip is going to find out. How embarrassing. I'll be in next week's school paper. "Class Valedictorian had a panic attack at Disneyland." Lowering my head, I think, "I'll never live this down." Guaranteed, this will be brought up at any future class reunions.

I look over at Sarah. The concern on her face is still there, but the sun is in a position that hits her hair, causing it to glisten. It is an even more bright shade of red. It's radiant. How did I not notice her before? It reminds me of the time she saw me have my first panic attack. I was glad she was there back then. I'm glad she is here now. I should have remembered her name.

While waiting for Mrs. Anderson's directions, I take note of my surroundings. Looks like I am still inside the park and near the entrance. Suddenly, I realize how exposed I am at this Red Cross station, being that it is half inside and half outside. I take a moment to adjust to my location. Mrs. Anderson purses her lips, hanging up her phone. She goes on to explain to Sarah and me that she won't let us out of her sight. Sarah shoots me a look. We share a very concerned glance. There is no way I'm getting out of this one, not without help, anyway.

The medic zips his medical bag and bids us goodnight, disappearing behind a counter.

Rather than giving up, Sarah whispers, "Hold on." She grins slyly. "I think Wes needs to use the restroom," she tells Mrs. Anderson. Brilliant idea. "Don't worry, I'll escort him," she says, wrapping an arm around me. I go with it and allow her to pretend to help me walk. What is surprising is that I feel fine, great even. However, it is a tad bit fun to pretend otherwise, especially since I get to lean against Sarah. The feel of her shoulders underneath my arm is making me a bit lightheaded. In the best way.

"Now, wait just a minute," Mrs. Anderson starts. She is quickly interrupted by her ringing phone. She answers it in a fluster and gives us the signal to leave. She holds the phone slightly away from her as she says, "I'm not letting you out of my sight. I won't keep you from using the facilities, but best be sure, I'll be waiting right here when you're done. Understood?" Mrs. Anderson assures us before bringing the phone back to her ear.

I smile widely. "You got it, Mrs. A." I wink. She is once again too preoccupied to notice. That gives me hope we will be able to slip her attention again. Thank goodness she is not very observant.

The restrooms are in eyesight of the medic station. Escaping is going to be near to impossible only if Mrs. Anderson is looking. We look for one of those unisex bathrooms to enter. I'm assuming so we can hatch a plan. Sarah lets me go in first so as to not draw attention to ourselves and to make sure Mrs. Anderson does not see us. Once she's inside, I feel myself relax a little. I approach the sink and splash some water on my face. Taking a paper towel, I pat down my face, hopefully wiping away some of the sweat beads. Sarah leans against the sink counter near the door, looking very concerned.

"So, are you ok, Weston?" she asks, moving part of her hair behind her ears.

"Yes, I'm fine…." I inhale, "I'm fine," then exhale.

Her brows draw together. "That was pretty scary."

Frowning, I admit, "It's not the first time." Sarah's eyes widen. "As you already know…." I wave my hand.

"You remembered?" She relaxes her face.

My eyes meet hers through the mirror. Seeing her now, knowing her real name, I can honestly say I'll never forget her again. "I'm sorry I ever forgot," I confess, lowering my head, ashamed.

She turns to face me so we are eye to eye. "It's ok."

"No, it's not ok." I stand facing her. "You were there for me back then, and I forgot your name. That's really messed up."

"I forgive you, Cogsworth." Sarah smiles, referencing the first time I had a panic attack and the only time I was ever cast in a school play. I shudder. Never again. Sarah's cheeks turn a bit pink. She adds, "It was a long time ago, and-and you're popular. You have like a zillion friends." She throws her hands up. "I don't hold that against you."

I return the grin. "Well, I'd like to make it up to you," I say, tilting my head down. Our eyes stay locked on each other.

"Oh really? How?" she asks alluringly. Her breath quickens.

I reach out my hand to take hers, but just before our fingers touch, I recall Mrs. Anderson saying she called my mom. I freeze, pulling back my hand. Ma! Oh crap. Remorsefully, I reach into my pocket for my phone. With a hand in my hair, I exclaim, "My mom's going to kill me. I have ten missed calls. Shoot, she's calling me now." I lift my gaze to meet hers, not wanting to ruin this moment. She can clearly see I'm not lying.

Sarah lowers her head. "You should answer that," breaking my vacant gaze.

My hair feels like it's a mess. I let my hand drop. "I know…" The moment drops with it.

Taking a step toward the door, she adds, "I'll see you outside," then proceeds to walk out of the restroom.

"Sarah, wait," I call out after her, but she's already halfway out the door. At the same time, my thumb instinctively taps on the green button of my phone screen.

"Ma?" I answer.

"In-Su? In-Su? Hello? Can hear me?" She sounds worried.

"Yes, Ma, I can hear you."

"What happened?" she asks, switching to Korean.

"Nothing, I just-"

Before I can get out another word, she's already saying, "Don't worry I'm coming to pick you up. In-su, did you really abandon your teacher today? I raised you better than that," she groans. She pauses for half a millisecond before continuing.

"The GPS says I'll be there a quarter after ten. So, I want you to stay by your teacher until I come, and don't go on any more rides. Is that clear?"

Pressing a finger to my temple, I reply with a soft and polite, "Yes, Ma." Without letting me explain myself further, she hangs up. The fact that she still treats me like a child is baffling. However, rather than fighting with her, like Brenden, I sit there and take it because I could not fathom disappointing her. I shove the phone back into my pocket.

It's been quite a day. I take in a couple deep breaths. I sigh, looking at myself in the mirror. There's a tousled piece of my hair standing up near my cowlick. Dang, I always have trouble with that. I run a hand under some water to fix it and pat it down. Looks decent enough. Exhaling, I see the teacups in my mind's eye. The spinning really got to me. Obviously, I didn't handle that well.

An image of Dad pops up in my head. I haven't thought about him in a while. There goes another ripple in my chest. I shake my head, causing the image to disappear. I do not want to think about that right now. Soon, I'll start feeling dizzy all over again. Can't let that happen. The first thing to replace the thought is the message in my yearbook. The message spells itself out before me in the unique handwriting of whoever wrote it. "Meet me at the castle." That's it. I pull out my phone. There's still time. This is my last chance to find out who wrote that message.

My thoughts about the mystery girl are interrupted by a knock at the door. Must be Sarah. She is probably wondering if I'm coming out. The knocking gets louder and more erratic, almost like there are multiple—

"Oh," I say, prying open the door.

Stumbling out of the bathroom, I am immediately greeted by my friends. Crap. They found me. No. No. No. This was not a part of the plan.

Trey grabs onto my hand, pulling me in for a bro hug. "Bruhhh, we heard what happened."

"Yeah, are you good?" Gabe asks.

"We heard from Kat White that you fainted?" Jeb places his hands on the top of his head.

"That's crazy, bro." Drew mirrors the same sentiments.

Without revealing the truth of what triggered the attack, I tell them what happened. Not even Sarah knows the truth. Wait, where is she? I look around for her face but she's nowhere to be seen. I look past Trey and the guys, but all I spot are pink mouse ears. I clench my eyes shut. That's just great. Not only do I have to deal with having had a panic attack, now I must interact with my ex again. I wish I could go back to this morning when I started following Sarah around.

Where is that girl?

Hannah and Kaite both approach me, caution in their step. Hannah looks torn like she wants to commit to being angry with me, but at the same time is super concerned about my well being. Kaite is completely unbothered, as always.

"So what happened to you?" Kaite asks, pitifully. I stare down at her lamentably.

Hannah has her hands wrapped around herself like she's a wounded animal. "Everyone is talking about your fainting spell. Is that true?" Her voice is soft and sincere.

I shove my hands into my pockets. "I didn't faint. I mean, kind of, but I'm ok."

"She wasn't asking if you were ok," Kaite blurts.

Hannah gives her a look of disdain. Meeting my gaze again, she says, "I was worried about you."

"Thanks," I say. Kaite scoffs. It takes a lot of self control for me to not roll my eyes. Since they are both here, I decide now is as good a time as any to deal with the aftermath of our breakup. Focusing back on Hannah, I ask her, "Look, can we talk for a second...*Alone*," I propose, reaching for her hand. I try to hide the contempt in my eyes as I glower at Kaite. It's time I put an end to whatever she thinks is still going on between us. What I ultimately want to get across is that I never wanted to hurt Hannah. She was a good girlfriend and deserves to know that.

"She doesn't want to talk to you, cheater," Kaite barks at me in disgust.

Trey and the guys back up very dramatically with their hands up. Cowards.

"Uh-oh. Someone's in trouble," both Trey and Gabe jab.

Hannah pushes out her bottom lip, nodding at Kaite who storms off unhappily. I have to hold back a grin. My eyes shift back to meet Hannah's. Her blue eyes beam up at me a little too eagerly. Well, that's strange. I always thought her eyes were extraordinary. Now that I'm looking at them again I can't help but wish I was staring at the various gold flakes in Sarah's brown irises. I shake my head, moving us away from the bathrooms. Forget Sarah for a second. Time to focus.

"Yo, Wes, no ghosting us this time, alright?" I hear Trey shout.

Gabe and the guys chime in with a resounding, "Yeah, you're stuck with us now!"

"Chill, I'll be right back," I say, turning my head. Trey and I share a glance. I lift an eyebrow, shifting my eyes from Hannah back to him. He nods at me, understanding I'm just going to talk with my ex.

A few paces away, we stand near a food cart, still in view of Mrs. Anderson and the guys, but far enough that we are out of earshot. A yellow picture of ice cream catches my eye. I suppress a grin when I notice we are standing near a food cart selling Dole Whips. Most coincidental.

"Well?" Hannah exclaims daftly.

"Right." Suddenly, I forget why I'm standing here. My head slightly jolts. "Let me set the record straight. I'm not seeing anyone else," I begin, thinking it's a good place to start. "That girl you saw me with is just a friend." I bite the inside of my lip, hoping she bought it.

Her eyebrows shoot up. She places a hand on her hip. "You expect me to believe nothing is going on between you and that weird redheaded girl?" she exclaims angrily with one finger in the air. "Weston, you were holding her in your arms when I saw you." Her mouth curls downward. She yanks her hand away from mine. Not good.

"So, you don't believe me?" I grind my teeth, bringing a hand to my forehead, not knowing what else to say.

Something is definitely wrong with me today. Instead of speaking or thinking with any logic at all, everything in my head is a missorted, jumbled mess. I feel like I'm in art class with Mr. Kendricks who's trying to explain abstract paintings. There are no formulas, no solutions, and no limits. There are only feelings and emotions, a skill in which understanding them is something I cannot list on a resume yet. I'll have to see if Harvard has a communications class that can turn me into a proper empath.

"You are unbelievable," Hannah spits out. "It's like I don't even know you anymore." She starts sniffing. "I just-I can't believe you already found someone else." She takes a step back.

"No, it's not like that," I say, reaching out for her hand again. Tears begin to well up in her eyes. The last thing I want is her crying, but my initial reaction is to tell her she's being ridiculous. Yet, something Sarah said comes to the forefront of my mind. I immediately act on impulse and pull Hannah in for an embrace. She wraps her arms around me, tight. "It's not your fault, ok," I say, patting her head. "This-this has nothing to do with you." My voice weakens. Just last week hugging her was the best part of my day. Now I cannot wait to let her go.

She lifts up her head from my chest. "What do you mean?"

I clear my throat. "Ehm, nothing." I press her head back into the now wet spot on my gray Thrasher brand shirt. "What I mean to say is, you were the best girlfriend any guy like me could ask for, you understand?" I step back, separating us, and lift her chin. No matter how bitter the words I'm saying taste, I still mean them. Her eyes shine even more through the tears. I wipe one away from her cheek with my thumb. She really is a beautiful girl. Any guy would be lucky to date her. I lick my lips. "I know how much this trip means to you." My eyes fall to the ground. I sigh, not knowing what else to say other than, "I'm sorry, Hannah."

She is taken aback for a moment, but her face is beginning to soften. The glitter on her cheekbones shimmers elegantly in the sun. It just adds to the natural beauty of her flawless porcelain skin. I admit there is a physical attraction between us. I must be an idiot to have broken up with the hottest girl in school. She puckers her rose pigmented lips, batting her long lashes at me as she squeezes my hand. I know what she wants, and this would be the perfect moment to do it. The temptation is there, but something in my gut tells me to step away.

My arms settle at my sides. "Look, can we just forget about the girl, forget about the past, and put all this behind us?" I press my lips together, not believing what I'm about to ask. "And make the rest of this day," I pause, forcing a grin so wide it makes my cheeks hurt, "a magical one?"

Hannah beams. Her tears practically disappear when she pulls me in for another embrace, placing a soft kiss on my cheek. "Oh, Wes. That's all I wanted to hear." She lets me go. "Will you come on some rides with me?" She smiles at me with bright, hopeful eyes, making the offer impossible for me to refuse. "I mean, if you're up for it. I don't want you to faint again."

I chuckle. "Nah, I'll be fine." See? I'm not heartless after all. Sarah would be proud.

A knot in my stomach twists. Oh god. I really don't want to go on another ride unless it is with— no, I really can't do another one, no matter who I'm with, but what choice do I have.

It's either that or I'll have to stay here with Mrs. Anderson. That cannot happen. Going on more rides with my ex is the lesser of two evils.

Still, I have to find a way out of it. The fireworks will go off in precisely one hour and 43 minutes. I have until then to find this mystery girl, which could be Sarah or Hannah. I sneer. God, I hope it is not Hannah. The truth is, part of me wishes it to be the girl I hardly know but spent almost the whole day with. I look around for any sign of her. Where did she go? I only see Mrs. Anderson yapping with a few of the medical personnel. Behind her is the counter with a black bag sitting on top.

"Hold on," I say, touching my shoulders and chest. "I left my backpack."

"She seems distracted enough," Hannah states, following my gaze. "If you go now, I'm sure you can swipe it without her noticing."

"Yeah, ok."

"I think Trey and the guys were talking about going to the Matterhorn," she mentions, checking her phone. "Looks like the wait time is going up so we gotta hurry." She blows me a kiss before heading over to Kaite. "You coming?"

"Yes, I'll be right there," I say in all earnestness because if I owe the girl anything, it's at least one ride at a place she loves. Hannah winks. Something in the glint of her eye gives me the impression she does not understand we are still broken up. I wave at her as I begin backing up. I would clear things up, but I'm so over it.

My pulse quickens as I pass behind Mrs. Anderson. I let out a breath. She is too wrapped up in conversation with a medic, a different guy than the one who assisted me, to notice I'm nabbing the bag. Hold on, this isn't mine. It has a red cross on it. It probably belongs to the medic. I scratch my head, looking around for my own black backpack. In fact, where is Sarah's? They were both in this vicinity. Unless someone stole it, but there are so many authority figures around, it seems unlikely. Then again, maybe the person who isn't here is the one who took it. Did she really take off with my stuff? That's what I should be concerned about-my stuff. I should not, however, be anxious about seeing her again.

Mrs. Anderson is still deep in conversation, but she spots me at the counter. "Oh, good. I almost thought you wandered off again," she exclaims. Oddly enough, the medic she is with promptly resumes speaking with her. Maybe he's the supervisor? I don't know. He seems into her though. I have to suppress a grin. They are chatting like old friends, laughing at jokes I do not understand.

Once Mrs. Anderson's head is turned again, I bolt towards Trey and the guys. Hannah and Kaite are also with them, looking impatient to leave this part of the park. I nod at them, pointing and signaling that we need to go now.

"Let's gooo!" Trey says a little too loudly.

"Come on, now's our chance," I say, rushing past the group. They follow me hastily.

"We're going straight to the Matterhorn, right?" Hannah asks, matching her walking pace with mine. I have to ignore the scoffs coming from Kaite's direction as she tries to keep up.

"Yeah, that's where you want to go, right?" I say.

Gabe comes up behind us and puts his hands on my shoulder and hers. "You know, it's good to see you guys back together." The ears from his baby Yoda hat are hitting my neck.

"We're not back together," I state as nicely as possible. "B-but we are friends, right?" I quickly add.

Hannah sighs like she is disappointed, but reluctantly agrees. There. That settles it. Even if she ends up being the mystery girl, I think she knows we are officially over.

"Aww, that's too bad. You guys made a cute couple." Gabe smacks his lips. "But, uh, so Hannah, are you free tomorrow night?" he cackles.

I jab him lightly on his side. "Stop."

We both hear Kaite blurt out, "Idiots."

"Had to shoot my shot," Gabe says before retreating to the back of the group where Drew and Jeb are walking. The nerve of that guy. I mean, it's not like I care if he wanted to ask Hannah out, but right in front of me? Geez. What a jerk.

Trey shuffles up to me, nose deep in his phone. I'm leading the way with him on my left and Hannah on my right. It suddenly feels like we are back in school. This is my squad. I wonder if this will be the last time we will all be together. My stomach feels a bit hollow. Not sure why I care, I'm ready to leave town. Yet, it makes me wonder if I'll see any of them again after graduation is over. There is a high probability that I won't, which is kind of depressing.

As much as I am looking forward to Harvard in the fall, I really think I'll miss this chapter of my life. That's probably why I wanted the summer for myself. Because maybe I want to be a kid just a little bit longer. I've never been the type to run around, being irresponsible and having fun with my friends, but it's starting to sound really good.

I know life doesn't work like that. Better to stick to the plan than act irrationally and mess it up.

How do people live like that anyway? Makes me think of that saying, "seize the day." I may not know her super well, but I can already tell Sarah seems to flourish living by that kind of philosophy. Part of me wants to experience that for once. It reminds me of my brother except I wish it would stop getting him into trouble. That is not sustainable.

CHAPTER 8
Distraction

We make our way to the Matterhorn quickly. In line, Hannah and Kaite whisper about something. I don't care to know. I just hope it isn't about me. I look back at the guys who are all on their phones. Typical. I pull out mine, but it's no use. My mind can't help but wonder about Sarah. Where is she right now, and did she, in fact, take my stuff?

If we were in line together, she'd probably make some kind of interesting commentary that would help take our minds off the wait. Darn it. I should have gotten her number. Why didn't I get her number? Idiot. If I had it now, I could text her to meet up. Sighing, I rub the back of my neck. Too bad. I wish she was here, though. Then again, looking around at my friends, I think the vibe would be way off if Sarah really was here.

Now that I know who she is, I recall passing her in the hall a few times after gym class which is next to the auditorium. She would be classified by Hannah and the cheer squad as a theater kid. We don't mix company with the theater kids. There's nothing wrong with them in my opinion, but our friend groups don't mesh. It has always been that way. For four years.

They are considered weird. It's part of the unspoken rules of high school, I guess. People on the cheer squad and people who play sports don't hang out with anyone outside their own confines. It is stupid and very shallow. I'm not ignorant. I know I am considered popular and therefore do not hang out with people like Sarah, but these rules should not apply to me. Since I was in so many clubs I feel as if I do not fit into one mold. I am not just a jock, I am also a debate captain. Not only can I make a 3-pointer on the court, I can also give directions to the nearest restaurant in French. Being a part of these clubs was not exactly my idea, but because of them I made friends with a lot of interesting people. Just because they are not in my inner circle shouldn't make them any less cool or important. Knowing my friends think otherwise does make me feel guilty. That might be why I try to go out of my way to be nice to everyone in passing down the hallways. This pseudo hierarchy is one thing I won't miss about high school. I just hope college isn't as superficial.

By the time we are next in line, the ride goes by so fast. I didn't have time to process it. Hannah was in front of me screaming her head off, but I was too preoccupied with the jolting turns that resulted in a headache. To my relief, however, at the end of the ride, my stomach contents remained inside. I'll take the win.

As we exited one by one, Trey and the guys began discussing what our last ride will be since we only have time for one more. Everyone seemed to have an opinion about which one to hit before closing. Since I seemed ok enough riding the Matterhorn, they asked me what I'd like to go on next. I just agreed with whatever Hannah said. The least I can do is keep her happy. Besides, I lack the enthusiasm to actually pick a ride. Not to mention, my mind is in a haze. I can't stop thinking about Sarah and the mystery girl who left the yearbook message. Are they the same girl? There's also the matter of my backpack. I'm not too concerned because I get the feeling that if I find it, I'll also find Sarah.

Gabe claps his hands together upon getting everyone to agree to return to the Star Wars area, Galaxy's Edge. He is such a nerd, which is not a bad thing. Though he claims it is not true. But, I swear, if he wasn't on the basketball team, I'm sure Hannah and Kaite wouldn't bother to put up with him in our friend group.

Trey and Drew laugh at a joke at Gabe's expense. I try to chime in at the last second, hoping none of them notice I missed it. I'm so very out of sync with everyone today. Thankfully, we start walking back toward Fantasyland without anyone saying a word about my phasing out except Trey, who grabs my shoulder, pulling me to the back of the group. He must know something is up.

"Yo, what's going on with you, bro?" he asks. "And don't say nothin' because I know you too well for that."

My mouth turns upside down. He does know me. I wouldn't consider him my best friend if he didn't. It's time to spill the tea, especially since I'm running out of time and he definitely deserves an explanation for me ditching them for the better part of today.

"Alright, look," I start, looking down at my feet, "I may have…met someone." My eyes flash to his.

His brows shoot up. "You met someone?" he says a little too loudly.

Drew looks over his shoulder at us. I pretend to laugh like Trey just told a hilarious joke. Drew smiles as if he heard the joke too then stares ahead. I put my hands on Trey's shoulders, shaking him. I could choke him right now. He laughs, shrugging me off. The last thing I need is for Hannah or any of my friends to overhear what I'm about to say.

Taking in a breath, with my hands at my sides, I speak in a

low tone that only Trey can hear as long as he is paying attention. "It's like this," I begin and proceed to tell him about this morning, including what led up to my panic attack.

"Ok, ok, now I get why you ditched us." He chuckles. "I would have too."

I can feel a bit of heat rise in my cheeks. "Her name is Sarah Lackey, do you know her?"

Trey thinks for a moment. "Mmm, nah, I don't think so." I deflate. This girl really flew under everyone's radar. If she was this unnoticed in school, how am I ever going to find her in an amusement park with over 46,000 visitors a day? Talk about a needle in a haystack. Trey adds, "But, hey, what about the yearbook message? Did you ever figure out who wrote that?"

I shake my head disappointedly. "No, but I kinda thought it might be her?"

"You really think so?"

"Yes," I say confidently, "No." I lower my head, shrugging. "I don't know, but I gotta find her."

Trey raises a brow. "Who? The mystery girl or, what was it, Sarah?"

Nodding, I admit, "Both?"

We walk side by side behind our group. They are none the wiser. We say nothing for a few minutes. Trey finally breaks the silence by saying, "Look, why don't we ask the guys if they know her? You know Gabe knows everybody. He'll probably have her number or know someone who does. Then you can just text her." He talks smoothly like this is such a simple solution to the problem. It is logical, I'll give him that. But I definitely didn't want to involve Gabe or any of the guys for that matter. Odds are one of them is bound to tell Hannah and I cannot have that. We just got on good terms.

"No," I shake my head, huffing. "Ugh, this is all so high school."

"We are in high school...at least for one more week." Trey takes a step back. "So make the most of it."

I run my hand over the back of my neck. He may have a point.

Trey sucks in a deep breath. "Let's look at the facts," he starts, "You spent half the day with a girl you hardly know and rode that teacup ride you hate." He exhales. "And ever since you've been with us, it's like you're not really here." He smacks his lips. "Bro, it's obvious you don't want to be here, so go get her already."

He thinks it's that easy. I scoff. "I can't just ditch you guys again." I bite the inside of my cheek. "And I'm not about to go running off after some girl I hardly know. That's so...so irrational."

"Boy, I don't know what's up with you today," Trey states plainly. "But this is our senior trip. We're supposed to be acting irrational, so for once in your life, take a risk, cuz I ain't never seen you this dazed and confused over Hannah or Shey or any of the other girls you dated in school."

I stare at the ground. He's right. Sarah is out there somewhere and so is the girl who wrote me the yearbook message. And I'm not going to find either one of them by staying here.

Abruptly, I turn to Trey with an inspired realization. "I want to remember this night," I say, knowing full well this may be my last opportunity to act like a seventeen year old.

Trey grins. "Let's gooo!" he says in a hushed yell. He taps on a notification from his smart watch, which reminds me of the time.

My heart thuds. "Oh no, the fireworks are starting soon," I say, checking the time on my own watch. I bite my lip. "How the heck am I gonna get out of here?"

Trey looks down, then up again. Snapping his fingers, he says, "You need a distraction."

"Ok, but how?"

He grits his teeth. "I don't know." His expression quickly changes from contemplating to something resembling an evil genius. Oh no. I don't like that look. A wide smile spreads across his face. "Leave it to me." He slaps my chest before walking a bit faster.

Matching his speed, I ask concernedly, "Wait, what's the plan?" Our pace slows, as Trey tells me what he has in mind. I look ahead to see if anyone is in earshot. Drew is now next to Jeb, who is walking with Gabe. They haven't looked back to check on us once. This is good.

When Trey tells me his idea of a distraction, my eyes nearly bulge out of my head. I am horrified but a bit curious to see what will happen. I can't believe it involves Gabe. If it does work, I will never look at him the same way again. No matter, I give Trey the green light. He speed walks ahead of me and nonchalantly places himself between Jeb and Gabe. I watch as he whispers to Gabe the unimaginable. I try not to gag as I think about what Trey might be suggesting. Whatever he's saying, I have complete confidence he is not mentioning anything that has to do with Sarah.

There's no telling if Gabe will go along with the plan. All I can do is watch him from behind. The ears on his baby Yoda hat bob up and down with each step, making me anxious. Oh no. Gabe stops. My stomach lurches. Drew and Jeb make eye contact, then glance over at Gabe and Trey. They must know something. I plant my feet where I am a couple yards back and watch as they huddle around Gabe and Trey. Soon their faces go from confused to extremely amused. I exhale, wishing I knew what they were saying, but the further back I am the better chance I have at slipping away without them noticing. Thankfully, the girls, walking ahead, haven't noticed yet that our group has temporarily paused.

The guys break out into heinous laughter. Trey nods back at

me, as do the rest of the guys. That's when the girls finally spin around, raising their brows in unison at the loud noises coming from behind them. I smile and act like I am hurrying to catch up. That is until Gabe straightens his back, takes off his backpack and starts walking over to Hannah and Kaite.

My pulse quickens. Trey raises a brow at me, giving me the signal to leave. It's the perfect opportunity, but there's a problem. My feet aren't moving. I can't look away. All of us, in fact, observe in horror as Gabe maneuvers his way around Hannah only to approach Kaite dead on. My throat tightens. It's like I am about to witness a car crash into another car, except it's much more terrifying than that.

Gabe awkwardly grabs Kaite by the face. The look in her eyes is borderline murderous. I close my eyes, only to open them a second later. Is he really going to go for it? Yep. Her frenzied expression doesn't deter him. Rather, he proceeds to plant the wettest kiss on her pink lip glossed lips. My eyes widen. I have to restrain myself from gagging. This might actually make me throw up. Absolutely disgusting. What keeps me from bending over is the repercussions. Kaite cannot condone what Gabe just did. She's going to hit him for sure. That I gotta see.

Kaite, most predictably, pulls away from him and shoves him backwards so briskly he almost falls. I bite back a smirk. He asked for it.

Pointing a finger at him, she yells, "Ugh, how dare you!" She groans in disgust. Yet, not a second later, she grabs him by the collar of his shirt and pulls him back to her. She violently kisses him.

What? I'm so confused. I blink, not once but three times. Do I need to get my eyes checked? I can't believe it. Kaite and Gabe are into each other? Am I seeing this correctly? Sure enough, they kiss and caress each other, quite aggressively, and so much so that Gabe's hat falls off. I shut my eyes as fast as I can. There's no way I can stomach another minute of their strange altercation.

Trey turns to meet my gaze just as I do. He raises his eyebrows up and down and mouths that it's time to go. I nod. He's right. This is my chance. Backing away, my eyes shift over to Hannah. I need to make sure she's not looking. After all, that's basically what this whole distraction was for. She's not, thank god. Her eyes are glued on Kaite and Gabe. Her expression mirrors my own. Horror, absolute horror. She can't stop staring at her best friend. Neither can the rest of our group.

Grinning, I have to hand it to Trey for coming up with the wild idea. That was one heck of a distraction. How he found out that Gabe has had a crush on Kaite, and for years apparently, I'll probably never know. All that matters is, it worked. Turning around, I make a full on sprint toward Fantasyland, not letting his efforts go to waste.

CHAPTER 9
The Castle

The sign to Fantasyland appears after annoyingly dodging multiple groups from school. All the chaperones must know by now that I'm supposed to be with Mrs. Anderson and that I have since disappeared. Good god, I'm going to get in so much trouble for this, I think, sucking in a breath. For once, I don't care. Graduation is one week away. Whatever means of punishment they give me can't go on my permanent record now, at least I hope. Is this what it feels like to be invincible?

A small frown spreads across my face as I pass the teacup ride. I want to look away, but wait. I pause, standing in front of the ride. My hands aren't shaking. I don't feel any type of panicking anxiety. Quickly, I resume walking. The teacups slowly fade out of view. My lips curl into a grin. It's just a ride. Just a harmless ride. Recognizing this makes me feel like I can finally breathe in this park. I take in a deep breath. The air is fresh and it smells so sweet, like churros.

The closer I draw to the castle, the less I feel worried about anything. Meeting this mystery girl, whoever she may be, will be worth whatever consequences I have to face when this day is over. Alas, I think of Sarah, causing me to pause mid-step.

What if I show up under the castle arch and she's not there? A big part of me doesn't believe in magic or that true love nonsense, but I have to admit there is a small piece still hoping for it. Who knows. Maybe Disney will prove me wrong?

And that's just it. At the end of the day, it really doesn't matter who wrote that yearbook message. The fact is, I want it to be her. I want the mystery girl to be Sarah. I think, if I want it enough, it could be true. Sort of like wishing on a star that turns out to be a satellite. It is not real, but maybe if you wish hard enough, the odds of it turning true might be in your favor.

I bet, if Trey were here, he'd tell me to stop overthinking it. Better yet, if Brenden were here, he'd also tell me to get out of my own head. They'd both be right.

My phone vibrates. I see a text from Trey.

"You at the castle?"

I quickly type in response, "Almost," then add, "BTW, ur the real MVP bro. I owe you."

"Duh," he texts, adding a shaking hands emoji.

He's also going to be in so much trouble. Dorothea and Ma are so similar. At least I don't have a license that can be taken away. Although starting work in the summer is going to be punishment enough. I really have to make tonight count, since it could be the last chance I have to act like an irresponsible teenager.

Passing a princess store, I look up. There it is. Sleeping Beauty's castle. I hate that I know that. I stalk through its archway, careful not to run into anyone from school. This is a popular spot. I'm sure some groups are here taking pictures. My eyes frantically search around for any familiar faces. There's a mental checkmark in my head as I rove over the girls, who are definitely not who I'm looking for. Nope. Not her. Not her. No.

Don't know them. Gosh, there are too many people. I'm losing hope that I'll find her.

As stealthily as possible, in a crowded amusement park, I pass through the archway and cross the stone bridge connected to the main courtyard. I check my phone for the time. Three minutes until the fireworks. My heart starts pounding. Ok, calm down. There is no need to get worked up over something like this. Besides, Sarah is all about "Disney tradition." I'm sure she'll be here on time. When I do the math, there is a very high probability of her showing up within the next minute, if she shows up at all and if the mystery girl is indeed her. I let out a breath and can feel myself relax. I roll my shoulders. All I have to do is trust the math.

I situate myself near the bridge. This should be a good enough spot to wait out the parade. I lean against the railing in a corner just out of the way of passing families getting ready for the show. The lanterns are being turned on. The sun is finally setting.

Everything is ready. My chest rises and falls with my steady pulse. I cross my arms over my chest. My eyes pinpoint one of the lanterns across the courtyard. I stare at it, breathing in and out. In my mind's eye, I am the picture of serenity. Yes. I can do this.

In one minute, the show will start. I'll be reminded of every hopeful promise taught to me by Disney. It will no doubt remind me of the one person who isn't in my life anymore. I should be freaking out right now, but instead, I'm unnaturally calm and sort of curious to see what I've been missing out on all these years. Where there should be dread, there is hope.

The music begins playing. My fists loosen. I look up at the lights with a quiet caution. It's been so long since I've seen one of these light shows. The streets are glowing with artificial light. My hands fall to my sides. I shove them into my pockets. Suddenly, characters I forgot I loved so much as a child are being shown in the sky. The musical score moves along with them until the story changes, as do the characters. It brings back old memories, good ones. I am riveted by how spectacular the show is. I have to stare down at my feet and focus on the reality of the situation. My hatred for Disney is waning.

As the show nears its end, my stomach begins twisting into knots. That means the fireworks will start going off, and I'll finally find this mystery girl. I look up to the sky, which is now dark enough to see stars. I suppose this would be quite the romantic scene if this weren't Disneyland. I gulp as I anticipate the sound of the first firework being shot into the sky.

This is it. This is the moment I've been waiting for. At once, I cross back over to the bridge. If this girl is a fan of fairy tales, like I think she is, then I know exactly where she will be waiting. I run to it. Whether or not I believe in fairy tales, I know too well that tonight is going to be one to remember.

As anticipated, it is completely crowded under the arch. The odds of recognizing anyone, especially now that it's dark, have substantially gotten worse. I'm suddenly afraid I'll never find this mystery girl. I huff, then hear a soft voice, making me spin around.

"Weston?"

She stands in front of me, clutching onto my backpack, in the middle of the archway. She stares at me, grimacing. Her cherry red hair is just as bright as ever, even in the shadow of this tunnel.

I take a step towards her. "I knew it was you." I breathe out slowly. "Sarah, Dole Whip Girl." I wink at her.

Her bright smile trembles just a bit. She giggles, "Heh-what do you mean?" Her backpack slumps a little off her shoulders.

"Uh-" I look down at her, frowning. Wait, is she not the mystery girl? Did I assume wrong? Staring at her, I really think she was the one who wrote the yearbook message. The fact she's denying it catches me off guard. For the briefest of moments, I look around us, then back at her. I smile. "What I meant was, I'm glad to see you here…with me."

She lifts her head. "Really?" Her tone is so full of hope, I realize I don't care if she didn't write the message. I wanted it to be her. That's all that matters. What bothers me is I should have made it a point to remember the name of the girl who gave me the purple card. I should have befriended the same girl who saved my reputation from tarnishing during a school play.

She doesn't back away as I lift my hand to brush a hair from her face. Even though the yearbook message wasn't written by her, this day still turned out to be one of the best I've had in a long time. I just feel bad I wasted so much time not knowing her. My lips part. It's not like I haven't thought of her since we first met. Even if I didn't know her name, I still remembered the girl in pigtails from third grade. She has to know that. Clearing my throat, I tell her, "I'm sorry for not remembering your name before." Her lips curl downward. Sensing her disappointment, I add, "But I still have that purple card."

Her eyes shoot up at me, perplexed. "What?"

I shove a hand into my pocket. "You were the only one who understood what I went through." She opens her mouth, but before she has a chance to say anything, I interject, "Losing your dad is not something a lot of kids can relate to." She nods slowly and her eyes soften. "And I never said thank you." The corner of my mouth curls.

She blinks. "For the card?"

"Yeah," I say sheepishly. "And for not ratting me out freshman year." I smile down at her.

Sarah's brows pull together in unison. She smiles back at me and says in a teasing yet sympathetic voice, "Sure thing, Mr. President."

I laugh, rolling my eyes. This girl really is something else. "I'm so glad you're here," I exclaim, reaching for my backpack.

She lets me take it. I set it down beside us, then suck in a breath before grabbing her hand.

Her breath trembles. "Weston…I need to tell you something —" She looks away, cheeks reddening.

"Tell me what?" My fingers twitch against hers. How is she so soft?

Her eyes shift nervously from the ground to mine. She inhales. "I-I've had a crush on you since third grade." She breathes out and bites her lip.

I step back, dropping her hand. Why does it feel like this is the second time this has happened to me today? Hannah briefly pops into my head. I'm getting the feeling of deja vú. I don't like it.

She lowers her head, "Oh, I knew this would happen," looking utterly defeated. I shake my head, suddenly noticing that I dropped her hand. Oh no. That was not my intention. This looks bad. I step forward to grab it again.

"No, I'm sorry; I was just taken by surprise," I say, trying to rectify the situation. Although on the inside I'm starting to feel panicked. The last thing I want to do is hurt this girl just like Hannah.

A million thoughts are buzzing around in my head. This can't work. I don't know this girl. What would my friends think? I blink and force myself to stop thinking about anything else that could ruin this moment. Her eyes beam in the light of the hanging lamps and glowing wands. "You know what, I kinda already knew."

She smiles and covers her face. "Oh god, was I that obvious?"

"Well, you could say that or I'm just very full of myself," I joke. She runs with it.

She uncovers her face to poke me in the arm. "Of course you're full of yourself, Mr. President."

I poke her back. "Well, I was the Prom King, you know?" All

jokes aside, it is one of the perks of being popular. You can tell who loves you and who doesn't fairly easily. Her confession is valid.

She continues to laugh. I take that as a sign this moment is salvageable. To keep the playful vibe, I ask, "So how did we both end up meeting here, under the castle arch?"

Twirling a piece of her hair, she starts to answer, "Well, it's obviously-" She tilts her head.

"Disney tradition?" I say, finishing her sentence.

She quips, "You did not just finish my-"

"Sandwiches?" My hand flies to my mouth. "Did I really just quote one of the songs from Frozen?" I let out a sigh. "I can't."

"Oh my gosh that's what I was gonna say!" she squeals, grabbing onto me. "Hey, I think I'm rubbing off on you."

She is standing so close I could place my hand on the small of her back if I wanted to. I refrain as I'm sure my face is beet red. I don't want to give her the wrong impression. However, she lets out another hearty laugh. It doesn't make sense, but I think I could listen to that sound all day. Our eyes meet. I'm all too aware of how close our faces are to each other. There's a significant rise in my pulse.

Looking down into her big brown eyes, I'm compelled to reach for her hand again. Instantly, I recall how she was not the one who wrote the yearbook message. She is not the mystery girl, but I'm too entranced to care who it actually is. They missed their chance. Standing here with her makes me not care about anything else. Even if I am at Disneyland, the place I've sworn to hate. All I care about is the person standing in front of me. My brain cannot comprehend anything else.

We flinch suddenly at the sound of the fireworks setting off. Simultaneously, we lift our eyes to the sky and watch them as they burst into a kaleidoscope of colors. I admit, it's pretty spectacular. Disney sure knows how to make you feel captivated. I'll give them that.

After a moment or two, I peer down at Sarah. She is completely mesmerized by the scene. I squeeze her hand, signaling her attention. She looks up at me. I am enamored by the way the fireworks dance in the reflection of her eyes. I wish I could stop time here and now. There are no debates about hierarchy or how it would work. We wouldn't have to grow up, and I wouldn't have to think about what's waiting for me at home. We could stay like this forever, just a boy spending time with a girl. That sounds pretty good to me.

With a strong determination to immerse myself in the enchantment of the moment, I place a hand on her back. I pull Sarah closer. Confidently, she wraps her arms around my neck at the same time I lean my head down. I feel every tiny hair she touches with her hands. It sends the ripples in my stomach to swim up into my chest. Fluttering anxiety is seeping into my bones, making me pause for the briefest of seconds. There's no need to panic. This is not bad anxiety. Without overthinking it, I continue to bring my face closer to hers. Our noses touch, and after a moment of hesitation, her eyes close. Fireworks continue to boom above our heads as I close my eyes, then bring my lips to hers. My heart quickens with each second our lips remain together. There are no words in the English language to describe the feeling of a perfect kiss. Perhaps this is what Disney calls magic? I may be inclined to agree.

CHAPTER 10
Speechless

Sarah and I walk hand in hand towards another ride she manages to drag me on. It's just the Star Wars one we had missed earlier so I go with it. I frown, thinking about how Ma is probably almost here by now. No. Stop. All I want to do is enjoy the hour and a half we have left without some sort of negative thought to ruin it.

Is that too much to ask? I aim my thoughts towards the universe.

In line, Sarah tells me about her large, blended family including her pet turtle, Simba. She really is an interesting girl. I listen intently because I want to know everything about her. Apparently, there are a total of six kids in her household. Sarah is second to oldest. She tells me it's three girls from her mom, two boys from her step dad and one baby boy from both of them. It sounds like a wild, chaotic, but happy kind of family.

It's so different from my own. It leads me to wonder what life would have been like had my parents stayed together. Would my brother and I have other siblings? Pretty sure it would still just be me and Bren. From what Sarah explains about her mom and stepdad, I can already visualize how different their relationship is compared to my parents'. Thinking back, I doubt they had ever shown affection in front of me. How opposite our childhoods must have been.

She continues talking with such enthusiasm about her life. I'm positively enthralled, but knowing that the night is almost over is killing my vibe. I search for an excuse in my head to make it last. Yet, I keep coming up empty. My eyes close for a brief moment because I'm dreading what's possibly coming tomorrow. I open my eyes and see a special girl who's describing her dream of visiting Bali and being discovered for her singing at a hotel there.

As I listen to her, I forget about my problems. The way she is talking so passionately gives me the urge to wrap her up in my arms, but I don't. That would be weird. Even after we kissed underneath the castle. That seemed like an exception. For now, just listening is all that makes sense.

"Hey, wait a minute," I exclaim, stopping in our tracks. "Did you say you wanted to be a singer?"

Her face turns a light pink. "I've never told anyone that before." She breaks my gaze, turning her head away.

Now, I definitely envy Brenden who can play the guitar like it's no one's business. It takes a special type of bravery to possess a talent like singing or playing an instrument and then getting up on stage in front of everyone to show off that talent. A shudder runs through me. I'm not cut out for that life. Thinking about how I have to go up on stage in a matter of days to give my valedictorian speech is something I cannot handle at the moment. I close my eyes. There is no need to think about that right now.

"You ok?"

"I think you're brave for having that dream," I manage to say as I pry open my eyes. She is looking at me again, flushed cheeks and all.

Sarah leans her head on my shoulder and sighs. "Do you ever wish you could be a child again?" That was an interesting change of subject. I go with it because I really want to avoid thinking about getting up on any stage.

"No, absolutely not," I answer fast and deliberately. Though my childhood wasn't the worst by any means, it certainly wasn't the best. I had no control over my life. Now, as I stand on the precipice of adulthood, I contemplate what it would mean to be completely independent of my mother. I'd be free to make my own choices. That would feel so good.

Sarah lifts her head to meet my gaze. "Wow, that was a quick answer."

I give her a light nudge with my arm. "Yeah, well, not all of us have parents that let us do whatever we want."

"Is that a hint of jealousy I hear, Mr. President?"

"I'm not ashamed," I say, grinning. Her fingers slightly bend in my grasp. "You haven't met my mother." We move up a couple spaces in line.

"Tell me about her, oh and your brother," she asks, her eyes beaming up at me. She is not going to let that go, is she? I hate that it's dark now. The lines around her mouth will be harder to stare at.

I run a hand around the backside of my hairline. "Eh, what do you want to know?" Talking about my family is another skill I currently don't possess. Honestly, it's not one I want to possess. Now I'm starting to sound an awful lot like Brenden.

Maybe that's where I get it from?

"Well, I've only seen your mother once when she was a chaperone at our eighth grade Spring Dance." She chuckles sprightly. "Remember she caught Freddie Hertz pouring gin into the punch bowl?" She covers her mouth.

"Heh, I actually remember that," I exclaim, recalling the memory. "Wasn't Freddie expelled freshman year?" What a character.

"Yeah, you're right," Sarah answers. "So other than having a really good eye for mischievous tweens, what else does your mom do?"

My jaw is tense. I owe her an answer. She's been telling me all about her family and her life, no less. So why is it so hard to tell her about mine? "Look," I shove my free hand into my pocket, "I just want to enjoy right here, right now." I lock my eyes onto hers. "Let's not ruin it by me talking about how controlling my mother can be, and let's avoid the whole Asian guilt topic." Stating that reminds me of this morning.

There's a dull ache in the pit of my stomach. Ma knows I didn't sign those employment papers on purpose. If I know her like I think I do, she's stopping at nothing to rectify the *"unacceptable"* situation. Sometimes I wish I were Brenden, someone with no expectations or a good record to maintain. My eyes fall to Sarah's, and instead of looking at me with judgment, she stares back with an understanding.

"I get it. Moms are…tough." Sarah waves a fly away. "It's just that for me, this is the first time I've been on my own without her…without them…" She pauses. "I guess I kinda miss them."

The corners of my mouth tug. "I haven't been away from my family for more than a weekend," I admit.

She smiles. "That's cute."

Not as cute as you is what I want to say but resist because that's so cheesy. What has come over me today? I really don't recall sounding this juvenile when I was dating Hannah or Lilith or Macy. None of the girls I liked before made me feel this way. I blink and try to refocus.

Maybe I didn't like them enough?

It doesn't matter. None of it matters. That's why I'm trying to remain in the moment, because the second I start thinking about reality, this infatuation will be sure to end.

Sarah moves ahead of me. Looks like we are next in line. Good. Hopefully this conversation about my family is over. There are just some topics I'd rather not discuss, at least not yet.

I follow Sarah to the back row. She's been on this ride a million times, so I let her lead the way. It is quite entertaining to see her squirm in excitement. During the ride, my head tilts in her direction. She's fully immersed in the simulation being portrayed on the screen. The seats move to make a fun effect, like we are actually rebels running away from the bad guys. I may not be a fan, but the way Sarah is enjoying this is making me want to watch some of the movies, just the old iconic ones. Who knows. Maybe I could get into them.

Before I know it, the ride is over. I realize I didn't get motion sick once. It could be because it isn't super fast or on water. Although, I have the strangest intuition it has nothing to do with the ride.

Sarah nudges me with her elbow. "So, how did you like it, Mr. President?"

I stiffen, turn to her with a serious expression and say, "You better stop calling me that." A wicked smile spreads across my lips. After a second or two, her eyebrow raises on one side.

She backs away with her hands in her pockets. "Oh yeah, what are you gonna do about it, Mr. President?" Her mouth curls into a teasing grin.

Setting down my backpack, I bring up my hands slowly as if I am surrendering, then I leap for her. She lets out a playful scream as she moves just out of my reach.

"You better watch yourself, Dole Whip Girl," I taunt, using her nickname. She continues to laugh, skipping away from me. I catch up to her easily and grab onto her waist.

"No!" she yells gleefully.

My face heats up as I wrap my arms around her and spin. With her in my grasp, I twirl us around in a circle. This is another moment I wish I could pause in time. I inhale the scent of her cherry red hair that lightly brushes my nose, a fresh vanilla scent with a hint of rose. Her laughter is delightful. There's a whirling sensation in my gut. My lips spread into a wide grin. If I could choose to have an out of body experience, now would be a good time. I want to remember what it looks like for me to have fun.

Mid twirl, I pause at the sight of a few familiar faces walking in our direction. The first thing I notice is the green Yoda hat. The ears are bouncing up and down. They are being closely followed by unanimated sparkly pink mouse ears. My heart stops. I immediately let Sarah go. She stumbles a little bit but finds her balance. I turn so I'm looking at them head on. I blink rapidly. It really is them. My entire squad. Of course they are here. This is Gabe's favorite section of the park. Heck, they were probably on the same ride as us. I was just too preoccupied to notice.

Quickly, I lift my backpack from the ground and hand Sarah hers without making eye contact. I am too focused on my friends coming toward us to deduce what she might be thinking right now. Acting as nonchalantly as I can, I shove my hands into my pockets and wait for them to approach. I suck in a deep breath. Mixing companies like this is not a good idea. Especially since Gabe doesn't look too happy despite what I had witnessed earlier. The image of him and Kaite together flashes back into my mind. That new memory is going to take a while to fade. I just hope it didn't turn into a core one.

Hannah and Kaite walk up to us linked arm and arm. Kaite is on Gabe's left, followed by the rest of the guys. They don't seem to notice where they are walking until Gabe, Hannah, and Kaite come to a complete stop, practically causing them to run into each other. Trey almost knocks into Jeb who bumps into Drew.

"Hey, what the—" Trey mumbles, steadying himself on Jeb's shoulder.

What are they doing here? What will they think?

The creeping sense of dread that I experienced on the teacup ride is back. I swallow some excess saliva that has pooled under my tongue. The temperature on my forehead rises. Not good. I clutch my chest.

Gabe waves. "Well, well, well, look who it is?" His eyebrow raises.

My attention is glued to Hannah, who is mad dogging me. I can't help but feel a little guilty for ditching her and the rest of the group earlier. I guess I owe them an explanation. My throat feels so dry though. I think I hear Sarah whisper something like, "Oh no." But I'm not sure.

Noticing Sarah, Gabe's mouth drops open. "Sarah?" he utters with a hint of confusion.

Wait, does he know her?

"Dude, who is that girl?" Drew calls from behind Gabe. Jeb, of course, echoes the same question.

My eyes blink in rapid succession. "Oh, um, this is Sarah Lackey, guys, from school." She gives a light wave. I shift my feet uncomfortably, moving a bit to the right. This is not me. Normally I'm very cool, calm, and collected, but right now this feels like an ambush. It's making me very uncomfortable.

"Do you know her?" I ask Gabe, jaw slack.

"Yeah, I know her." Gabe cackles. "She's my neighbor."

My stomach drops. Sarah is Gabe's neighbor? How is that possible?

Sarah seems visibly uncomfortable. She rocks on her heels, probably waiting for someone else to say something. I look back at Gabe, speechless. Imagining them as neighbors is throwing me for a loop. If it is true, then that means we have crossed paths more times than I could count. There have been so many parties and hang outs at Gabe's throughout the years.

Was she there?

Every time we were playing basketball in his driveway, was she nearby? She could have been in my life sooner if only I had looked around. But it leads me to wonder, would I have even noticed her?

Sarah and Gabe stare at each other for a brief moment before Hannah speaks up, breaking her arm link with Kaite. Both of them look exceptionally pissed. I purse my lips, not wanting to hear whatever is about to come out her mouth.

With her eyes on me, she says, "Who cares who she is. I think we all want to know what you are doing with her?" The disgust in her tone is palpable.

Kaite takes the red lollipop from her mouth and leans over, whispering something in Hannah's ear. My brows furrow. That girl is more than irritating. Gabe inches closer to her, and following her lead, joins in a secret snickering. Hannah's incredulous eyes stay glued on me.

Trey slides around Drew, who moves aside so that now they are all standing in a spherical shape. We are all facing each other. I don't like this. The vibes are way off now. Hannah gazes at me, then at Sarah, then back at me. That's not a good sign.

"Eh, yo, is this the girl you were looking for?" Trey blurts, looking between Sarah and I, as if he just had an epiphany.

Grinding my teeth, I glare at him. How could he say that in front of everyone right now? I'm going to strangle him. He puts a hand dramatically over his mouth. Clearly, he forgot to keep that between us.

"Wait, wait, wait." Gabe looks my way. Smirking, he asks, "You were looking for *Sarah* this whole time?" The tone of his voice when he says Sarah's name gives away his obvious opinion of her. "Is she the one who wrote the yearbook message?" He bends over in a laugh. Jeb and Drew follow suit. They are absolutely hysterical.

"Shut up, Gabe," Sarah barks, giving me the impression she doesn't like him very much.

"Oh, I'm sorry."

Judging by the sarcasm in his tone, it would seem Gabe isn't fond of her either. Perhaps it's not completely my fault that I didn't meet her sooner. Panicking, my eyes flash from Sarah's back to Gabe's. My mouth opens but no words come out. What do I even say right now when it seems all my friends are against this girl?

"What yearbook message?" Hannah asks, sounding hurt, like I betrayed her. Which is preposterous.

Kaite interjects, "I told you, he's a cheater." She starts tapping her foot, looking absolutely annoyed, and continues sucking on her red lollipop.

My hands are slowly turning into fists. I don't know what to say at this point that will be in my favor. So I remain silent.

Looking directly at Sarah, Gabe asks, "So, what, did you follow him all day long or something?" he sneers.

Sarah folds her arms, responding with a biting, "No." Ok, woah. It sounds so weird to hear her talk to him like that.

How familiar are they?

Ignoring her, he turns to me and snarls, "Were you ditching us to be with...*her*?" They really must not like each other. That baffles me.

"Yeah, seriously, is this why you kept ghosting us?" Jeb asks sincerely.

"Answer the question, bro," Drew says.

I shake my head, blurting, "It's not like that." I feel on trial here and the jury is way too judgmental to make an unbiased and just verdict.

Drew inserts himself, "What is it like then?"

"Excuse me, what yearbook message?" Hannah asks again.

Trey interrupts before I can respond. I'll have to thank him later for that. He raises his hands and lowers them. "My dudes, let's not fuss over where or who our boy has been with, alright? Let's just go on one more ride before we have to go. We still have time."

"Whatever, Trey," Gabe yells. "I know you helped him."

"That's it. I'm out," he exclaims, walking away. He really doesn't like confrontation. Neither do I.

In my peripherals, I see Sarah who looks just as concerned as I feel. Sensing that I am getting nowhere, my jaw clenches shut. I stare down at my feet. This entire altercation is progressing from bad to worse. I am silent as stone.

Kaite stops tapping her foot. She takes a few aggressive steps towards me and says, "Give me your yearbook," with one hand outstretched while the other is placed on her hip.

"Why?" I retort sharply. This cannot be good.

"Just give it to me," she demands.

I instinctively look over at Sarah, searching for some sort of explanation as to what's going on; she gives me none. Her eyes simply meet mine, then they quickly peer at the ground. A bad feeling creeps into my chest, making my pulse quicken.

"Wes, look man, I don't know what she has told you, but she is a psycho-like freak, who's been obsessed with you since elementary school," Gabe says.

"Are you joking?" Hannah blurts.

A swift feeling of rage overcomes me when I refute, "Shut up, Hannah." The words come out sounding more aggressive than I intend. I part my lips ready to apologize, but nothing comes out. I think better of it. Maybe I'm not sorry? She glares at me, mouth open. I never snapped at her like that before. I definitely feel bad, but I'm more concerned about why Kaite wants my yearbook. What could that possibly mean?

"I'm telling you right now, you don't want to mess with her, bro," Gabe admits. I notice him glancing at Sarah before adding, "She's like a stalker, dude. The girl is obsessed with you."

"Shut up, Gabe!" Sarah yells, fear in her eyes.

"Heh, I bet she even has a diary that she writes in every night, Mrs. Sarah Hill-Cho," Kaite spits in a mocking tone.

"That is not true," Sarah huffs.

Drew adds between laughs, "Yeah, bro, and she probably has pictures of you hanging on her wall that she kisses every day."

Sarah shakes her head, stammering, "No I don't," her voice cracking on the last word.

"She probably drives to your house and watches you while you sleep," Jeb feels the need to add.

She turns to me, pleading, "Weston, they're lying." Her eyes grow wide. I can tell she's afraid, but of what? None of this can be true, can it?

The guys continue laughing along with the girls. I clutch a hand to my chest, not knowing what to feel right now. Dread? Panic? No. Shame, but whose?

Hannah passes Kaite and takes my backpack out of my hands. I'm surprised I let her. A cold wave of fear settles upon me. What, in fact, is she trying to show me?

"Let's put an end to this," she says, pulling out my yearbook.

Time stands still. Hannah hands the book to Kaite who flips to the back where the signatures are. Her eyes search the page. She smirks at something in particular, points to it and flips the book around. Beneath her finger is the yearbook message.

"Meet me at the castle when the fireworks start," she reads in a mocking tone. "You wrote this, didn't you?" she asks Sarah pointedly.

Sarah's face is panicked. Every muscle in my face tenses. She shakes her head and her lips part to speak, but nothing comes out. She goes quiet.

Courage envelops me briefly. "She said she didn't write it," I state definitively.

"She's a dirty little liar," Kaite accuses.

Now, I'm really mad. "You have no idea what you are talking about," I say, snatching the book from out of her hands.

"Oh really?" she scoffs. "Then why did I see her write it yesterday?"

Brows furrowing, I face Sarah. It can't be true. Our eyes meet. Instead of saying out loud, "You told me it wasn't you," I wait for her to deny the claim.

Begrudgingly, she sighs. She dips her head and relents, "It's-it's true. I lied, but-"

"Ha, told you," Kaite spits out. "Gabe is right, she is a stalker."

"No," Sarah attempts, looking only at me. "Look, I didn't mean to lie, I just-" She stops herself, noticing I broke eye contact. I can't bring myself to look at her, not right now. She literally lied to my face about writing the yearbook message.

Why would she do that?

I shiver at the recollection of her confession. She's had a crush on me for so long. I shuffle my feet, staring down at them. Something is not adding up, but I am done overanalyzing. I'm done with my friends. I'm done with this day. I just want to go home already.

Realizing I won't be saying anything else, she huffs, "You know what, it's not even worth explaining since it seems like you've already made up your mind about me."

Slowly, I bring my eyes up to find hers. She crosses her arms after tightening the straps on her backpack. I can tell she wants to leave but waits a second, giving me a chance to speak up. Like an embarrassed coward, I remain silent. She spins to walk off. I don't try to stop her.

"See you at home," Gabe yells after her, snickering.

"Hey wait, why don't you meet me at the castle, pookie?" Jeb slaps Drew's hand, proud of the jab.

A sad truth hits me. These jerks are my friends. How disappointing.

Hannah and Kaite slowly move back, allowing space for Gabe to come up to me and put an arm around my shoulder. "I'm sorry you had to find out this way," he exhales, "but she's a loser and you are the king, bro. You deserve better."

"Dude, I think she was in my Spanish class sophomore year. Girl is creepy," Drew tells me. "She was giving major stalker vibes."

"Yeah, you better be careful cuz she could, like, kill you with her weird obsession with you or something," Jeb laughs.

Both of them think they are so funny. Well, I'm not laughing. "You guys are douchebags."

They hold up their hands in defense. "Woah, that was uncalled for." I hear Drew scoff.

"Yeah, what the heck, bro?" Gabe says. "Don't get mad at the facts. Aren't you all about that?" He is not wrong.

Speaking of facts, "Did you actually see her write this?" I question Kaite, holding open the yearbook.

She nods. "Yep."

I stare at her as if for the first time. She goes on to say how she saw Sarah snag my yearbook when she thought no one else was looking. According to her, she even kissed it. I'm not sure what to believe at this point. It all sounds so absurd.

"I didn't tell you because even though Hannah and I thought it was weird, we forgot about it. And she's a nobody. The last thing I expected was to see you with her today." Kaite definitely has more to say. I remain silent until she lets it all out, that is until Hannah buds in.

"Can we just forget about that weirdo? Ok, this was supposed to be our trip, Weston. You were supposed to be with me." Her eyes begin to water. Normally, it would move me to comfort her, but right now I just don't care.

I pinch the bridge of my nose. "We are not together anymore,

Hannah," I say pointedly. "I'm sorry I broke up with you before this trip, but it is what it is. Get over it." The sting of my words makes the water in her eyes start to fall. It's fine. She'll find comfort with Kaite anyway.

I take one last look at her, at all of them. They just destroyed what was shaping up to be one of the best days of my life. I really despise them for this. Admittedly, Hannah is right about one thing. If it wasn't for me making a grand romantic gesture, then I wouldn't be in this mess. There would be no drama, and I wouldn't be at Disneyland. I'm aggravated with everyone in this friend group, except for Trey. Groaning within myself, I cannot emphasize enough how badly I want this day to be over already.

Eager to get away from them, I toss the yearbook into my bag.

Before I say something I'll later regret, I simply state, "I have to go," then walk away.

As much as I wanted to keep reality from taking over this moment, it has found its way to me. I shake my head, irritated with myself. I should have known better than to waste time in this godforsaken park. This is why Disneyland is the unhappiest place on earth. Only bad things happen here. I should have known.

I drag my feet back to the spot where the buses are lined up. I'm so ready to leave. There, I notice Mrs. Anderson, who is standing near Trey, waving me down. Great, I think, lowering my head. I really don't want to deal with a lecture right now. Grimacing, I have no choice but to tread over to her. I hold my head up high and keep my hands in my pockets. Whatever consequences are in store for me I will handle with professionalism, like an adult. That's what I'm expected to act like now, right?

"There you are, Mr. Hill-Cho. You have a lot of explaining—

Hey, Victor, we do not climb on bus windows. Get down right now!" She rushes off towards the second bus in the lineup. It is almost comical how easily distracted she gets.

"Eh, uh, sorry for bouncing," Trey says, slinging his green headphones around his neck.

I shrug. "It's all good. I got out of there shortly after you left."

"You good, bro? You look pissed."

I take my hands out of my pockets and stare at the ground. "Nah." I cross my arms.

Trey laughs and asks me to explain what happened after he left. I tell him, all the while, my insides are swirling with anger and confusion. This night ended up a disaster all because of me. Heat swells in my chest. Not only that, my friends showed their true colors tonight. They are so immature and managed to shatter an adoring image of a girl I barely know. She was turning out to be perfect, until they ruined it. Now, I don't know what to think.

"So, Sarah is the mystery girl," Trey begins. "Even though she lied about writing in your yearbook. She's also Gabe's neighbor, who called her a psycho stalker freak," he pauses, "Is that right?"

"Something like that." I could do without the psycho stalker freak part.

Trey shakes his head. "Man, and this was supposed to be such a sick senior trip," he groans.

My hands ball into fists. "Yes, I know. It's all my fault."

He shakes his head. "That's not what I'm saying."

I sigh, "I know."

"Don't beat yourself up," he refutes.

Staring at the ground, I want to say, "That is easier said than done," but instead, I fold my hands on the top of my head. Gabe's words are still ringing in my head. "She's a stalker, loser, freak." What a poor choice of words. He shouldn't call someone a freak just because they are different. Still, I'm left feeling confused.

One thing is certain, though: I'm angry. Angry that my day was ruined. Angry that I had a panic attack. Angry that Brenden can do whatever he wants. I'll always be angry about dad leaving. I'm angry that Ma won't let me make my own decisions. My hands start shaking.

"Hey, chill out," Trey says. "I mean, I'd be mad too, but you don't want to have another panic attack, do you?"

I kick my foot at nothing in particular. "Gabe just makes me so upset. He is such a jerk sometimes. They all are."

"Yeah, yeah, I know," he agrees with me. "The boy has issues. I mean, he's got a thing for Kaite." He shudders. "What does that tell you?"

A light chuckle comes out. "You got that right." Exhaling, I nod as my hands fall to my sides. "So much for making memories on our *epic* senior trip," I say, laying on the sarcasm.

Trey tilts his head. "You know what, I wouldn't say that necessarily."

I fold my arms against my chest. "Why not?"

"Because we all had a good time at one point or another throughout the day, and you found out who the mystery girl is," Trey states. "And Gabe kissing Kaite is something I'll never forget." I scowl as the image of the two of them pops back into my head, but it does put a smile on my face. He's right. I'll never forget that. "And at least we are going home soon."

"Yes, finally."

He grabs onto his headphones wrapped around his neck. "Hey, looks like they are letting people on the bus. Imma go get a spot. You coming?"

I tuck a hand into my pocket. "Nah, I gotta wait for my mom."

"Alright, later, bro."

We bump fists as he turns to leave. He enters the first bus on the right of the sidewalk and I remain standing, trying not to wallow in self pity.

This entire day was a rollercoaster. If anything, it made me feel ready to move to Harvard sooner than later. So much for wanting a free summer to myself. I'd rather be swamped in work than have to waste time doing something so juvenile ever again. They say this is part of growing up, but I want to skip all this nonsense and just enter adulthood already, I think.

I stand with my arms at my sides next to one of the buses, waiting for Mrs. Anderson to come back. No doubt she will have plenty of choice words for me. My charm won't do anything for her now. I wonder if this means I don't get to be valedictorian anymore. A slight flutter of hope enters my chest. Maybe I won't have to get up on stage and give a speech after all? That would be a dream come true. I frown. To be honest, that's the least of my concerns.

Mrs. Anderson has her face in her phone, walking back to me. "As I was saying, Mr. Hill-Cho, you are in some serious trouble," she threatens, looking up to point her phone at me.

My eyes grow wide in a panic. "Am I going to be suspended?" That's where my mind goes. But they can't suspend me for running off like that, right? Almost everyone ditched their chaperones today. Honestly, I don't even understand why they would even assign us one when we are all on the brink of graduation. Most of us are 18 anyway. Suddenly, I wish my birthday was in May.

"Suspension?" she huffs, throwing her head back. "Hardly. We will see what Principal Hickman has to say about it, but plan on spending quite a few days in detention, young man."

I exhale a long sigh of relief. "Ok, that's fair," I relent, really meaning it.

They only have a week to put me in detention before graduation. Typically, I'd be in distress over my permanent record, but since I was already accepted to Harvard, there's no need to panic. I'd say sneaking off was worth it.

"I'm sure your mother will give you enough grief over this whole ordeal," Mrs. Anderson mutters. "Alright, enough dilly-dallying, everyone, get on the bus." She raises her voice and waves at some girls from my grade who are standing idly nearby.

"Wait, have you heard from my mom?" The back of my throat feels sore.

"Yes, as a matter of fact, she should be in the parking lot right now."

I gulp and watch silently as the rest of my classmates pile into the buses. There's been no sign of Gabe, Hannah, or anyone else. Sarah's face pops into my mind. I haven't seen her either. My stomach sinks. The probability of her not wanting to see me right now is high. I still can't believe I said nothing in her defense. How low am I?

My eyes shut as I let out a rather disappointed sigh. I grit my teeth thinking about what happened earlier. It's perplexing to say the least. I may not know Sarah well, hardly at all even, but she's the same girl who covered for me when I had my first panic attack. She's also responsible for giving me the purple card at just eight years old when my dad had walked out on us. That same thoughtful girl is supposed to be my stalker? I shake my head. It can't be true.

Not once throughout the day did she ever give me that impression. In no way, shape or form did she give me the ick. Yet, there's something I can't understand. Why did she lie about writing the yearbook message? I think back to this morning when I first saw her by the Dole Whip cart. Was that interaction planned or was it serendipitous like I had originally thought? I was convinced it was something similar to fate, if I believed in that sort of thing. Now I'm not so sure.

Mrs. Anderson calls another chaperone, telling them she's

going to escort me to the parking lot now. I grasp the long straps of my backpack and follow her, breathing out a sigh of relief. Finally, this night is coming to an end. As much as I had wanted it to last, my senior trip did not go according to plan. Everything that happened was unexpected. Best to try and put this day behind me as fast as I can.

I spot my mother's silver Volvo right away in the parking lot. It is parked right in front, not far from where the buses are lined up. She waves her hand out of the window at Mrs. Anderson. I swallow a bitterness in my throat as our eyes meet briefly. Her hair is still tightly pulled back into a low bun. Not one hair is out of place even after a long day. She catches my eye and her sharp gaze lets me know I'm dead.

Mrs. Anderson lays a hand on my backpack. "Sorry for making you drive all this way, Sharon."

"It's no problem," Ma tells her.

"Weston is in one piece."

I force myself to smile. "Yep, all good," I say, opening the passenger car door.

"Thank you," Ma exclaims as I shut the door.

"Alright, you take care now." Mrs. Anderson leans down to wave goodbye to Ma. Before Mrs. Anderson leaves, Ma says, "I apologize he ran away. Please say what he can do for punishment."

My face sours and I have to resist the habit of correcting her English in front of my teacher. I do find it interesting that's the first statement out of her mouth when I literally was unconscious for a bit. I fasten my seatbelt, frowning at my feet.

"I'm going to talk with Principal Hickman first thing on Monday, but don't worry, I'm sure it's just going to be a couple days worth of detention."

Ma responds with a simple, "Good."

Mrs. Anderson backs away from the car, already on her

phone again. Ma turns on the ignition while waving goodbye to my teacher.

"Safe drive," I hear her call out.

Ma pulls the car out of the parking spot without so much as a word to me. It's a good thing since I don't want to talk either. We sit in complete silence until we reach the exit of the park. I turn my head to look out the window in order to gaze at the lit up park now behind us and start to wonder how this night could have ended if my friends hadn't shown up at the very end. Many scenarios circulate in my head. Not one of them involves this outcome.

CHAPTER 11
Seeing Red

On the freeway, my mom finally breaks the silence between us by questioning me about the fainting spell. Oh, so she does care, I think sarcastically, closing my eyes. But it is the last thing I want to talk about.

"In-Su? What happened? Tell me now," she demands in Korean. She knows I prefer English. I reply in the language I'm more comfortable with just to annoy her, very unlike me.

"Nothing happened. I just passed out, that's all, but I'm fine," I say, opening my eyes. Sarah's face flashes quickly in my mind. I can only assume what it means, but I'm brought to a pause as my mother's words hit me like a brick.

"I signed the papers for you. You're all set to work for Uncle Henry."

My brow arches in the sudden change of subject. I scoot up, adjusting the seat belt. "Ma, you can't do that. That's illegal." The audacity she had to forge my signature.

She blinks. "It is just to get your background check through. You can sign the rest of the onboarding paperwork when you arrive," she says as a matter of fact, like she did nothing wrong.

Even from her side profile, I can see a grin beginning to spread on her lips. Here I thought she was so mad the entire car ride was going to consist of her scolding me. "Uncle is very excited for you to be working with him this summer. He is even paying to fly you out right after graduation," she adds. "You work hard to show appreciation," she says, switching back to English.

My pulse skyrockets. "Wait, what?" I cling onto the side of the car door, shifting to face her.

One corner of ma's mouth curls into a smirk. "I knew you would be excited," she says in her mother tongue. She takes one hand off the wheel to pat my arm. "I took care of everything. No need to worry about your mistake this morning."

It takes me a moment to swallow what this means for me. I suck in a giant breath and let it out slowly. I start to state the facts of my situation to rationalize what just happened. My high school days will be officially over the day after I graduate. I'm starting work this summer and won't be getting a break. When I arrive in Boston, I'll say goodbye to my adolescent phase. My heart rate beats sporadically. I breathe in and out. Stating the facts normally calms me down. Not this time. The fact is, this sucks. I really thought I had more time before the future was supposed to start. I don't want to grow up. Not yet. Unexpectedly, time has run out.

Turning my head, I stare out the window. The road beneath us travels so fast. I breathe out. No. I breathe in. No, I can't. This is not the plan. I don't like this. I can't do this. My breath starts quickening again. Cars pass us from one lane to the other. The temperature is rising in my cheeks with each passing vehicle. My head feels like it's spinning, like I'm back on that teacup ride.

Next thing I know, I shout, "I'm not going!"

My mother turns her head. "What?" Her tone is harsh.

"Ma, the road!" I yell as our car drifts into the right lane. She looks out to the freeway. The car is coming so close to grazing the blue Forester beside us. Mother screams, letting go of the wheel. Panicking, I tug back on the steering wheel and pull it as hard as I can the other way. Thankfully, it swerves into the correct lane. Heaving, Ma pulls off onto the shoulder, slamming hard on the brakes. For a long minute, we both sit in silence, catching our breath.

"Are you ok?" I hear her ask between shaky breaths.

I nod my head calmly, looking down at my hands. That's odd. I stretch out my hands and notice they aren't shaking. Right now, they seem steady enough to perform heart surgery, if I had that skill. Inhaling, I look up at my mother. She is not ok, but I'm too distracted with how calm I seem to be. For almost getting into a car accident, I feel pretty serene. There's almost a sense of tranquility that is settling upon me. Like a heavy weight has been lifted from my shoulders.

"I'm sorry," Ma says, blotting her face in the mirror with a napkin. She's trying to compose herself. She is completely disoriented. I haven't seen her like this in a long time.

"It's ok, Ma," I say calmly in Korean.

She inhales slowly, then turns to me. "In-su, you are going to Harvard this summer," she states, placing her hands on the steering wheel. "The decision has already been made."

I shake my head. "No, I'm not going," I say, surprising myself. Something about today has really turned me upside down. I usually steer clear of any kind of argument with her, but this time, I'm not backing down. This is my life. My decision.

She shifts towards me, taking off her seat belt. "Where is this coming from?" she asks, astonished. "It has been your dream to go to Harvard." Her voice is high, shaky.

"I know. I know," I say, reassuring her. "And I still want to go to Harvard. I just-" I pause. My eyes drift to the ceiling. I have to stop myself from admitting my true feelings because I lack the courage to express an opinion different from hers. That talent seems to come easily to Brenden. Not me. Yet, something deep down is pushing me to say what I truly mean, regardless of the consequences. Taking in another deep breath, I swallow, then clear my throat before admitting, "I want the summer off."

She bores her eyes into mine, brows furrowing. "Do you know what your uncle had to do to get you this job? I will not have you disrespect him like that and embarrass me. Do you want to end up like your brother?" Her voice is stern, unmoving. The jab to Brenden is unexpected, but I ignore it and stand my ground.

"I never asked for that!" I glare back at her.

She sighs one of those, "I'm extremely disappointed" type of sighs. It's what my mother does to try and guilt my brother into submission. It hardly works. I tend to avoid it by always agreeing with her. It's a different feeling to be on the other end of it, knowing I'm the one causing her the distress instead of Brenden.

The lines between her forehead relax a little. "Where is this coming from, In-Su?" Her eyes narrow on me. "You can talk to me."

I break her gaze, running a hand around my neck. She doesn't realize this is something I have been wanting ever since senior year began. Well, longer even. How do I tell her that? She will never understand.

"It's a girl, isn't it?"

My eyes flicker to her. "No," I grumble, folding my arms. "That's absurd."

Ma turns her attention back to the dash and says in a monotone manner, "It's always a girl."

My cheeks flushing, I say in a sudden burst of annoyance, "You don't know what you're talking about." Oh good god. I've heard those words before. I slump in my seat. Maybe I am turning into Brenden.

"A mother knows, son," she exclaims somberly, reaching for her seatbelt. "Now I understand completely why you don't wish to go."

I sit back up and calmly unfold my arms. My lips remained pressed together even though I want to say, "I am not Brenden," but aiming another low blow at my brother when he's not around to defend himself seems wrong. I refrain.

My mother brings her eyes to mine again. She's looking at me like I have something to hide. Her pouty lips signal a wave of guilt into my gut.

Knowing it's partly true, I sigh and unwillingly explain, "Alright, I did meet this girl today, but she has nothing to do with the reason why I don't want to go to school this summer."

The continuous heat in my cheeks is betraying me. I've never talked to my mother about a girl before. Even when Hannah and I were together, I kept our relationship low key, only interacting at school or out and about, never at home where Brenden or Ma could engage with us.

"It's all over," she mumbles, facing the steering wheel.

My eye twitches. "What are you talking about? Nothing is over. I still want to go to Harvard. I still want to get a good education," I reassure her. Closing my eyes, I decide here and now to say, "I just want the summer for myself."

When I say it out loud, it doesn't sound so irrational, after all. Everything after graduation is already planned out for me. My whole life is set. All I ask is for one free summer before this happens. Surely, it doesn't take someone with a PhD to understand why.

Ma turns on the ignition. Her lips are pressed together. I imagine she is done speaking. I lean over to try and meet her gaze, but she looks out the window, avoiding eye contact.

"Ma." I touch her shoulder. "Ma, it's going to be ok."

She still refuses to look at me. Anger begins to climb its way back into my fists. It's so ridiculous she can't even discuss the option of giving me the summer off. I have never been more upset with her in my life.

After looking over her shoulder, she pulls the car back onto the freeway. A minute or two down the road, she finally speaks up, saying, "She's already changed you."

"Ma, I barely met her today," I debate. "How could spending one day with a girl change anything?"

Ma drowns out any input I might have on the matter with one simple statement. "One day can change everything."

The rest of the car ride home is quiet. Ma doesn't talk anymore, and for once, I don't try to grovel for her acceptance. In fact, as soon as she parks the Volvo in the garage, I rush inside and proceed to lock myself in my room. Tomorrow she can try to convince me otherwise, but for now, my mind is made up. I'm staying here this summer, and there's nothing she can do about it.

Upon entering my room, I start getting ready for bed. I can feel how late it is without looking at my watch. Today has been a long one. So much has happened. I don't want to think about how I left things with Sarah. Reflecting on the day's events is making my stomach feel uneasy. It's either that or I'm starving. Though it is late, I should probably get something to eat.

After a quick shower, I leave my room very quietly. There's gotta be some food in the fridge for me to munch on. In the kitchen, I pry open the refrigerator door as softly as I can, hoping it doesn't disturb Ma or Brenden, if he is home. The last thing I want to happen is to wake her up, if she's even asleep, and start the argument all over again. There's nothing in here that looks very appetizing. I resort to making another PB&J and munch on some chips from the pantry.

I head back to my room and plop myself down on the bed.

Two bites later and my appetite is gone. I really ought to go to sleep. That is exactly what I'm gonna do. I set the half eaten sandwich on my nightstand and lay down. Sleep does not come. I have to force myself to close my eyes and try to trick myself into sleeping. Immediately, I'm met with Sarah's face again. Only this time, I see Gabe and Kaite too. They called her a stalker. A loser. A freak. I can't believe it.

Another memory from today enters my head, taking over the yearbook message debacle. I'm on those teacups again, swirling around and around. My heartbeat skyrockets. I turn over in bed and try to reset my mind. Think of the number pi. 3.14159-it's not coming to me. Usually going over these numbers puts me right to sleep. My eyes open. Tonight is simply not working.

Almost instinctively, I bring myself to a sitting position. I get out of bed to walk over to my door and unlock it very quietly. The hallway is dark. There are no sounds coming from Ma or Brenden's room. I don't know why, but my feet start walking towards my brother's room. At his door, I give it a light tap. He's either dead asleep or not home yet. When I enter, I find that he indeed is not home.

Besides the surfboard being gone from the spot above his bed, everything looks as it did this morning. A mess. There are clothes, CDs, and vinyls everywhere, and his comforter has remained on the floor. His acoustic guitar sits nicely in the corner, being held up by a black stand. It's probably the most expensive thing in his room. Come to think of it, how did he afford to buy that? It's not like he can hold down a job. Ma certainly doesn't give him money. That's one mystery I don't feel like solving.

Nosily, I look around the room at the posters of bands plastered to his walls. It seems like these have been up for ages. Everything in here, actually, looks pretty similar from when we were kids. Even amidst the tangled mess of video game cords is that same old Nintendo console sitting right next to his Xbox.

Seeing it makes me think back to the last time I came in here, unannounced.

That time, I overheard Ma yelling at dad over the phone. It was shortly after he left us at Disneyland. I could be remembering it wrong, but it sounded like she had a restraining order against him. A shudder runs through me. She had no right to do that. I missed him so much and never understood what exactly happened between them. That was the last time I cried. I couldn't stop the tears from streaming down my face. Dad was my hero. My best friend. Then he was gone. Why did he have to leave? It dawns on me that *she* made him go. I do not understand why.

All I remember was feeling so angry, I came running into Brenden's room looking for something. There wasn't anything I needed in here though. What I do know for sure is instead of kicking me out, I recall being handed a controller and playing those old games like Super Smash Bros until the morning came. Before then, I didn't know what it meant to be awake past my bedtime. I fix my eyes on the old thing and sit down on the floor. Robotically, I reach for the controller and turn on the console. It still works. This ought to shut my brain off.

Time seems to go by fast. I don't know how long I've been playing when I hear a rattling noise coming from Brenden's window. I look up in a trance, eyes hazy. Then it starts opening up. Shaking myself out of the trance-like state I was in, I pause the game and stand up to see a white surfboard being shoved through the window. Am I dreaming? The board falls to the ground, knocking over Brenden's vintage stereo from the windowsill in the process. I move out of the way at the same time he comes in. I do nothing to help.

He crawls through the window smoothly, like he's done it a thousand times.

"What the heck?" Brenden exclaims upon seeing me. He lands on top of his bed, then jumps down to pick up the fallen board. "Are you kidding me?" he declares solemnly at the sight of his now broken stereo. He pushes the surfboard aside to pick it up. "Just freaking fantastic," he mumbles angrily. I feel kind of bad but say nothing.

"Weston! What are you doing here?" he huffs, moving the broken stereo to his bed.

There is nothing I could say to defend myself for trespassing. I shrug, looking at the floor. My gaze shifts back onto him. I watch as he grabs his surfboard. He wipes off some sand and hangs it back above his bed. His long hair is completely tousled, probably from a day of surfing. I hate that he got to go to the beach while I had to go to Disneyland. Yet, at the same time, the thought of not going and not meeting Sarah makes me almost glad I went. Almost.

Brenden brushes off some stray sand particles from his t-shirt. He arches a brow and says, "What is wrong with you?" Soon after he asks, a faint smile creeps across his lips. "Wait, how did Misery-land go?"

"Like you care," I reply scornfully. He would like to know. I bet he lives for my unhappiness.

"That bad?" he chuckles maniacally, shuffling over to the mini fridge he keeps in his closet. My eyes wander curiously over to it. I wonder why I don't have one of those. Where did he even get that? Ma sure didn't buy it for him. Half the things in his room seemed to have just shown up out of nowhere. Brenden takes out an energy drink, opens the can and takes a few swigs before asking me if I want one. Surprised he even asked, I still shake my head no. I get enough heart palpitations as it is without the help of any stimulants.

"Whatever," Brenden says, setting it down on the wide ledge of his bed frame. He walks over to what used to be the area where he had his dresser. It is now a bean bag littered with a pile of clothes. Do I see some guitar picks in there? I repress an eye roll. Why does he feel the need to live in such slovenly disorder?

It truly baffles me. What time is it anyway? There's no clock in this room, and my wrist is bare.

Regardless of me being here, Brenden proceeds to change by taking off his black t-shirt. Does he really not care that I'm in his room or is he going to get me later? What game is he playing at? His nonchalant behavior is starting to tick me off.

Searching for an excuse to irritate him, I tap my foot. "Does Mom even know you snuck out again?"

He darts a look of annoyance at me while replacing his jeans with shorts. "You gonna tell, snitch?"

I narrow my eyes at him, ready to quip something back, but I notice the lipstick stain on the side of his face. So that's what he's been up to, I think insinuatingly. I wonder if he ever went to the beach. Maybe the sand on his board was all just a ruse to throw me off? I grit my teeth. Wherever he may have been, he was still having fun. Just the thought of him with some girl or with his friends irks me. Why is it that he can do whatever he wants with no consequences, but I have to behave perfectly? The reality of the situation is suddenly too much for me to handle. Rather than slink away into my bedroom in defeat, I feel the urge to blame him.

I fold my arms and snarl, "You know, maybe I will tell Mom what you've been up to."

He casually picks up his drink from the bed frame, unfazed by my attempts at picking a fight. "You have no idea what I've been up to."

My brows furrow as I clench my fists. "Whatever it is, I'm sure it can't be good."

He laughs. "You've got nothing on me, In-su." His lips curve.

Irritated that he used my Korean name, I threaten, "I'll tell her you got home late and about all the times you snuck out this week." That was a shot in the dark, since I haven't paid attention to anything else going on in this house during finals. After taking another long swig of the energy drink in his hand, he stares at me with those black eyes of his, not saying a word.

Mad he's not giving in, I groan. It's not like him. Also, I'm not acting like my typical sensible self. Have we switched somehow? While he is cool and collected, I can feel something irrational inside of me, wanting to take over. It is boiling in my stomach, creeping its way up into my chest. As much as I want to suppress it, I'm afraid I don't have sufficient willpower to do so.

Brenden blinks. "Go ahead, tell Ma. See what happens," he says, returning the threat.

Finally, he's starting to sound like himself. But I know he won't touch me. To be honest, he's never actually beat me up. Maybe that's why I taunt him sometimes. He's all bark and no bite.

Calling his bluff, I raise one eyebrow, saying, "Watch me," then promptly spin around. A full on deliriousness overwhelms me. From behind, I hear Brenden set down his now empty drink before darting after me. I sprint past my own room, heading for Mom's.

"You're dead," he yells out, not even trying to be quiet. It's too late for his empty threats, since I'm already knocking on Ma's door.

In a maddening haze, I shout, "Ma, Bren snuck out—"

Her door bursts open by the third knock. "In-Su, you are out of control," she says with no hint of sleep in her voice.

Has she been awake this entire time? It's the middle of the night. What is she doing? I stare blankly at her; at the same time, Brenden stops in his tracks. He doesn't dare to say another word and neither do I.

Out of nowhere, she grabs onto my arm, pulling me in the direction of the living room. "Go to bed, Min-Su. I know you've been sneaking out. I'll deal with you in the morning," she orders

Brenden. I feel like I'm five years old again having just tattled on my brother.

I turn around and notice Brenden, instead of retreating, is leaning against the wall most casually. He must be snickering at my expense. This is only making me ten times more upset. I'm so sick of this family. Forcefully, I pull my arm away from Mom, as I am done being treated like a child.

"Stop," I yell. "I'm not doing this right now. I'm going to bed." I am beyond exhausted.

"Excuse me?" she questions, her eyes furious.

"You're such an idiot," Brenden heckles.

Ma points a finger in his direction. "This does not concern you, Min-Su."

I snap, "Of course it doesn't. It never does. He can do whatever he wants and stay out till dawn doing god knows what, but not me."

Brenden pushes himself off the wall. "What are you talking about, Prom King?" I think I've ticked him off this time. "You get everything you want."

Frustrated with him and Ma, I run my fingers through my hair. It's still a bit damp from the shower I took earlier. I leave my mother in the living room and pass Brenden on the way to my room. He curses and mumbles something I can't make out. I don't want to deal with either of them right now.

"Just leave me alone!" I shout, attempting to shut the door, but Ma is right behind me. She follows me into my room and stands with her arms crossed next to my dresser. Alright, I guess we are doing this now. My throat tightens. There's no escaping this. A tightening sensation grows in my chest again.

"If I can't sleep, you can't either," she starts.

I inhale rapidly. "Why can't you just let me be, Ma?" I exclaim, desperation in my voice. I travel to my bed and sit down. My head is starting to pound, probably from all the yelling in Korean.

She moves to the edge of my bed, uncrossing her arms. "In-Su, the decision has been made for you. You are working for your uncle this summer, end of discussion."

"That decision was not yours to make," I say, standing up. My hands automatically ball themselves into fists. I'm absolutely furious. She can't make me give up my summer. I will not let her.

"What's done is done," Ma adds coldly. "You better start packing," she commands, walking away. "Because maybe I'll have you go early."

Was that a threat?

She can't do that to me after everything I have done these past four years. I sacrificed plenty of hang outs and parties with my friends just so I could get extra homework done. I stayed after school to tutor other kids, participated in clubs I don't care about, signed up for extra credit. During the course of my entire young adult education, I've gotten straight A's. Does she understand how hard that is to maintain? I was the perfect student and got accepted to an Ivy League school, but I guess it wasn't good enough. No. I'm not good enough.

There is a burning sensation in the center of my chest. My nose is practically flaring. It feels like my entire body is shaking. There is a colloquial saying about seeing red when one is mad. I didn't think that was possible until right now. Red is everywhere. On the walls. Over my bed. In Ma's eyes.

I suck in a quick breath and blurt in a fury, "Just say it to my face, I'm not good enough for this family, just like dad wasn't either."

There it is. The truth I've been afraid to admit for so long. Brenden, standing in my doorway, shoots me a look. He is stunned. Ma's jaw drops. Her brows unfold as her eyes grow wide. The devastation in her face is clear. I blink rapidly. Ma turns around fast, heading into the hall. I rush out after her, still so furious. Ma flees to the restroom just outside her door.

"Wes, stop." Brenden stretches out his arm, stopping me in the hall. "You really need to chill," he says in a soothing tone. His eyes are full of concern.

My eyes flicker at him out of spite as I try to wriggle past him. "Let me go, Bren."

He knows he can't stop me; I'm much taller and stronger than him now. Wait, where have I seen him do this before? My eyes grow wide. Wait, is he trying to protect her? That is ridiculous. Angry, I slam my arm down and break through his hold. He staggers backwards into the hallway and I head straight to the bathroom. To my surprise, I find Ma leaning over the sink, hyperventilating.

She is clutching her chest, heaving. I'm horrified. I've never seen her like this before. Her face is so pale, and her eyes are stricken with fear. I glance down at my hands balled into fists. The red I've been seeing starts to fade as I realize how intimidating I must look. Her breaths quicken, reminding me of a panic attack. I understand now. Every muscle in my body suddenly feels weak. I go back out into the hall. My legs nearly give out from under me as I lean against the wall and slide down to the floor. Shaking, I think, "Wow. My mother is scared of me."

"Joesonghabnida," I whisper, head in my hands, though I know she won't accept my apology. I say it again in English, "I'm sorry, Ma."

Her breaths seem to stabilize. Brenden quickly enters the bathroom. I hear him say calming things like, "It's ok. You're fine." I have not heard him talk so kindly to her in such a long time. It is so strange. Once her breaths sound a bit more stable, he leads her back to her bedroom, one hand on her back with the other holding her hand.

What a terrible night this turned out to be. I lean my head against the wall. Ma's words from earlier echo in my ear. "One day can change everything." I fear she may be right.

Not more than a minute later, Brenden returns. He sits beside me on the floor. I don't look at him. My eyes stay glued to the smoke detector on the ceiling with its flashing light blinking green. Somehow, it reminds me of the teacups, spinning round and round. They spin in circles constantly with no end in sight. It's sort of like that rabbit hole from Alice in Wonderland.

How did I end up back there?

"So what just happened?" Brenden asks, breaking the silence.

My lips remain closed. There is no excuse for my behavior so I will not speak. About a minute or two later, I think he catches on. But just because I don't speak doesn't mean he won't.

"Do you remember what really happened that day that Dad left us?" he says somberly, surprising me with a sudden change of subject.

I lift my head but still don't answer.

He brushes some of the long brown pieces of hair from out of his face. Exhaling, he says, "He had come back from god knows where." He lays a hand on his propped up knee. "I was only eleven, but I remember he told Ma that he won it big in Vegas. We both knew better."

My lips part. "I don't remember this."

Brenden sighs. "Of course you wouldn't. You were only six. Anyway, come to find out, he gambled away their entire life savings, including my college fund."

My jaw clenches. I may have been a kid, but I wasn't completely clueless. How did I not know this?

"That lowlife even had the audacity to ask her for more money that day for some prior debts he accrued." Brenden scoffs, continuing, "But she had already filed for divorce and got a restraining order against him."

"Wait," I blink, "So, all those times he left before, he was actually out gambling?"

"And cheating."

That doesn't make sense. I sigh, "But if Ma knew, why did she stay with him for so long?"

Brenden's eyes shift to the floor. He lowers his head and replies, "For you."

My hands rest on my knees. "I don't understand."

"Do you really not remember how differently he treated you?" Brenden says, exasperated. "You were his little genius, but me and Ma were…not." His voice cracks, lowering his head. We haven't spoken like this to each other since I don't know when. I'm still in shock by how much he is opening up to me. Brenden is a lot more vulnerable than I give him credit for, more than me even.

Combing through the memories, I see my father in my mind's eye. He was tall and strong. I don't remember too much about him besides that he was from Colorado. What I mainly recall was our relationship. He used to pick me up and put me on his shoulders, running around acting like a wild animal. It was the best. We spent a lot of time together at the mall and he taught me a secret language of sorts. They were hand signals that only he and I could understand. It was like a game. We really did have a special bond.

Parents say they don't have favorites, but they lie. It was no secret that dad preferred me to my brother. I think it's because I found him hilarious and Brenden did not. He also took me to places I don't think he brought Bren. One place that comes to mind was in a small room with a giant fish tank at the back of a store of sorts. I don't exactly remember where he took me, but I always had a good time. For the most part.

He used to sit at a big round table with his friends. They would play games. When they would allow me to come in and watch, I would sit in the back of the room and speak our secret language by sending Dad hand signals that matched the cards in his friends' hands. If I did a good job, we would go out for ice cream. If I got a signal wrong, he would get furious.

Now that I'm really thinking about it, I realize that secret place was merely a poker game in the back of some seedy bar.

A lump in my throat appears. I swallow and look over at my brother. "So, those special places he used to take me were…"

"Probably poker games."

"You're sure?" The thought of him taking me to those games makes me sick. I was only six or seven years old. How could he do something like that?

Brenden sighs. "Yes. Ma and I found out after the fact."

Balling my hands back into fists, I ask, "And those hand signals he taught me weren't just a special language between he and I, were they?" My stomach churns.

Brenden shrugs, looking down at the hardwood floor. "I don't know. I never learned it but probably."

One distinct memory is forming a picture in my head. I scoff. It's so obvious now why he took me to those poker matches in the first place. I was using those hand signals to help him cheat. Why did I not see it before? I should have known from how upset he became when I would mess up. He would yell and scream. It scared me. The thought of our special game turning out to be a way for him to win money makes me sick.

My mouth curls downward. I ask with caution, "Is that why Ma got a restraining order?"

His face is turned away. He doesn't say anything at first, but after a few seconds of silence, he says, "No."

My brows pull together. "If not that, then what?"

"You know why."

My eyes shift back and forth. What could he possibly mean by that? I rack my brain, searching for something that I'm missing. Then it hits me. I'm too stunned to even speak. All those times Dad had lost his temper, my mother rushed me into my room. Each time he and Ma were arguing, I was given headphones. Looking back, I seemed to have been protected from my fathers anger and my mothers suffering. But where was Brenden? Now I remember. He was there right in the middle of it.

I knew something was going on, but each time it happened, I was distracted by a new puzzle to solve or a new rocket to assemble. There was so much I didn't see. Maybe, deep down, I didn't want to see it. There's an overwhelming emptiness in my gut.

I say with trepidation in my voice, "He hit her." I swallow. "And…you?"

Brenden folds his arms across his chest. "Only when I got in the way," I hear him mutter, anger riddled in his tone. "Which was a lot," he exhales.

I swallow the lump in my throat. "I didn't know, Bren. Not really."

He slides one hand over his hair, unfolding his arms. "I know; we tried to keep it that way."

My heart thumps slowly with the seconds ticking by. I do not know what to say so I stare at the floor. The longer I stare, the more the pieces start to come together. Then my mind wanders back to that fateful day at Disneyland. It all makes sense now. A big part of me could not understand why Brenden didn't shed a tear when Dad left. I might have even held it against him, subconsciously. Yet, now I get it. He was happy that the monster who hurt him was leaving.

"That's why she told him to leave," I say. "At the teacups."

Brenden nods. He brings his knees to his chest and rests his head on them like a little boy.

"Why didn't you tell me?"

He tilts his head. His black eyes, like Ma's, meet my gaze. "Because it doesn't matter." He shakes his head.

"It does matter and I've been a complete self-involved idiot." I let out a long sigh. "All this time, I've been missing someone who hurt you and Mom." I pause, then add gingerly, "And I blamed you for not caring."

"I don't care, not anymore," is all he says in response. He lifts his head up. "And don't you dare say a word of this to anybody, you understand?"

Nodding, I quickly add, "I blamed her, Bren, this whole time." I utter a groan. "And now she's scared of me."

He raises a brow. "You think you scared her?"

"I know that's what happened. My hands were like this," I demonstrate, holding my tightly bound fists out to him. "She has to know I'd never hurt her," I say with slightly hazy eyes.

He waves a hand. "Nah."

I let out a warm breath of irritation. "I'm serious, Bren."

"No, like you actually think Mom was scared of you?" He looks at me like I'm a fool. "You're joking?"

"Forget you," I say, standing up.

Brenden follows suit. "If you actually think that, then you need to be for real." He leans his back against the wall. "Ma knows you wouldn't hurt a fly."

"But she was clutching her chest and practically shaking!" I exclaim in a huff with my hands spread out.

"She was having a panic attack," he says as a matter of fact.

"Since when does she get panic attacks?" I thought I was the only one in the family with that defect. How does Brenden know? It's like they have a secret club or something where they decide to not tell me certain things.

"Look, just because I know that, it doesn't mean anything." Brenden folds his arms. "Don't worry. You're still her favorite."

"Not after tonight."

"Come on, even if you don't go work for Uncle Henry, you're still going to college to be a lawyer, and for that alone, you can do no wrong," he states, looking away.

I stare at my brother, the person I've misjudged for so long. He won't like it, but I say anyway, "You could go back to school, you know. I could convince Ma to give you half of my tuition money."

He smirks at me, moving his hands into a finger gun. "Gee, thanks for the offer, bro." He clicks his tongue.

"Bren."

He sighs, letting his hands fall to his sides. "Don't worry about me. Alright? I've got everything under control."

From the looks of those shadows under his eyes, I highly doubt that, but I don't press. I simply say, "What are you going to do then?"

"Enough." He stands up straight, moving off the wall. "This isn't about me." The side of his mouth curves into a grin. "The real question is, are you going to take the summer off or not?"

That is my dilemma. The probability of Ma getting her way is high. After tonight's events, I'm not sure I want to fight her anymore. On the other hand, do I really want to give up my summer? This was my last chance to prolong my childhood and have some real fun. Maybe I could actually hang out with my brother and help him figure out what to do with his life. Seeing this unguarded side of him makes me think I really don't know him at all. I want to change that.

Perhaps this summer I could really try living in the moment, actually seizing the day, much like Sarah. There's only one way to find out if it's worth the risk.

"You gotta help me sneak out," I interject, having decided.

His jaw drops. "What?"

Without elaborating more, I spin around and head to my room. Quickly, I change out of my lounge wear and back into some regular clothes. I settle for some gray shorts and a basketball jersey. Brenden follows me. I pick up my phone and see that it's 1:45 am. It's late, but I have to do this now or else I'm afraid when I go to sleep, I'll lose the nerve.

Brenden is silent until he sees me checking my phone and that's when he blurts, "So, what's her name?" He is next to my desk, arms folded across his chest. "I didn't know this was actually about a girl." He smirks.

My brows shoot up. "It's not. Wait. How did you know-" I stutter, slipping on my jersey.

"Please. I wrote the book on that." He lifts a brow, grinning on one side of his mouth.

He does have rizz. This, I do know well. It is actually kind of obnoxious how girls seem to go feral over him. It is not like I'm immune to having girls like me, I admit, but the difference is I have to work to be charismatic and he doesn't have to try at all.

Sneaking out is another thing that comes natural to him. It's not like I haven't thought about sneaking out before, but between Ma, my friends, and Hannah, I never seemed to have the reason to. Not to mention how dead I'd be if I got caught. I hate to say it, but I'm not as slick as Brenden. Tonight, however, I'm going to have to take a page out of his book and do something that requires his expertise.

He follows me stealthily down the hall and into the kitchen. I wonder if Ma's asleep already. On a normal night, she'd be in her room by ten. I hate that we fought. Part of me wants to march back in there to fix things, but I know that wouldn't be a smart idea. It's probably better to reconcile tomorrow when both of us are in a better head space. Besides, for once, there are others that take precedence.

I shake my head as I reach for the keys to the Volvo, in disbelief that I'm doing this.

"Are you sure you want to steal her car?" Brenden quips as he saunters to the garage door, opening it as quietly as possible.

Even I barely hear the hinges squeak. He is good.

"No. I'm not sure." My fingers tremble, shaking the keys. I bring them to my chest to muffle the noise. "Maybe I should wait until tomorrow. Sleep on it," I say as my feet stiffen by the door.

Brenden throws back his head like he knew I'd chicken out. "Wes, do you like this girl?"

If my immediate answer is not yes, then I better put myself

to bed. A grin forms on my lips. "Yes, yes, I do." It's not logical. Nothing about this day, this night, has been logical. I don't care for once.

"Then go." Brenden pulls back the door wide enough that I can see the Volvo from where I stand in the kitchen. "Showing up in the middle of the night, throwing rocks at her window. You can't lose."

He's absolutely right. Things would have gone a lot differently with Hannah, had I not broken up with her before our Disneyland trip. Then again—My mouth opens slowly as I realize something important I had forgotten. I changed the plan. Because I knew I couldn't give her what she wanted, I had to break things off. Now here I am, about to run into the arms of another girl who probably wants the same thing, but, sadly, nothing has changed for me. The facts are the same. I'm going to Harvard. That's almost 3000 miles away from Los Angeles.

I close my mouth, shaking my head. Parting my lips, I say in a low whisper, "I can't go."

Brenden arches a brow. "Don't be such a pansy."

"I don't want to lead this girl on." That is the truth despite how her name creates a rippling sensation in my chest.

"Must you always overthink everything?" he says in an equally low whisper. He lets the door close about halfway, keeping his hand on it so that it doesn't make a sound.

"No, it's not like that," I say, then start explaining the events of the day. I tell him the shortened version of everything.

Brenden makes a face and brings a free hand to his chin. "What I'm getting from this is," his hand falls, "you're worried this girl might be a stalker, but she is possibly the nicest, most thoughtful person you've ever met?"

"No, I'm not worried she's a stalker. That's what my friends think."

"Yeah, and you believe them?" he says poignantly.

"No," I say. "No, I don't." I look down at the car keys in my hand. "I just don't know if I should go to her house when I can't make any promises."

"Well, assuming she would even want to talk to you after you let your friends roast her," he scoffs, "let her decide how she feels about it. Stop trying to control everything. For once in your life, live in the moment."

He sounds just like Sarah, who wants to give up a full scholarship for her dream of the moment — to go live in a camper van in Bali. She's ready to take chances for what she wants.

Maybe I should too?

"Alright, I'm going," I say definitively.

Brenden pushes the door open, allowing me to walk through briskly. Before hopping in the Volvo, I notice out of the corner of my eye, a very nice looking red BMW in front of our house. It's parked sloppily behind Brenden's beat up sedan.

I raise a brow. "Whose car is that?" I ask, jumping in.

Brenden shakes his head. "Don't worry about it." He looks away. I wish I could read his facial expression, but I can't.

Putting on my seat belt, I ignore the inclination to press him further about it. Come to think of it, I've been seeing a lot of random luxury vehicles parked near our house lately. I never thought anything of it because, well, I've got other things on my mind, like graduating for one. My jaw tenses. I just hope they don't have anything to do with Brenden. My chest rises and falls. I'll press him about it later. All I want to focus on is getting out of here without getting caught.

Placing both hands on the wheel, I take in another deep breath and sense my heart rate slowly speeding up.

"Relax, Wes," Brenden says, hand on the garage door opener. "I'll cover for you."

I nod, trying not to think about the misdemeanor I'd be charged with for driving as a minor and without a license. He presses the button. The door rolls up. It's so loud, Ma is sure to hear, but it's now or never.

Before I get to backing out, my brother rushes over to tell me to shift the gear into neutral and wait until I'm out of the driveway before turning on the ignition. I do as he says. The car rolls out of the garage so quietly, it's no wonder he got away with doing this for so long. Perhaps Ma won't know about this little escapade after all?

CHAPTER 12

Apologies

I've turned down this street probably close to a hundred times. It's only 15 minutes from my own neighborhood. Routinely, I park in front of Gabe's house. His new white G-wagon sits quietly in the driveway, a graduation gift from his dad's dealership. It makes me wonder, if my dad was still around, what he would have gifted me? Shaking my head, I forget the thought. It wouldn't have been worth it for all I know.

Turning off the car, I look out at the neighborhood. Such a shame I've been here countless times, all the while not knowing Sarah Lackey lived just next door. My head shakes. How was I completely unaware that she lived so close? I'll never know. Pulling out my phone, I check my messages again to make sure I have it right.

"I need to know where Sarah lives," I text Gabe. "Which house is it?"

He probably won't answer, as it is well past two in the morning. His large white and tan house is dark. There are no lights on of course. Same goes for both houses on either side of him. I suck in a breath. There's no guessing which one is hers, but I at least have a 50/50 shot. Smiling, I think, the odds are in my favor tonight. Then again, if I knock on the wrong door, things could go south quickly. I've never been much of a risk taker, but tonight is the exception because I have to find her. I scratch my temple. This is so crazy. By far, it's the most impulsive thing I've ever done. I lick my lips and whisper into the night, "Here goes nothing."

With my hand on the door, I pull the handle, then immediately stop. What in the world? There's someone running over to Gabe's car, very stealth-like. I must have been too dazed to notice where they came from and there doesn't seem to be any other cars parked on the street. Did that person walk here? I swallow. Who is this guy? What are they taking out of their pocket? I squint my eyes. Oh no. What are they doing? Are they breaking into Gabe's car?

Slowly and quietly, I make my way out of the Volvo, crouching down beside it. I think I'm successful in not being heard because the person doesn't look my way when I shut the car door. Quietly, I creep around the back side of it. That's when I hear a strange hissing noise. I stand up just enough to get a glimpse of the guy. My brows shoot up. It's hard to tell, but I think they are spray painting Gabe's car with no signs of trying to break in. Alright, that's my cue. I better be a good friend and chase them off before they do more damage, even if Gabe doesn't deserve it.

"Hey, yo!" I yell, revealing myself from behind my mom's car.

Startled, the dude drops the paint cans in a panic and starts running. I bolt after him. My eyes flicker over to the front porch, where the Ring camera is. Yes, I sneer. He's caught. The guy darts through Gabe's lawn, heading for the house on the right. I follow him. The guy is rather small. I think I can take him.

All those years of basketball drills made me really good at sprinting. I catch up to him real fast. Almost out of breath, I grab him by the arm. He yelps in pain. Wait a second. My heart stops. The voice is female. I loosen my grip as I turn her around to face me directly. Fear strikes my eyes, causing them to dilate.

"Sarah?"

"Wes?"

I let her go. She stumbles back, rubbing her arm. I bite my lip, hoping I didn't hurt her too badly. We stare at each other for a long minute, both wondering, I assume, why the other person is here. I open my mouth to speak, but close it when a light brightens the left side of her face. She looks different somehow. In a good way. Has she always worn glasses? The light is shining from Gabe's porch. Crap. I gotta get her out of here. She has the same thought and tells me to follow her. We sprint towards the house to the right of Gabe's. Her black hood falls, revealing a little red pony tail. She leads me to the far side of the house.

Safe in the shadows, she peeks her head out from the corner, no doubt attempting to see if we were indeed caught. I position myself right behind her and lean my head out to see as well. No one is outside yet. Only the damaged G-wagon sits in the driveway for now. The corner of my mouth curls upward. I can't believe she spray painted it. Wait. Now that I'm really looking at it, there's something not quite right about the spray paint. Actually, it's not painted at all.

"What is that?" I accidentally whisper.

"I silly-stringed his car," Sarah admits, gasping.

Her words sink in as I gaze upon her work. A small laugh escapes me. "Silly string?" I tilt my head downward. She looks up, eyes meeting mine. A small thud comes from my chest.

Extraordinary.

"I wanted revenge, but I couldn't bring myself to actually hurt the beautiful car."

I stifle a laugh. This girl is something else. I can tell she's trying hard to suppress a laugh herself but succumbs anyway.

Snickering, I put a finger to my mouth. "Shhh." Now I'm the one about to give us away. She covers her mouth, giving over to the laughter. We hear commotion coming from Gabe's driveway and quiet ourselves. We look around the corner and see Gabe's dad, Jaime, emerging from the garage.

Sounding beyond angry, he shouts, "What did you do to your new car, Gabriel?"

He walks back in the garage to yell for his son to come downstairs. He sure is loud. I'm pretty sure the entire neighborhood can hear him. This is hysterical. Leaning against the house, I can sense how close Sarah is to me. I could very easily lay my free hand on her shoulder but refrain. It just wouldn't be appropriate.

Gabe emerges from the garage, looking confused as ever. He's in white boxer-briefs. Boy didn't think to throw on some clothes. What an idiot. I roll my eyes and sigh. That's embarrassing. Sarah snickers. At least she finds it amusing.

"Are you serious?" His jaw drops at the sight of his car. With his hands above his head, he exclaims emphatically, "What? No. I didn't do this." I almost feel bad for him. Almost.

Jaime points. "I don't care who did this, you clean it up right now." He walks over to the left side of his house, disappearing from view, shortly returning with a hose. "Wash it." Oh, he's not playing.

"But it's the middle of the night," Gabe whines. What a loser.

"I don't care if it takes you until the break of dawn, you're cleaning that junk off," Jaime huffs before retreating into the garage.

"But, Dad, I didn't do this," Gabe refutes angrily. "Whoever did is sooo dead. Hey, wait, check the Ring camera." He looks back at his dad who is already inside. He lifts his eyes in dismay to the empty space in our direction. Sarah and I jump backwards, fast. Nah. There's no way he could have seen us. My heart rate speeds up. Shoot. I slap a hand on my forehead. What if he saw my mom's car? It's still parked right in front of his house. There's no solution to that problem. I just have to rely on the fact that Gabe might be too delirious to notice. The panic in me quickly subsides at the sound of a hose being turned on. I exhale with a hand on my chest, thinking we are in the clear. That was close.

Sarah buries her face in her hoodie. I grin knowing I'm an accomplice in…what is this?

Mustering up the courage, I ask in a low whisper, "Why'd you do it?"

As soon as I say it, I recall what happened, not merely four and a half hours ago. She stares at me as if to say, "You know why." I give a slight nod before inching back over to the edge of the house, craning my neck far enough to catch the pissed off look on Gabe's face. Serves him right. Sarah peeks again, too. She muffles another laugh. His aggravated mumbles start up again, but so far, it looks like he hasn't put two and two together. I think we are in the clear.

Sarah walks past me to the fence near the back of her house. She gestures with a wave to follow her once again. I do. Through the darkness, we traverse her backyard riddled with toys that are everywhere, and I mean everywhere. I step on one, causing me to almost trip and crash into her.

"Ah, sorry," I mutter softly. Good thing I have excellent reflexes.

Sarah giggles, "No I'm sorry it's such a mess," and walks over to the sliding glass door. "My mom owns a daycare."

"Oh, that's interesting."

The sliding door opens up right into the kitchen. We step inside. I look, wide eyed, around the room. The feeling of being in Sarah Lackey's house has me completely enveloped. I shove my hands into my pockets, wondering what it would be like to be here during daycare hours. Would it be chaos? Probably, though it sounds utterly charming.

"I shouldn't turn on any of the lights down here or Gabe might suspect something," Sarah says. "But follow me."

"Smart," I reply with a grin. She smiles back at me. I'm glad my eyes are already adjusted to the dark.

Quietly, I follow her up to the second story of her house. It's bigger than I thought it would be. The layout is similar to Gabe's. Yet somehow better. It is wide and spacious. There is a large living room area with a huge L-shaped couch and a TV hung on the back wall. The pillows on the couch are all brightly colored and mismatched. There are even more children's toys up here than there are in the backyard and stuffed animals are sprawled everywhere.

The decor is somewhere in between farmhouse and midcentury modern. I only know that because Ma has a list of what styles people are into when they are looking to buy a house. It helps her create a vision for prospective clients. Sarah's house has a very unique style. It's nice. Aside from the living room, there is a balcony that overlooks the downstairs foyer. I breathe, taking it all in and smelling a mixture of baby powder and vanilla. I can almost imagine what it would be like to see Sarah and her entire blended family at home. There are pictures on the walls of her siblings, I believe. Not to mention the many shoes and toys I had to step over along the stairwell leading up here. It's such a different vibe. There's a more cozy atmosphere that my family missed out on. Well, it comes as no surprise, since we are a different sort of family.

Sarah walks up to the furthest white door at the end of the hallway. It must be her room.

"So, this is it," she says, entering it. I go in behind her.

She sits on the twin bed closest to the window and turns on a lamp. I tread lightly through the door, unsure of what to think at this moment. I get a strange feeling. I mean, it's not like this is my first time in a girl's room, but being in hers is quite a surreal experience, especially since Sarah and I only met a short 12 hours ago. Now, here I am in the most intimate space she could share with a person, and she chooses to share it with me.

My eyes rove the quaint room. There is a clear divider by means of a curtain in the middle, but it's pulled back, letting me know it has an occupancy of two individuals. I don't have to wonder which side is Sarah's. The bed on the right side is made up of many stuffed animals, most of which are cats. The corners of my mouth curl. There's a dresser over there, too, with multiple items of clothing, fit for a child, spilling out of its drawers.

Sarah's, on the other hand, seems cluttered at first glance but with a closer look, it's actually pretty put together. Everything has its place, like the huge bookshelf in the corner, which is stacked full of novels, and do I see anime, or manga, I mean? I suppress a grin. Looking closer, I notice a book that went mega viral last year, "My Shining Star."

Pulling it out from the shelf, I don't hold back from teasing her, "Of course you would have this book."

Sarah sits down on her bed that is less than a foot away from the bookshelf. "And why not? It's so good. It's one of my favorites. Have you read it?"

"Nah. I wouldn't call myself a reader unless it's a scholastic journal or something of the nonfiction genre," I explain, flipping through the pages. A small picture of the famous actor, Taylor Kingston, falls to the floor. I chuckle, "Oh, what do we have here?"

Sarah's face blushes. "Shut up." She gets off the bed, bending down to pick it up. "So what, I'm a big fan."

"Yeah, you and every other teenage girl," I goad, snatching the picture from her.

"Hey."

I place the picture of the famous actor, and supposed heartthrob, back in the book that his wife wrote.

"Ugh, I just love him," Sarah gushes. "And isn't it so sweet she wrote that book for him after they had lost touch?" Her eyes flutter. "They were high school sweethearts, you know, who actually got together. I just think it's so romantic," she swoons.

This, I know well. Everyone was obsessed with their love story. The video of how the actor's wife proposed was everywhere on social media. Then her book sold out. I don't keep up with celebrities or anything like that, but I know everything there is to know about Taylor Kingston and Amy Sparrow, probably since they both happened to be from California.

"I guess you're right about that," I mutter, scratching my chin. I've never considered myself a romantic, but I can see the importance in trying. I'll have to make a mental note of that.

Moving on from the books, I gape at her vast vinyl collection. She has it neatly displayed atop her dresser right next to the record player. Wow, I don't recognize any of these bands, except one. I think I may have seen it before in Brenden's room, if I'm not mistaken. We don't usually like the same type of music, but maybe I ought to give this one a listen. I make another mental note to add the band to my Spotify.

On the wall above her dresser are various polaroids of her and her friends, I think, hung from twinkle lights. From the looks of the pictures, those were probably taken a couple years ago. Sarah looks different, yet the same. Her hair is longer and brown instead of cherry red. She has her glasses on. I wonder if she has contacts and that's why I haven't seen her with them until now.

Very interesting.

"You can sit down." Sarah points to a small white chair that faces her bed. I notice the large fish tank in the other corner of her room. I smile. That's gotta be where she keeps her turtle.

"Ah, yes, what was this guy's name again? Simba, right?" I strut over to the tank and lean down to see him. What a neat pet. I was never allowed to have animals growing up. Ma was allergic. Although, now that I think about it, Brenden may have had a snake at one time. I wonder what happened to it?

Sarah is quiet. I sit myself down on the chair. Our eyes meet, and suddenly, I feel awkward being in here.

She breaks my gaze. "So, see any pictures of yourself?" She crosses her arms. Her eyes pierce mine and just like that the mood shifts. There is a weird tension in the air. My jaw tenses. It builds the longer I stay silent. My lips part. I need to say something, but what? What I do best is relay the facts. But what are they? Firstly, I am horrified she was bullied by my so-called friends. Second, I hate how she looked at me when they were tearing into her. What's worse is I didn't even back her up. She has to know what they said is not at all what I think. My shoulders slump. More importantly I need to apologize, not only for my friend's behavior but for mine. That is why I came here anyway. I just didn't expect to jump into the topic so fast.

Gripping the edges of the chair, I say solemnly, "Sarah, I'm sorry."

She looks away and shifts uncomfortably on the bed. Her lips purse. I sit up straight, frowning. She doesn't believe me. Why should she? I just stood there and let those guys insult her. Well, I have to make it up to her. Taking my hands off the chair, I place them on my knees and tilt my head up. "Sarah, you have to know, I never thought you were-were…" My voice trails off. How can I say it without it sounding so god awful?

"A stalker, right?" she interjects.

Her eyes are so full of hurt, but I sense a hint of insecurity in her tone. I need to reassure her. But how?

I say immediately, almost cutting her off, "No. You're not a… a…s-stalker." My mouth trips over the word.

Sarah practically leaps off her bed. Oh, great. Is she angry? I need to explain more, but she's crouching down and grabbing something from her side table. She opens a drawer, pulls out a blue book with white daisies on the cover, and closes it. She stands up, reaching out her hand. It is obvious she wants me to take it.

"Here. Read about how obsessed I am with you," she says, face flushing. She stands in front of me, waiting for me to look inside.

With a horrified expression on my face, I grab it, then immediately try to hand it back to her. She refuses. I look down at it, perhaps a bit curious to see what lies beneath this feminine cover. I must have a death wish because my fingers intrinsically open the journal. I read the first line to myself. "Today, Monica and I went to the mall and guess who we saw? Weston-" I shut the book. "No, I'm not going to read this," I say, extending it back to her again, but she refuses again.

She puts her hands on her hips. "Wes, you have to read it. See for yourself how I am some weird stalker girl who's obsessed with you," she states sarcastically. Her eyes are glowing in the yellow lamp light.

I lay the journal down at the foot of her bed. "I don't care."

Sarah clutches her chest. "What?"

I blink. "Sorry, that was a poor choice of words," I say, shaking my head. I look up at her, and this time, I say what I really feel. "Let me try again." She nods slowly, giving me the chance to make things right. Clenching my fists together, I open them up and breathe in and out. She's making me nervous. No need to get all worked up, just relay the facts, I repeat to myself. My eyes begin to widen. "Look, I'm sorry about what happened back at Disneyland. You're not a stalker. You're not anything Gabe said you were and I'm sorry for not defending you. Especially after the more than interesting day we had." Her furrowed brows seem to relax. "If it's any consolation, I blew up at everyone after you left."

Sarah takes a tiny step towards me. Her eyes light up, and the corner of her mouth curls. "Really?" Her voice sounds hopeful.

I take a step near her, nodding. "Yeah, if you can believe it." I take another step until we are maybe three inches apart. "Sarah, my friends are idiots. What they said was really messed up. That's not how I feel about you, though." She stares up at me, confident. I can't stop gawking at her eyes. They are exceptionally brown. I think those glasses may even enhance the chestnut hue in her irises.

"How…do you feel about me?" she asks, shyly, her breath unsteady.

Her lips look so pink. She can't be wearing lip gloss though or whatever girls wear to make them so pigmented. It doesn't matter. I don't know why they have me mesmerized. I've forgotten what I'm supposed to say next. All I want to do is lean down and recreate the moment we shared under the castle.

What was I saying again? My heart is pounding. The heat is rising in my cheeks again. It's embarrassing, but it doesn't stop me from bringing my face closer to hers. I swallow. Her brows relax completely. She tilts her head up just slightly. Our lips are a few centimeters apart. Yep, this is happening. I close my eyes. Not a second later do I pry them open. My phone is vibrating like crazy, causing me to abruptly pull away from Sarah. Darn it. Way to ruin the moment. I take it out of my pocket and see it's Brenden.

"Cover is blown. Ma is furious," he texts.

I turn away from Sarah, hoping to hide my annoyed scowl. So much for my brother covering for me. I grit my teeth and suck in a breath as I look back to see Sarah inching away. She is now back to sitting on her bed, looking incredibly disappointed. She has no idea how much I am too. Gosh. Seems like no matter how much I want to prolong this day, it has finally come to its end.

Gutted, I run a hand over the back of my neck. "I'm sorry, but I gotta go."

Sarah sighs. "It's ok. Really."

I groan. "Ugh, I feel like such a jerk."

"You're not," she assures me, smiling. "You came here in the middle of the night and apologized. That's not jerk behavior, Mr. President." Her teasing smile is something I could get used to. Nodding, I shove my phone back into my pocket and head for the door.

"Make sure you go out the way we came in," Sarah says, standing up. "We have a Ring camera. My mom and stepdad would flip if they saw a guy come out of their house at 2:30am."

"Fair enough," I say, lingering in her doorway. There's still so much I need to tell her.

"So, will I see you tomorrow?" Sarah wraps her arms around herself, waiting for me to answer.

I am reluctantly looking up to meet her gaze. Her eyes are big. They are filled with the kind of hope I recognize. I've seen it before in Hannah, and Lacy, and a few other girls I've been involved with. My chest feels like it's being squashed by a very heavy boulder. The reality of the situation comes crashing into me. I'm not sure where I'll be tomorrow, but what I do know is I'll have a mess to clean up. Where that leaves Sarah, I'm not sure. I shut my eyes as another vibration from my phone goes off.

"I really have to go," I say, opening them. I hate that I cannot answer her. Sarah slouches. Her dainty smile slowly disappears. My heart drops. "Sorry," I whisper.

My feet manage to drag me out of her room and back down the stairs. I can't believe I'm ending the night like this, but I have no choice. Ma is probably calling the cops to have me arrested for stealing her car. Insane, yes, but I wouldn't put it past her.

"So that's it then?" Sarah exclaims, following me downstairs. It takes everything in me not to respond. Upon reaching the kitchen, I make my way to the sliding glass door we used to enter her house. My resolve practically shatters when I catch a glimpse of her sulking figure in the reflection of the door. That's it. I freeze. Call me illogical or impulsive, I don't care anymore. It feels good to act irresponsibly. I spin around.

"Let's go somewhere," I exclaim, heart pounding.

Sarah almost bumps into me. She takes a step back, balancing herself, then shoots a look of confusion at me.

"Go somewhere? Now?" She adjusts her green rimmed glasses.

I grab her hand. "Yes. Come with me, right now. There's a place I want to show you." Forget Ma. I'll deal with her and the consequences later.

Her brow arches. "But I thought you had to leave." She's testing me.

"Yeah, well, I can't get in any more trouble than I already am." I smile and slide open the door with my other hand. "Will you come with me?"

She grins. I extend my hand to her and she takes it. A rush of adrenaline hits me as we step outside. I smirk. If only Brenden could see me now, and Trey for that matter. Talk about living in the moment. I think I could get used to this.

We trek stealthily, hand in hand, to my mother's car which is still parked in front of Gabe's house. I really should not have parked there. Oh well. Mistakes were made. I open the door on the passenger side for Sarah, who is covering her face. I keep my head down too, hoping Gabe's ring camera cannot make out our faces.

Hopping in the car, I turn on the ignition and say, "For the record, I don't care that you wrote the yearbook message. I wanted it to be you."

CHAPTER 13
In Theory

I t's been a long time since I've been here. I take note of the sign as I pull the car into the parking lot at Elysian Park. Everything looks pretty much the same. Come to think of it, I haven't been back here since the start of junior year. It was such a safe space for me to escape to every now and again. I hope Sarah likes it. To my knowledge, no one knows about this place except for a few locals.

In the lot, we exit the car. I look around as if for the first time. It's nothing impressive yet. We walk over to the dirt path that is not very well lit. I grit my teeth, nervous about how this looks.

As if reading my mind, Sarah jokes, "Are you going to murder me, Weston Hill-Cho?" She smiles teasingly.

"I know this looks suspicious but I promise it'll be worth it," I say in reply. It's either really stupid or brave of her to be here with me now. "Ok, grab my hand. This next part might be a bit dangerous." Let's hope this act of irresponsible behavior pays off.

"I can handle anything," she says a bit cockily while taking my hand. What I thought would be a rush of electricity flooding into my veins is merely a feeling of warmth. A comforting temperature from the touch of her hand on mine. It is familiar. I did not expect that.

"There's a big wooden swing at the end of this trail," I explain as we walk hand in hand up the small dirt path. "It overlooks the city."

"Wow, that sounds magical."

That word typically makes me cringe, but after the events of today, it doesn't seem like a bad way to describe it. In fact, it reminds me of the way she looked when the fireworks exploded above us. I'll never forget it.

"Alright. A couple more steps and we are there." I can almost see the large tree at the top of the hill. Its large branches are enough to hold a ton. It's really a remarkable tree. Actually, it should be coming into view now. Wait. My eyes rove the premises. There's nothing here. I scratch my head. "Is it gone?"

"Maybe we are on the wrong trail?" Sarah suggests, biting her lip.

I let go of her hand to explore, searching for any sign of the old wooden swing. Why is it gone? It has to be here. That was the most remarkable thing about this place. Sarah walks where the tree should be and over to the edge of the hill.

She inhales, looking out at the city lights below and exclaims, "Woah, this is quite a view."

Abandoning my search, I join her in staring at the indescribable view. In my peripherals, I notice her content expression. She stands there in her black hoodie with her hands in the pocket, listening to the hum of cars driving in the distance. Looking at her, I conclude, swing or no swing, this was the real reason I brought her here.

My head tilts down. "You like it?"

She cackles. "Of course. It's breathtaking." She keeps her eyes fixed on the view. "How did you find this place?"

"It was by accident," I tell her. "Ma made a wrong turn, and me, being an impatient ten year old, had felt like we had been driving for hours. I needed a break. So, I made her pull over. This was the first place she found."

"That's pretty serendipitous."

This girl doesn't cease to amaze me. I smile. "Yeah it was."

We both let the silence ensue as we stare out into the valley. This would be a great end to an incredible day, minus a few mishaps, but there is a faint tapping in the back of my mind. The longer this moment continues, the more romantic it's going to feel. It'll be next to impossible to say what I need to say. Alright, better do it now before I lose the nerve.

"Sarah?" I start, turning to her. "I'm leaving after graduation."

She turns her head just enough to meet my gaze, while still being able to see the incredible view. "I know that, Harvard boy." She smiles at me lightly.

I lick my lips. "No, you don't understand. I'm leaving like two days after graduation. I had hoped for the summer off, but unfortunately, that's not going to happen."

"So what does that mean?"

"It means I won't be around this summer, and when I leave, I don't know when I'll be back."

Her smile melts as it begins to set in. "Oh, I see." She looks back out to the city. "I'm guessing that wasn't a part of your plan, huh?"

I shrug. "Plans do change sometimes." I lower my head a little more. "But this time, it's out of my control." As I say the words, I can't believe them to be true. Would fighting about it more even be worth it? I suppose there's no harm in trying. However, I get the feeling that wishing for a free summer would just be delaying the inevitable. There's no stopping my mother when she sets her mind on something. She is awfully stubborn.

Sarah and I stand so close I can sense her every movement,

as I'm sure she can sense mine. My eyes shift downward. "It's not my choice."

"Of course it's your choice, Wes," Sarah interjects, moving backward.

I blink. "But it's not."

She exhales a long sigh, then sits on the ground. "And why not?" I would prefer to not get dirt on my shorts, but I sit beside her anyway.

"Because there's no reasoning with my mother," I tell her, sitting cross-legged.

She looks back out to the city and says, "Have you tried talking to her?"

"Yes, sort of," I say, my knees bouncing. "Trust me, if you met her, you'd understand that she always gets her way, and there's no point in fighting it because-"

"Because you're scared of letting her down?" she adds.

Slowly, I nod. "Something like that." Admitting this is easier than I thought.

"Well, if you ask me, that's kind of messed up." Sarah tugs on the left string of her black hoodie. "If she loves you and you tell her you don't want to go, she should respect your wishes, right?"

"I don't have that kind of luxury in my household."

She just doesn't understand our background or our family dynamic. Defying my own mother is simply not done in my culture. Brenden clings to his American heritage so he can get away with his acts of rebellion, but I see how it takes a toll on Ma. To make things easier for her, I deem it my responsibility to acquiesce to her every request. Sarah may have a point, though.

She turns her head. "That sucks."

"Tell me about it," I complain. "But look, enough about my mother." I let out a light chuckle in an attempt at softening the mood. "I wanted to show you this place because-because..." I trail off, nervous about what I'm getting ready to say.

"You don't need to tell me that we'll just be friends. I already know that," she huffs, crossing her arms.

Shaking my head, I lay a hand on her back. "No, that's not what I was going to say at all."

Sarah breathes out like she's been holding it in for a long minute. "Really?"

Before I say something else, I think for a minute about why I broke things off with Hannah. It was much for the same reason I'm feeling so apprehensive now. Pure logic drove me to the conclusion that we wouldn't make it. We are going to be living almost 3000 miles apart. To make it work, we would have had to continue our relationship long distance. But long distance relationships never work. I didn't want to risk it. That is what my head was telling me then. Now, I fear, my heart is telling me something completely different.

Swallowing, I start to say, "Look, I can't make any promises." Sarah stares out at the city lights, her chest rising and falling with each breath, as I confess, "But I want to get to know you better."

Sarah is silent for a long time. I can only assume what she is thinking until she finally speaks.

"Today was amazing," she says. "For me, it was almost fairytale-like." Her lips form into a soft grin. She playfully nudges me with her elbow. "I know you probably hate to hear that, but it's true. I mean you're Weston Hill-Cho, you're the Prom King. Well, more than that, you are the class president."

My cheeks feel a bit warm. I shake my head. Such nonsense.

Sarah continues, "And you noticed me today." She sighs. "You saw me." Her eyes bore into mine, almost as if she's looking through me, like she's searching for something that's hidden.

A surge of emotion overpowers me, moving me to place a hand on top of hers and say, "I wish I had seen you sooner." My head instinctively leans over to plant a light kiss on her forehead. As I pull away, for a brief second, I get the urge to lean down and kiss her on the mouth, but I hold myself back. One corner of my mouth curls. I sigh. She looks like she's holding her breath. Her eyes look away from mine as she exhales. Just like that, the moment is gone. That's the thing about moments: they end, just as fast as they begin.

She pulls away, smiling. "I'll never forget this day."

See, I don't want this to be the end, but I can feel her pulling away. I smile back at her with a bittersweet taste in my mouth. She leans her head on my shoulder, and we look out at the city lights below us. We stay like this for some time. I lose myself in thought, going over every possible scenario in order to logically continue this relationship, even as friends.

My mind wanders back to long distance relationships. I don't want to do long distance, even if it is done all the time. I don't think it works out in the end. Well, I guess sometimes it does, but statistically, the odds are against us. Then again, it's not like we couldn't try. She could always move to Boston. That's an idea. She's not set on UCLA anyway, so why not? Good lord. I can't believe the thought crossed my mind. The notion is ridiculous. We barely know each other. Why am I already thinking about the future?

Jarring myself out of my thoughts, I inhale quickly and exhale. Hold on. That is exactly the problem. I'm already thinking about what could happen before it has even begun. I know Trey would tell me to chill. We are just kids, anyway. There is no need to figure everything out right now. What happened to having fun? If I do end up getting to stay for the summer, that's exactly what I want to do. Have fun. Even if I don't get to stay, the fact is, I still want to get to know Sarah better. Where is the harm in that?

"Sarah?" I utter in a soft tone.

"Hmm?"

Turning my torso to face her, I grab her hand in mine and

say, "This is going to sound kinda wild. Frankly, it's illogical, I mean, we barely know each other." I'm stumbling over my words. She chuckles and does not interrupt me. She is patient and lets me get out what I'm trying to say. "But we should see where this thing goes."

With her hand still firmly in mine, she admits, "You say we don't know each other very well, and that may be the case for you, but I've known you for so long and I..." She shakes her head. "Now, this will sound actually wild. I might be crazy for saying this." The pupils inside her brown irises grow wide as her gaze returns to mine. "But if we did get together and it didn't work out...." She bites her lip, pausing her thought. I swallow, not knowing what to do with those words. I search her eyes for a clue to try and understand what this means. She doesn't know what could happen— I certainly don't. Under normal circumstances, this would drive me away, but the sincerity in her eyes relaxes me. She is being honest, not crazy. I squeeze her hand. Before I'm able to speak, she quickly adds, "If we don't make it in the end, I don't think I'll survive the heartbreak."

I frown and pull her in for an embrace. The sweet scent of a vanilla fragrance coming from her hair takes me back to the moment we shared underneath the castle. If only we could recreate that moment.

Stealing a breath of courage, I state cautiously, "You're right; there's no way to predict the outcome of whatever this could be..." She pulls her head back to look me in the eyes. "But I'm willing to take the risk if you are." I can't believe those words just came out of my mouth. This is the beginning of a new version of me, I think.

"But you're leaving," she states pointedly.

"I know, but I don't want this to be the end." I laugh at how dumb I sound right now. "I know, we should probably just be friends, but let's not overthink it." My eyes frantically look every which way except her eyes. Right now, I feel so unhinged. It might be because it's almost 3 am. "I can't promise you anything." I force myself to look at her. "As much as I like to pretend I have everything under control in my life, I don't." I inhale. "My mom has my hands tied. I'm probably going to be in Boston this summer, and if by some miracle I do get to stay, well, I'm still leaving in the fall. We'll barely see each other, but let's not overthink it." The great part is we don't have to figure everything out. We are just a couple of kids, who will take it day by day. This might not be that complicated, actually, in theory.

My hands shake, maybe from the lack of sleep or the sheer nervousness of opening up to someone else. Sarah tries to stop herself from yawning but can't. It is so late, and it's been such a long day, she must be exhausted. Naturally, I stand to help her to her feet. Once we are both standing, it takes me a moment to notice how lovely Sarah beams, even in the darkness. Her entire mood shifts. Thankfully, she doesn't make me wait long before offering me a response.

Keeping a hold of my hand, she asks, grinning, "What would that look like exactly?"

As casually as I can manage, I shrug. "I don't know…" I pause, pulling her closer. "How about we start with you giving me your number?" The corner of my mouth lifts.

She lets me wrap my arm around her, as she pivots to take one last look at the view. "I guess that would be alright, Mr. President."

I grin down at her like a fool. "Is that going to be my nickname forever?"

Part of her hair softly grazes my chin. "Yes," she laughs, looking up at me. I give her a light squeeze with my arm. She is so warm.

With my arm still around her, I pull out my phone. We begin exchanging numbers, and I reveal her nickname under her profile I created. "Dole Whip Girl." She shows me the one she makes for me. We laugh, and god, do I not want this night to end. Yet, the horizon is starting to turn light. I don't even want to know what time it is, but unfortunately, that means we should probably go.

My arm drops from her waist. I lead us back down the dirt path. The closer we get to the car, the more certain I am that this day will finally come to an end. My heart pounds. What a way to end it. At the car, I let her in on the passenger side, waiting to shut the door until she's buckled. My chest rises and falls with each thudding pulse. On the outside, I'm trying to look patient and calm, but on the inside, my thoughts are whirling.

Graduation is only a week away. I have Sarah Lackey's number. I may or may not be leaving for the summer. What will I do? It's all so much, but I can feel my brain wanting to shut down. I'm not capable of thinking about it right now. I must sleep. Some things will have to be figured out tomorrow. Today has finally come to its unavoidable end.

CHAPTER 14

Hit Send

Sarah

Wes drops me off. I wave goodbye from the front door. My mother is going to freak out when she sees this on the Ring camera. I don't care though. The punishment they decide to give me will be worth it because I wouldn't trade this day for a million Dole Whips. I chuckle at the memory of him calling me Dole Whip Girl. That happened. Weston Hill-Cho actually gave me a nickname. My heart flutters. This whole day has been one long dream. Any minute now, I'm going to wake up and realize none of this has been real. I pinch myself, just in case. Ouch. My lips spread into a wide grin. It's real. It was real.

My phone wakes me up. Groggily, I roll over in bed to see a missed call from my mom. Eh, it's too early; I'll call her back.

The light from the screen hurts my eyes. Squinting, I see it's almost 2pm. Dang, that's late. I lay back down with my phone in hand. Sleep is still calling my name. If I were to close my eyes right now, I could probably drift right back into a deep slumber, but I don't. The events from yesterday come flooding back into me, like a freight train. I lay a hand on my chest and think of Weston. The Prom King from Thousand Oaks High kissed me. I could laugh in Gabe's face right now. A sour taste infuses my tongue thinking of my horrendous neighbor. Gosh, he really is the worst.

Last night, when I got dropped off from the bus, he was supposed to give me a ride home. The only reason he still gives me rides is because our moms wouldn't have it any other way. They think we are friends just because they are friends. If only they knew how much of a bully he really is. Then maybe they wouldn't make such a big deal over it. There's no point though. In his mother's eyes, he can do no wrong. His father, on the other hand, may be persuaded. I'll have to keep that in mind in case I need it. It's a good thing we are graduating soon. Either I'll move, or he'll move. Then we'll hopefully never have to see each other again.

Remembering how Gabe called me a freak and a stalker in front of Weston gets me all riled up again. My natural instinct is to bury myself in my books and shut down, but I can't give Gabe and his friends the satisfaction. Yes, I'm still mad. Yes, I feel utterly humiliated. These things are true. Yet, I refuse to break down. That's why I stormed off in the first place. I swallow the lump in my throat, as the tears well up in my eyes. No. I try to blink them away, refusing to cry. I'm not going to give in. He doesn't get the satisfaction of making me cry. Instead, I decide to pretend like nothing ever happened.

I just can't believe him. We've been neighbors for years, and I didn't do anything to him to warrant that kind of hostility. It's just not fair. He has watched me since middle school slowly become completely invisible. All the while, he gained popularity. If only Weston knew how truly pathetic Gabe is. Then maybe he wouldn't be a part of his posse. Who knows? Maybe, after yesterday, Weston will think twice about who he hangs out with.

The jerk also forgot about me last night. I saw him and his friends loitering where they normally do near the track and field fence. I waited at a bench by the entrance of the school until they were done messing around. I didn't want to get in his car, but he was my ride home. Fortunately for me, he and his friends piled into his car and drove off without telling me. He didn't try to text or call. I guess I could have waved him down, but, no, there was no way I was getting in that car. So, I watched him pull out of the school parking lot in his new G-wagon, leaving me stranded. What a sick whip though. It's a new one that his dad bought for his graduation. Lucky brat. A smile spreads across my face. I bet he had fun cleaning off the silly string.

Finding myself stranded at midnight, in the parking lot of my school, I felt not all was lost, though. I ordered an Uber with the emergency credit card Mom gave me and got home safe. Riding in that Uber was much better than going with Gabe. If I have any say over it, I'll never set foot in his car again. I doubt he would be willing anyway, if he ever finds out it was me who silly stringed his car. That's a win for me.

Breathing in, I decide to force myself out of bed. No doubt it will help me to forget about the bad parts of yesterday. It's not worth ruining a new day. My lips part to form a faint grin. Today, I might be able to talk to Weston for the first time on the phone. I wonder what that will be like?

I follow my normal morning routine of showering, brushing my teeth, putting in my contacts and feeding Simba before breakfast. I sigh, trying to forget about stupid Gabe and his stupid friends. There's a vibrating noise coming from my nightstand. My eyes shoot over to it. A jolt runs through me.

What if it's Weston? Oh, what a silly thought. It's probably my mom. I run over and see the face ID. Yep, it's her. Better answer this time now that I'm awake.

"Hey, honey, how are you? Did you see I called you earlier?" Her voice is calm and doesn't at all put me on edge, as if she's not mad about me coming home so late. Maybe she didn't notice the Ring camera? I can hope.

I smile and say, "Sorry, I was busy-uh-talking to Monica. Yeah, I was telling her about how Disney went." It's a white lie, one that I hope she's too busy to notice.

"No worries, honey, I'm glad you had fun." She chuckles at someone whom I can only assume to be Greg. "We are out by the pool today. Your Aunt Carol actually got everyone their own floaties. No arguing about sharing. Can you believe that?"

My smile broadens at the sound of them splashing in Aunt Carol's pool. I can hear their obnoxious screams through the phone. It sends a sharp pain through my chest, causing my smile to slowly turn upside down. Why didn't I go with them? It's not like any of my friends were able to go with me on my senior trip. I really tried to get Monica to come along, but she felt weird, being that she's a junior. My other friend, Teagan, is also not in my graduating class. So, why didn't I just skip it and go with my family instead? I guess I thought it would be fun to stay on my own for the first time. Silly me.

"Rocco, stop hitting your sister," I hear my stepdad, Greg, shout through the phone.

Knowing that Gemma wasn't going to be home made all the difference too. She's off living it up in Bali, and I'd be stuck with Aunt Carol trying to convince my mom to let me go visit her over the summer. I'll have to do that regardless if I went with them or not. Weston's beautiful face flashes in my mind. Yeah, I think I made the better decision. I can feel the heat on my cheeks. As much as I miss my family, I'm so glad I went to Disney. I would not have missed it for the world.

"So how was it, honey? Did you go on the teacup ride?" Mom asks, sounding distracted. She knows that's my favorite ride.

"Of course, I did. It's a Disney tradition," I say, sounding excited. I try to tell her about the rest of the rides and about the actual fun parts of the trip, but I can hear she's a little too distracted with my siblings at the moment.

"Hold on," she interrupts. "Stop hitting your brother, Agnes. Do you want a time out?"

"Do you need to go, Mom?" I ask, trying to hide my disappointment.

"No, no, it's just Agnes and Rocco again. I'm sure Greg can handle them." Baby Zacky's cries cut her off, followed by a shuffling noise. I hear Agnes grab the phone. "Shera, that you?"

"Hey, Aggie," I laugh at the sound of her trying to say my name correctly. She can't quite get it right yet. It's so cute. "Are you having fun at Aunt Carol's?"

My eyes flicker over to the bed across the room from mine. On a normal night, I'd be trying to get her to calm down before bed. She can be so rambunctious. I hardly succeed unless I bribe her with a story from one of her favorite books. Thankfully, it's always one that has some romance in it.

"Yesh," she states between small breaths. I smile as I can practically hear how wet she is from the pool. Rocco is suddenly nearby, saying it's his turn to talk to me. He's a strange kid, but I swear he and Agnes were twins in another life. Greg's other son Manny, on the other hand, is practically Greg's mini-me.

"Hey, Rocco, are you behaving?" I attempt to say, practically yelling so he can hear. My voice is drowned out by the sound of Manny trying to take the phone away.

"No, it's my turn," Agnes argues.

After a minute or two listening to the three of them fight, I hear my older sister wrangling baby Zacky and the coos of mom trying to get him to calm down. Doesn't look like Jill is going to talk to me, either. I frown, and Mom is definitely not coming back. I lift my brows. Maybe Aunt Carol is around.

"Hey, put Aunt Carol on," I request loudly, but I don't think anyone is listening anymore. "Hello? Mom? Jill?" My heart sinks. It's time to let them go. "Ok, I'll talk to you later. Love you," I say to anyone left listening, then hang up.

The silence from my large empty house swallows me up like a black hole. I fold my arms around myself. I really am alone. Alright, no need to be dramatic. At least they'll be home in a couple days. Until then, I'm sure I can find something to occupy my time, like hang out with Weston, maybe? Goosebumps run up and down my arms. Oh, Weston.

Looking down at my phone, I see many missed texts. I have a couple from Monica and Gemma. She probably wants to know if I really am going to visit her in Bali this summer. I hope I can. Then again, if Weston is staying, I'd also want to stay. Is that delusional? Maybe I should text him? No, that's desperate behavior. Or is it? I snap my fingers. Monica will know. I click on her name to FaceTime her. Unlike the lie I told Mom, we haven't actually spoken since early yesterday. She gave me advice on how to approach Weston at Disneyland. When I saw him sitting there on that bench, I completely froze. I think I was starstruck or something. Whatever it was, I had to get out of it because I knew it was my only chance to grab his attention.

In school, I'm not very brave. I tend to like being invisible for the most part. Monica on the other hand loves to stand out. She is very outgoing. She can walk up to anyone and start a conversation. If the kids in school didn't consider her a freak just because she likes cosplay, then I think she would be popular. It's a good thing she doesn't care about what other people think. So, of course, I had to get her expertise on the matter. Her advice was to just simply walk up to the Prom King. At first, I thought she was mad. One does not simply walk up to the most popular kid in school for no reason. That's social suicide for a girl like me. However, since none of his friends were around, it seemed like a doable idea.

The phone rings. I gotta tell her that it worked.

"Hey, what's up? Did your mom flip out about you sneaking out?" Monica answers, jumping right into conversation. She is straightening her dark brown hair in the bathroom from what I can tell.

I shake my head. "No, you know, I think she hasn't looked at the Ring camera footage all week." My stomach rumbles. Better go get something to eat. I leave my room and make my way to the kitchen.

"Well, that's a relief," Monica replies. "So, you promised you would tell me everything about what happened with you and the senior Prom King." She pauses from straightening her hair to look directly at the phone camera. "Do not leave out any details."

Beaming, I go on to explain everything that transpired between us from the moment I asked him for a dollar at the Dole Whip cart. My heart beats fast. I tell her about my stupid neighbor insulting me and how Weston took me to Elysian Park to apologize.

"Wait, then he asked for your number?" Monica shouts excitedly. She almost drops her hair brush.

I chuckle, "Yes." A long sigh escapes me. "And I've wanted to text him all day." I prop my phone up on the kitchen counter so she can still see me as I pour myself a bowl of cereal. You know, no matter how old I get, I think I will always love Cinnamon Toast Crunch for breakfast. I eat a spoonful. So good.

Monica starts braiding a small section of hair near her face. "So, just text the guy."

Coughing, I practically choke on my food. "Excuse me? I can't text him."

"Uh, why not?" she refutes.

"Because he should text me first. That's the rule," I say, wiping my face with a paper towel.

Monica rolls her eyes. She ties one of her braids with a small clear hair tie. "That's so dumb. There are no rules, S. If you like him, text him. Simple as that."

"Easy for you to say, Mon. You didn't get called a stalker."

"Oh please, from what you told me, he didn't even care." She does have a point. "Like, why would he give you his number if you're not allowed to text him?"

I bite another spoonful of cereal. "It's not like that," I say between chews. "I know I'm technically allowed to text him. I just don't want him to start thinking I'm actually obsessed with him." Saying this makes yesterday's events come flying back into my mind.

I shut my eyes, only to be met with Gabe's insults. He called me a freak and a stalker. Who would even believe that? But then, I remember Weston's face. He did. He believed them. Even if for a moment, he thought I was some crazy girl who's obsessed with him. Maybe I am.

At the end of the day, I'm just a girl who likes a guy. Despite that one awful interaction, the moment under the castle was real. Weston Hill-Cho wrapped his arms around me, his gorgeous brown eyes looked into mine. He kissed me, a loser. That happened. I did not just dream it.

"Sarah, look, the way I see it is, if you can't be yourself, even now, at the very, very beginning of this—I don't know what you want to call it—uh, situationship?" I laugh at the word, but she might be right, since I don't really know what to call this thing between Weston and me yet. "Then what's the point?"

"You're right," I say, gulping down some of the milk in my bowl. "You're always right."

Monica grins. "Duh. When are you going to just start listening to me?"

"Hey, I do listen to you," I admit. "And because of that, I

have you to thank for the magical and most romantic day of my life." I swoon, thinking about the view at Elysian Park.

"Ah, yes." She smiles. "Ok, well, I gotta finish doing my makeup, and you need to go text Weston," Monica orders. I swear, she could be my life coach. Do people need life coaches at 17? Well, I sure do. "And report back to me," she says before hanging up.

Her face disappears from my phone, and I'm left alone to finish my cereal. Once my bowl is empty, I put it in the sink, deciding to wash it later. Chills run through me. Monica is right. If I can't be myself now, then what was even the point of me leaving the message in his yearbook? I want to text him so I should. There are no rules here. Alright. I'm gonna do it. All I have to do is tap on his name and send him a text. Yeah. Easy peasy. It's what I want to do. So, why can't I?

My heart is pounding like crazy. Why is this so hard? Ok, I just gotta do it fast. I pull up his profile. I tap on the message icon. I suck in a breath. Quickly, I type a simple message and hit send before I have time to change my mind. I exhale and bite my nails. There's butterflies fluttering inside my chest. I can't believe I just did that. Oh, I hope he responds.

CHAPTER 15
Fro-Yo

Weston

Ma waited up for me to get home last night. I thought I was going to be walking into a battlefield. To my surprise, when I walked through the door, she did the strangest thing and hugged me, looking genuinely concerned for my well being. She, of course, checked the car for scratches afterwards, but I was pleasantly surprised that she did not blow up at me about our fight or about me stealing the Volvo. Instead of getting into it about working this summer, she let it go, allowing me to go to sleep. This morning, she even woke me up at noon having made a typical American breakfast that she absolutely thinks is unhealthy. Pancakes and sausage. I know it was her way of apologizing, without actually saying the words. I accepted by eating what she cooked. It was delicious.

During the meal, I came to find out Brenden had covered for me after all, telling Ma how much pressure I am under. To her, this explained my recent erratic behavior. I'll have to remember to thank him for that. Earlier, I went into his room to ask how it all went down, but he seems to have disappeared again, as well as his surfboard. It doesn't bother me that he's gone. He really came through for me last night.

Now I'm back in my room, sitting at my desk, trying to finish up a last minute assignment for the school newspaper. I'd rather do this than have to deal with all those text messages I woke up to. There's probably ten alone from Hannah. I think I saw six from Gabe. There were some from Trey about the grad party, since we are combining ours in order to throw one massive party. I groan, not wanting to deal with any of them right now. I turn it off. Watching the phone screen fade to black instantly makes me feel better.

Time to focus on something I know I can handle, like homework. It could very well be my last assignment in high school, too, which is very weird to think about. I don't feel I'm ready for this next phase of my life, but it's going to happen, regardless. I breathe in, as this was all a part of the plan.

I hear a knocking on my door. Ma enters shortly after, shuffling inside like a quiet mouse. She is off work today and is less on edge. The air around her is tangible. I stand to let her sit at my desk in the only chair I have in my room. Her hands are clasped together neatly on her lap. She looks down, brows slightly raised. When she finally meets my gaze, I know what is about to transpire. My stomach sinks.

Ma twiddles her thumbs then says in Korean, "In-su, we need to talk about your summer plans."

Unfortunately, there's no getting out of this conversation. I swallow and continue to stand uncomfortably in front of her. "Yes, Ma," I reply back to her in Korean. I don't want to set her off. Maybe this will go better than expected if I speak in her preferred language.

"In-su, you know we both worked very hard to get you to this point in your life," she starts. "I know you have made a lot of sacrifices to be accepted to Harvard, and I have too."

Starting off strong, I see. I resist breaking eye contact.

She continues, "And your Uncle Henry is very excited to have you work for him this summer. It would be very disrespectful of you not to go." I lean my head down. Of course, she would bring up respect to try and guilt me again. "But," she pauses, her voice ending on a high note. I tilt my head up, eyes flickering over to hers. "I don't want to lose you." Her eyes are starting to look a little glassy. Is she going to cry? Oh please, no. She sighs, "I put a lot of pressure on you because I know you will do great things for this family."

I chime in, "Ma, I-"

"Let me finish," she orders, but in a tactful manner. She frowns, unfolding her hands. She places them on her knees. "I'm afraid your poor brother is lost, but by your example, maybe he can find his way back." Half of her mouth curls, not exactly into a smile but not a scowl either. "Even though I want you to go, it doesn't mean that's what should be done. So, if you need a break, then I will understand."

My heart stops. I ask in disbelief, "What?" and my brows shoot up. Did she just say what I think she said?

Ma closes her eyes and exhales. "You can have the summer off, if that is what you wish."

Blinking, I stare at her in awe. Is this really happening? No way is this real.

"Are you serious?" I inquire, needing to know if this is a joke or not before I allow myself to make plans. Then again, my mother doesn't joke.

She nods, "Yes, In-su."

A rush of excitement flows through me. I can't help myself from bending over and squeezing my mother, even though we don't normally hug in my household. "Thank you," I exclaim, letting her go. For a moment, there is a hint of a smile creeping across her lips, but it quickly vanishes.

Her face is serious again. "As long as you promise me you

will enroll for fall classes as soon as possible, and you will start work for your uncle at the beginning of the semester. It's very important you make connections early before you go to law school."

"Yes, I promise." I'm still in utter disbelief. Did I really just get the summer to myself? I need to text everyone. Before I pull out my phone, I look down at Ma, who is staring at her hands. She seems so disappointed. It's probably because she doesn't want me to end up like my brother. Although, I'm starting to think that's not such a bad thing. Squatting before her, I add, "Don't worry, Ma. I'm still going to stick to the plan, and Min-Su will be fine. He just needs us to believe in him again."

She brings her head up slowly. "I hope you're right." She wipes her watery eyes, sniffing. "One more thing, In-su." She is serious, but her tone is light, unlike the normal harsh voice she uses to scold me. "Don't you ever steal my car again, you understand me? One misdemeanor could ruin your life."

"I know, I know," I nod in agreement with her. "That was dumb. I'm sorry. It won't happen again." This I know to be true.

Something did possess me yesterday. Under normal circumstances, I would never risk my Harvard acceptance letter being revoked. One misdemeanor could have ruined everything for me. Yeah, rest assured I'm not doing that again. That's another reason I gotta hand it to Brenden. He's got a lot of guts.

"So, for that, you are grounded until graduation."

"That's fair," I say.

Ma clears her throat and stands up. "Ok, I'll leave you to finish your project now."

As she exits my door, I get a surge of energy. The fact that I'm grounded until graduation has no effect on me. Who cares? Ma can have this week. This summer is mine.

With a free summer now ahead of me, I am renewed with a childlike vigor that I can't explain. There are so many fun things to plan that I rarely have the time for now. Like going to the beach, surfing. That reminds me, I need to call Brenden. He won't believe this turn of events. I can't wait to see his face when I tell him. Perhaps we'll get to spend time together this summer. Who knows, maybe I can convince him to go back to school or just do something worthwhile with his life? He's still young, barely turned 21. He's got time.

Oh, and Trey will absolutely flip out when I tell him the news. Now that I'm not leaving right after graduation, I can finally look forward to graduating, including the exquisite celebration he has planned for us next weekend. If there's one thing I know about Trey, it's that he knows how to throw one heck of a party. It is going to be fire.

That reminds me to turn my phone back on. As soon as I do, I am bombarded with the same 20 plus message notifications. I sigh and scroll past them, deciding not to answer any right now. I set down my phone on my bed. My phone vibrates again. Annoyed, I proceed to pick it back up to silence it, but I see a new message from Sarah. My eyes bulge. She texted me already? I'm so glad she did.

"Hey Wes, I had a great time last night. Hope to talk to you soon." She ends the text with a heart hand emoji. My pulse races with excitement.

I begin typing a prompt text back, "Me too," then hit send. There is obviously more I want to say, like how I'm staying for the summer, but it feels so impersonal to say over text. An idea enters my mind suddenly. I rush out the door into the hallway, yelling, "Ma, would you take me somewhere?" Surprisingly, she answers yes with the condition that I can't go anywhere else until after I graduate. She leaves me no choice but to agree.

Quickly, I return to my room and change into a more decent outfit, settling on a blue shirt with the name of our school on the front and a pair of black joggers. Ma meets me in the car as soon as I am ready to go. I tell her where to drive, and on the way, we make a pit stop. It takes no more than five minutes. Getting back into the car, a smile lights up my face as I begin to think about the endless possibilities of a free summer before college. It will be one to remember.

Ten minutes later, we are parked in front of Gabe's house. Ma reminds me that since I'm grounded, I can't stay long, and I'm fine with that. She just gave me the summer off. So, I'm not going to push it by fighting with her over how long I get to spend here. At least she gave me this opportunity to tell Sarah in person the good news. I wouldn't have it any other way.

Hopping out of the Volvo, I stride up confidently to Sarah's house. I hope this is a good surprise, I think, pressing the Ring doorbell. It rings and keeps ringing. I knew I should have asked first if she was home. I shake my head. The ringing comes to an abrupt stop. My stomach drops. Sounds like someone is answering, I think. Oh god, what if it's not her? If it's her parents, I'm going to be so embarrassed.

"Who are you?" a male child asks through the doorbell camera.

Nervous, I lean down and say, "Uh-hi-my name is Weston. Is-uh-Sarah home?" I'm met back with a rumbling and scratching noise. My face feels hot.

"What are you holding?" the child asks through the noise.

I open my mouth to answer, but I'm cut off by another kid, this time female, saying, "Shera?" Then the noise stops. My brow raises. What the heck just happened? Do I keep standing here? The front door flies open. Sarah runs out in a panic. She stands in front of the camera and bends down, yelling out of breath, "Hey Agnes, you better hang up now." She places a hand on the camera. "Everything's ok; I'll talk to you guys later. Bye." She spins around and tells me to come inside, quick. I do as she says.

Inside, she slams the door behind us and leans against it to catch her breath. "Hey, sorry about that." She bites the side of her lip.

"No-uh-I'm sorry for not using the back door?" I say, remembering that's what we did yesterday.

She smiles. "That's ok. I mean, I hope you didn't feel attacked or anything by my family."

"Oh, so is that who I was talking to?" I figured as much. Me coming from a small family and being the youngest makes me wonder what it would be like to have a big family with younger siblings. Sounds kind of fun and a little chaotic, if I'm honest.

A corner of her mouth curls. "Yeah, two of my kid siblings got a hold of my mom's phone. They really are troublemakers." I can't help grinning when she talks.

We share a brief glance in silence before her eyes find what's in my hands. "Wait, what is that?" She points to the white container.

"Oh, this is for you," I say bashfully, handing it to her. "I hope it's not too melted. It's the closest thing I found to Dole Whip outside of Disneyland."

Sarah takes it from my hands. Her eyes glow. "You didn't have to get me anything." Her cheeks are turning pink. The red in her hair enhances the rosy shade. It's oddly very attractive.

Breaking eye contact, I state, "I wanted to because I have some good and bad news."

"What does that mean?" Sarah raises a brow. "Oh, do you want to come in and sit down?"

Tilting my head down, I say solemnly, "That's part of the bad news." I pause, looking back up at her. "You probably won't be seeing me much this week because I'm grounded." It's so embarrassing, but I had to tell her. I wonder if she ever gets grounded by her parents? I'll have to ask her one day.

Sarah frowns. "Oh, that sucks. Sorry." She grips the frozen yogurt container. I really hope she likes it. I know from personal experience it's no Disneyland Dole Whip, but the flavor is close.

"Yeah, you probably already knew this, but I don't have a license." I grit my teeth. "Not yet, anyways."

"Me neither." We share an understanding glance that makes me feel a bit better. "So how long are you grounded for?"

"Until graduation," I say. Looking down, I pause for a second, then bring my eyes to hers. She must know how nervous she makes me. I can already feel my face heating up. "But the good news is I'll be around for the summer."

Sarah beams. "Really?"

"Call it a Disney miracle," I joke, disgusted it just came bellowing out of my mouth. Appalled, I cover my face. That was so cheesy.

Next thing I know, I feel a warm hand on mine, pulling it off of my face playfully. "Weston, that's so exciting," she says, letting go of my hand. I wish she would have held on to it. No matter. She is smiling at me, standing probably a hand-width away. Part of me wants to pull her in for an embrace, but I know it would just make me want more. She's not ready for that. Neither am I. We also decided to take things slow. That's exactly what I'm going to do.

She nods and realizes that I am leaving. "Right. Ok." She steps closer to me and turns to the side with one hand extended. I don't understand if she wants to hug or shake hands. So, I also turn with my hand outstretched. Sarah is still holding onto the frozen yogurt and looks like she's in an extremely awkward position. I don't want our final encounter until graduation to be this weird. At the last second, I pull her in for a proper hug. The fresh scent coming from her hair instantly hits me and sends me back to the moment we shared underneath the castle. What a moment. Maybe one day we'll go back there. Oh shoot, did I really just admit that I would be willing to go back to Disneyland? As a realization comes to me, I can't help but smile, letting Sarah go.

"I'll text you," I assure her, backing up towards the front door.

She laughs, "You better, Mr. President." She gives an understanding nod, opening the door for me.

I hate that I can't stay long, but since Ma gave me the summer off, I want to be extra compliant. Even more so than before. This was a huge step and I don't want to do anything to change her mind. Forcing myself to leave, I walk down the steps and wave at Sarah from the car.

On the way home, my thoughts continue to swirl around how much I used to loathe Disneyland. Just yesterday, I hated the thought of stepping foot inside that park again. Yes, it was my idea to go there for the senior trip, but I had regretted the decision ever since it was made, that is, until yesterday. I'm painfully aware that had I decided not to go to Disneyland, I would not have met Sarah. For this reason alone, I may be forced to change my entire outlook of the park. If I'm honest with myself and was asked to return to the park, I'm pretty sure I'd say yes without any hesitation, as long as I get to go with her.

CHAPTER 16
Awkward

Sarah

Monica and Teagan wave me down from our table. At lunch, we tend to sit at the furthest table in the corner, to the right of the stage and below the stairs. It's our table, well, only for two more days. Then, it'll just be Monica and Teagan's. I wish they were graduating with me. It's not fair that my only friends had to be underclassmen, but of course they are the coolest people I know in this school.

"Hey, besties," I say, setting my lunch tray down. Monica practically leaps over the table to demand I tell Teagan what happened at Disneyland.

"Oh my god, you have to fill her in." Monica grabs the apple slices from my tray. She gives me a Fruit Roll-up in return. She knows me so well.

Teagan shuffles in her seat excitedly. "Yes, spill the tea, girl. I haven't seen you at all this week."

"I know, I'm sorry. I had to finish a couple projects for Mr. Bellvale. So, I had to work through lunch every day this week," I say after biting into a turkey sandwich. Wes pops into my mind and how I ate this same lunch when we were at Disneyland. Does that make me too predictable?

Monica finishes chewing an apple slice, then adds, "T, they spent the whole day together, and then he showed up at her house in the middle of the night." Her eyes are super wide.

Flushed, I give her a look. "Shut up."

Teagan squeals, "Oh my god, tell me everything."

After taking a sip of water, I begin to tell her the story of how I spent the day with Weston Hill-Cho. Monica, being Monica, interjects with all the so-called juicy details that I just so happen to leave out.

"And then he takes her to this place in LA that was supposed to have this swing or something, but it wasn't there and then…."

"And then he took me home. The end," I blurt, cutting her off.

Teagan swoons, "Wow, and have you seen him since?"

"No, but we text…sort of," I say with a hint of disappointment in my tone. It's not his fault he got grounded. Well, I guess it is, but it doesn't matter. These things happen. I really appreciate that he came to my house to give me a heads up about it. I know he told me we wouldn't be seeing each other in person. I just didn't think it would affect how much we communicated over the phone.

When I told Monica the story, it didn't hit me as much as it does now. I stop eating and sit back in my chair. My eyes wander the lunch room, knowing full well Weston does not have first lunch, but I look for him anyway. We haven't had any classes together this semester. So, it makes sense that I haven't seen him in the halls. On Monday, I thought I had seen him with his posse. It was just Gabe, Jeb, and those other guys from the basketball team. I avoided them like the plague.

"Come on, tell her about the kiss." Monica pokes my arm.

I bury my face inside my shirt. I knew she was going to go there.

Teagan gasps, "What? No way. You kissed Weston Hill-Cho?" She covers her mouth.

Monica yanks on my shirt to reveal my face. "Sarah, come on. We don't have boyfriends. So, we're living vicariously through you."

"He's not my boyfriend," I remind her.

Teagan raises a brow. "Uh and why not?"

Monica places her elbows on the table and rests her head on her hands. "Ugh, it's so infuriating."

"What is?" Teagan looks genuinely concerned. Both of them are so dramatic.

I put my hands up. "Ok, chill, Mon. We are just getting to know each other."

"Explain?" Teagan pleads.

"Yeah, explain why you guys aren't a couple yet?" Monica adds.

"I already told you," I say, giving Monica a side eye. "He barely knows me. So, we are taking it slow. No need for labels."

"Ok, I get that," Teagan reasons.

"Yeah, but you've been obsessed with him for soooo long," Monica interjects.

"He didn't know that," I retort. "Besides, it's better to not put any labels or anything because he's moving at the end of the summer anyway."

Monica groans, "Boring. Who cares?"

Slightly agitated, I snap, "I do, and I'm not wrecking my chances with him just because you think it's boring."

"I'm sorry," she states, instantly changing her attitude. "I am rooting for you guys."

"I know." My eyes fix themselves to the table as I slouch down in my chair. "Sorry for snapping, I just wish I could see him again before graduation."

Teagan raises a brow. "You mean you haven't seen him since he came to your house?"

I explain how he got grounded because he snuck out that night to take me to Elysian Park and then came to my house the next day to tell me about it with fro-yo.

"Well, you got two more days. Then you'll have the whole summer to hang out."

"Oooh, maybe you'll have one epic summer romance before he leaves for Boston, and then you'll break up but, oh no, it's too much." Monica places a hand on her head, like she's pretending to faint. "So, you'll follow him out to Boston, surprising him, but-huh," she gasps, "He's got a girlfriend." Monica looks distraught as she finishes acting out a scene like it's straight out of an anime, exaggerated expressions and all.

Some kids around us roll their eyes. This is why we aren't sitting at the popular table. I don't care right now. Teagan and I both give over to laughter. I think Monica takes the romance books she reads a little too close to heart. Moments like this are what I'll miss from high school, though. Just acting wild with my girls.

"Oh my gosh, oh my gosh." Teagan covers her face with her hand. "Weston is right there."

My heart skips a beat. Cautiously, I turn around in my seat to see where she's pointing. Teagan is right. Weston is speaking to Principal Hickman. His hair is perfectly combed, and his outfit makes him look like an ivy league freshman already, very sophisticated. I hope he doesn't look over here and catch me staring at him. So, I turn back around.

"What are you doing? Go over there," Monica orders me.

Teagan blushes, shaking her head. "No, no, no. Don't do that. That's so embarrassing."

"I agree with T," I say to Monica.

"No, just go over there and stand near the vending machine. He will be forced to pass you."

"Uh yeah, and that's exactly why I'm not going over there."

Monica smirks. "Do it, or I'm going to yell your name to the entire cafeteria."

My eyes widen with fear. "You wouldn't," but of course she would. She has no shame. I groan. "Alright, alright I'm going," I say, standing up. "But if I do something embarrassing, I'm not talking to you for a week."

"If you do something embarrassing, I promise to babysit Agnes and Rocco for a week," Monica offers. I smile and give her an approving nod. Now I kind of hope my awkwardness seeps through, just to see her get tortured by those two.

At the vending machine, I pretend like I'm contemplating what to buy. Weston is within earshot and is talking to the principal about his upcoming Harvard classes. I try not to eavesdrop by staring at the options before me. Hmm, should I get some Skittles? How about a Hershey's bar? My stomach rumbles. Looks like I'm actually going to get something.

"Hey, Dole Whip Girl, need a dollar?" I hear Weston ask. My heart thumps wildly. When did he stop talking to the principal?

I turn around, as nonchalantly as I am able and say, "Oh, hey, what's up?" Did I really just say that? My brows shoot up at the recollection of when I asked him for a dollar at Disneyland. "Oh, wait, good one." I give in to a light chuckle. He does too. Am I crazy or are his cheeks a little red?

"You know you actually still owe me a dollar," he says coyly.

"Is that right, Mr. President?" I say back. He smiles, but then doesn't say anything else. I open my mouth then close it. No words come to me. Why does this feel so forced?

Everything seemed easier when we were in Disneyland. It is my happy place, after all. That's probably why our conversation flowed so smoothly. I felt much more confident there. I'm then reminded of how Weston and I only texted a couple times before seeing each other today. Part of me thinks the magic of Disney has worn off, or maybe it's because we are back in his natural habitat? I have to admit, he is different here. Now, he's more confident and seems less anxious. I feel the complete opposite. He did warn me that I wouldn't see him because of his grounding. Not to mention, he said he has detention every day until Thursday this week for skipping out on his chaperone twice during the senior trip. That didn't happen to me— perks of being invisible.

It's not that I'm upset that I haven't seen him. I'm simply-uh, I don't know what I am, actually. I think I just imagined being with Weston a whole lot differently than how this past week has been. I've practically thought about it every day since elementary school. Now that it almost happened, it's definitely not what I expected. I just didn't think it would be this hard to be together. Well, I know we are not exactly like together-together, but we are something. If it is tough now, I can't imagine what it will be like once he actually leaves for Harvard in the fall. At least, I won't have to think about that for a while. No matter how slow this goes.

Weston shuffles some papers in his hands, then tucks them under his arm, jogging me out of my own head. "So, um, how are you?" He seems nervous, which is very unlike the high school version of Weston. This makes me feel better.

"I'm good," I state blandly. "Just getting ready for my grad party, you?"

He grins. "Yeah, same here."

"Cool," I mutter, not knowing what else to say. Monica better get ready to babysit. I'm sure the color in my face will start matching the shade of my hair any minute now.

Weston looks down, then back up. He switches the papers from one arm to the other. The silence between us is so unsettling. I have to say something, but he starts speaking at the same time I do.

"Oh, sorry, you go," he says.

"No, no, go ahead." My eyes stare into his. A tiny bit of hope jumps in my stomach. Maybe he'll say something that lets me know what's going on in his head, like if he's thinking about me, for instance. The longer I wait, the longer the silence consumes us.

He runs a free hand over the back of his neck. "I wanted to say—"

The lunch bell rings. His eyes flicker to his watch. I look back over at Teagan and Monica who are packing up their things. It's time to head back to class. My gaze circles back to Weston, giving him one last chance to finish his sentence.

"I was, uh…."

"Yes?" I ask, silently willing him to say something, anything at this point.

He stares down at me, eyes bright. His mouth opens. My heart pounds anxiously with every millisecond he's quiet. He smiles and adds, "I was just going to say, see you at graduation."

I release the breath I was holding for what felt like five minutes. Wes moves past me, waving goodbye before heading down the hall opposite of me. I wave back, even though he's already turned around, and whisper, "See you at graduation, Wes." That did not go well at all.

Monica and Teagen have already headed to class. I'll catch them up later. I grab my backpack from the table and head to my least favorite class of the day, gym. Everyone knows I'm not very coordinated, but for some reason, the school makes people like me have to take this dumb class to graduate. I'm just glad it'll be over soon.

The rest of the day goes by fast. I can't believe I'll be done in just two more days. The reality that I'm graduating high school still hasn't sunk in yet. I don't think it's hit my mother either because ever since they got back from Arizona, we haven't had time to discuss what I'm going to do when I get out of school. I know she will want me to accept the scholarship to UCLA, but I really have my heart set on Bali. I'll have to talk to her later about it. Right now, I still have my party to think about. Everything is set. I even have my dress and shoes picked out. It's tiki themed, very Hawaiian, and I'm excited. I still haven't invited Weston, so maybe that's what I'll use as an excuse to text him.

Gabe gives me a ride home, even after I promised myself to not get in a car with him. It's only because over the weekend, he texted me saying he had a hunch that it was me who silly stringed his car and was going to make me pay. I then pulled an Uno Reverse card and threatened that I would tell our parents about the senior prank he has planned for this week involving fire. I overheard Kaite talking about it in the girls' bathroom. That shut him up. He hasn't bothered me since. Unfortunately, since I still need rides home from school, I have to get in the car with him. I'm just glad I only have to endure his driving for two more days.

At home, when I walk into the foyer, I'm bombarded by my crazy siblings, who have been bouncing off the walls since their return from Aunt Carol's. My older sister, Jill, is back at school up in Berkeley, so she isn't around to help corral them anymore. That wonderful privilege falls to me. I really don't mind since Manny, Greg's oldest, pretty much keeps to himself, and Agnes and Rocco tend to calm down as soon as I put on my favorite anime. Mom would help but is a little preoccupied with baby Zacky. Now, he is a handful. When he is asleep or chill, for once, I'm normally left to my own devices. Actually, I think I'm left alone too much. Sometimes I want to be more involved, but Mom is amazing. She can handle it all.

Agnes and Rocco finally calm down after eating their apple flavored snack pack. Instead of chilling with them and watching anime, I put on another show they like more. Right when the theme song comes on, they are completely entranced. Chuckling under my breath, I leave them to go upstairs to change. I throw on some yoga pants that cut off at the ankle, since it's pretty warm out. Greg doesn't like to turn on the AC until July. So, I make do by wearing something that is breezy. After throwing on a large vintage t-shirt with pictures of the late Latina pop star Selena, I sit on my bed and contemplate texting Weston.

I open my phone and see a missed text from Gemma. That's strange. I didn't even hear the notification sound. My phone must still be on silent. Oops. I'll fix that.

"Hey cuz. U decide to ditch and come to Bali?" I read. My chest slowly rises and falls. I groan and lay back on my bed. Gemma is persistent, I'll give her that, but there's no way I can think about Bali when there's still graduation to worry about. Not to mention how I already accepted the scholarship to attend UCLA. Mom and Greg would freak out entirely if I gave that up. Breathing out, I relax myself. No need to think about my future now. I just want to talk to Weston.

Rolling over in bed, I fix my eyes on Simba. He's just chilling atop his favorite rock, probably wondering what I'm doing. A long sigh escapes me. I tell him, "Bruh, I don't even know." I'm not weird for that, right? Lots of people talk to their pets. I don't know why, but it reminds me of when Weston was in my room that night after Disneyland. My face feels a bit heated. I can't believe I tried to make him read my journal. Speaking of which, I reach down to pull out my notebook from the bottom drawer of my nightstand. It's been a long time since I've looked through here, let alone written in it. I flip through the pages, mad Gabe had seen this once, a long time ago. It was bound to happen, ever since we moved next door. Our mothers would trade off babysitting whenever the other had a date night.

I grip the book hard and flip to one of the pages displaying my chicken scratch handwriting. Even so, I can make out the words, Mrs. Hill-Cho, coupled with some hearts drawn around Weston's name. I must have been eight or nine when I wrote that. I bring a hand to my face. Yikes, I could scream from the cringe. A long drawn out sigh pours out of me as I look upon his name. I rip it out. It's time to stop with this school girl crush. I want something grown up for once. Can anyone blame me? Every little girl had a crush on him back then, and they still do today. It's not weird. I just hope looking at this didn't change his mind about me.

Flipping through the book, I see there's another entry that has Weston's name written in hearts. I rip that one out too. Maybe Gabe was right. I am obsessed. Well, it stops now. Shaking my head in defeat, I put the journal back in the bottom drawer. Laying back on my bed, I lift up my phone to see if I have any new messages. I didn't hear it ring, but you never know. I unlock it and see no new notifications. My finger dances around Weston's nickname. After our awkward interaction today, I wouldn't be surprised if I never hear from him again. There's no telling what he thinks of me now. A smile creeps across my face. There's only one way to find out.

CHAPTER 17
Graduation

Weston

Ma sets the graduation cap on top of my head. "You look so handsome," she says, grinning. She also straightens the yellow ribbon hanging around my neck. I look in the mirror to make sure everything is where it should be. Not a hair out of place. It looks like I'm ready. Any guy like me should feel proud on his graduation day, and yet, I feel most unhappy. The corners of my mouth waver, then ultimately curve down. I don't want to feel like this, especially since today really has been a long time coming. I worked so hard to get here. I am finally graduating high school. It should be one of the proudest moments of my life. It's not.

"Yes, you look very nice, In-Su," Uncle Henry compliments. Ma had him flown out here to attend the ceremony, but he arrived earlier than planned and in a bit of a frenzy. I know why.

"Thanks, Uncle," I mumble in Korean while stepping into the hallway.

My stomach is in knots. I don't feel anxious though, just

miserable. Sighing, I walk into my room. It's not time to leave yet, and I need a minute alone. Inside, I stand in between my bed and desk, looking at nothing in particular, as if I'm in a daze. That's what this entire week has felt like, one big blur. I haven't been able to focus. My gut tenses. It's all because of my brother.

Instinctively, I reflect on everything that transpired over the past few days. I stare at the floor, wishing Brenden were here to see me graduate. It doesn't feel right without him.

Ma knocks on my open door. It must be time to go. Keeping my eyes fixed on the floor, I barely move an inch, probably looking lost and confused.

"You ready to go?" she asks in English, softly placing a hand on my back. I don't correct her. I lack the energy to do so.

Knowing there's no reason to wait at the house any longer, I shrug and say, "Yeah."

"I know you wanted him here, In-Su," she switches to Korean, "but you have worked very hard to get here. Enjoy it," Ma says in an attempt to make me feel better. It doesn't. She sighs, "In-Su." She is cut off by Uncle Henry.

He stands at my doorway. "Min-Su has made his choice," he says with an obvious distaste for my brother. "Let's not make today about him." Uncle Henry and Brenden have not exactly seen eye to eye in the past, and after what happened, his opinion of Bren must be even lower now. He arches his back and straightens out his suit jacket. "Come on, we don't want to be late."

It takes me a second to get going. Being on time is not something I am worried about today. I simply don't care. There are more pressing issues to worry about than showing up late to graduation.

We arrive at school quickly, and Ma and Uncle drop me off at the entrance. I tell them to follow the signs for the football field where the ceremony will be held. The knowledge of me getting up on stage in front of the whole school hits me like a ton of bricks. It makes me sick. Shouldn't I be used to this by now? I mean, I've given pep rally speeches in the gymnasium and made announcements from the principal's office. I should be fine. Somehow, this is different. It is not just some two-minute school spirit speech. It is the valedictory speech, the one my fellow students will remember for a lifetime.

Walking down the hall, my chest tightens. I better not have a panic attack. That would not be good. I groan. Instantly, Sarah's face comes into my mind. Yet, not Sarah from Disneyland, rather the one from freshman year. The girl who was in the closet with me, the one who really calmed me down. I hope I get to see her today.

Jarring myself out of my thoughts, I notice Trey hauling his big backpack out of his locker. "Bro, where have you been?" He slams the locker shut at the same time I open mine.

"I was getting ready." I fake a smile. "You know this pretty face takes time," I joke, hoping to ease any suspicion. He knows it's not in my character to be late.

He throws his backpack over his shoulder. "Of course, bro." We fist bump. "You gotta look good for your big speech," he chuckles.

My stomach rolls over on itself. "Yep, exactly," I say, grabbing my notes from a folder in my locker.

"Man, that sucks you're missing the party, though. Are you sure you can't stay one more day?"

I shrug. "You know my mom, she's pretty adamant about me leaving," I state, fabricating the truth. It sounds the most realistic, without me having to explain the real reason behind why I decided to go work for my uncle this summer. He's my best friend and all, but this is something I can't get into right now. Plus, word is bound to get out about why I changed my mind, and when that happens, I'd rather be halfway across the country.

"I get it, dude. I mean Dorothea is the same." He smirks, moving his backpack to his other shoulder. "Ok, see you out there?"

"Yup. On my way," I say, shutting my locker.

Without going into detail as to why I am leaving so soon, Trey took the news pretty well. Of course, he was disappointed that I'm missing our joint graduation party, but he gets it. He's a real one like that, and I know he'll have fun with or without me there. Maybe in a few years, we can host a class reunion of sorts to make up for this loss. That's if we stay in touch. The probability of remaining friends with the same people from high school is very low, but Trey Williams is my boy. I'm determined to be bros with him for life.

Stepping outside, I'm immediately overwhelmed by the hundreds of people in their seats. There's families upon families, waving and speaking amongst themselves, no doubt about their graduates. My eyes rove the crowd for my own family members. I spot them pretty easily, actually. Ma and Uncle are sitting under one of the balloon arches. They look so tense and bothered. I put a hand over my eyes and squint. There is one open chair next to Ma, which is most likely the seat that was reserved for Brenden. My jaw tenses. This sucks.

I peer out into the section where the graduates are supposed to be sitting. There are plenty of kids I recognize, but I'm only looking for one girl. As soon as I start walking over to the stage, I notice her. A peculiar redhead, who's taking pictures with some girls who I don't think are from our grade, is beaming. She looks so happy in her cap and gown, laughing with her group of friends. Suddenly, she turns to wave at someone in the crowd. I follow her gaze to a group of people in the middle section where the guests are seated. I see a tall man with gray hair and a middle aged woman holding a baby. She has to be her mom; they are almost identical. There are three rambunctious children right next to them. A smile spreads across my lips. They must be her family. I wonder if I'll get to meet them someday.

The strongest feeling of remorse hits me. Crap. She texted me a couple days ago inviting me to her grad party. That was so cute. I completely forgot about it and ghosted her without meaning to. What is more, I haven't had a chance to tell her I won't be around this summer. I keep putting it off. I bite down on my lip. I just hate that I'm going to be letting her down.

On my way over to the stage, multiple classmates ask to take selfies with me. I happily comply. There won't be moments like this at college, I imagine. We reminisce for a few moments about the past four years. It makes me wonder where we will all be in five years or so. After a few minutes of chitchat, we part ways and head to our seats. Mine is next to some other students who were chosen to speak. The rest of the graduating class are arranged alphabetically. I look out into the crowd and spot most of my friends, Trey, Drew, Gabe, Jeb. My eyes flash over Hannah, hoping we don't make eye contact. She's another girl I've ghosted but on purpose. I'm so over her clingy nonsense.

While I wait for the ceremony to start, I make small talk with Michael Henderson, who sits next to me. We talk until the principal gets up on stage. I listen attentively to the small speech he gives about our time as seniors. I do not, however, think about if Sarah has seen me or not. Of course she has. I really don't want to tell her the bad news when this is all over. There's no avoiding it, though.

Principal Hickman invites the assistant principal on stage. After another short speech from her, it is now time to receive our diplomas. She calls our names in alphabetical order. I better get ready to go up there since my last name begins with an H, regrettably. I'm actually surprised Ma didn't have our names changed after Dad left. Of course, before going to Disneyland, I would have never wanted that. Knowing the real reason behind their split now, I'd be fine with dropping anything having to do with him.

The assistant principal calls Gabe's name. Funny, I had forgotten his last name was Garcia. All this time, I thought I'd be one of the first from my friend group to officially graduate. Gabe, being Gabe, takes his diploma then bends over to flash the audience with his rear end. Typical. I roll my eyes. The audience laughs hysterically. I knew he was going to do something stupid like that. Now he's someone I definitely don't want to keep in contact with after I move. What an idiot. Principal Hickman has him escorted off stage. I cover my mouth, hiding my amusement.

One by one, students walk up to the stage, excited to finally graduate. Already, this moment seems so nostalgic. For four years, I've gone to school with these people, and now, I wonder if I'll ever see them again. Oh, sounds like my name is being called. I trepidatiously walk up on stage to grab my diploma from Mrs. Anderson. She looks extremely excited to be handing it to me. I take it, shake her hand, then walk back across the stage. Plenty of people in the student body scream my name, cheering me on. I wave to them, heart burning, knowing it is a nostalgic moment for them too, hopefully looking like the guy they have come to admire from a distance. I'll never forget the happy looks on their faces. If only I could stop time to immerse myself in this moment just a little bit longer.

Back at my seat, the time seems to be moving too fast. I stand up and shout for all of my friends, including Hannah, but definitely not Kaite. She's the worst, but wait. Did they just call Sarah's name? I applaud her too and watch as she takes the diploma from Mrs. Anderson. She looks so incredibly euphoric.

Eager for my speech to be over, I sit back down and wait until the last student is called. My knee starts shaking. It feels like the sun is beating down on me. It's so hot. I suck in a deep breath but fear I'm not getting enough oxygen. Why are we outside? I run a finger around my collar. We should be inside where there is AC blowing nonstop. Even though I'm wearing shorts underneath this gown, I can still feel the sweat dripping down my legs. I'm going to need to jump into some form of water after this. I wonder how fast my pulse is racing? My watch notifies me it is at an inclining 150 BPM. Woah, that's high. I really need to calm down.

Still looking at my watch, I notice I have one minute until my speech. Shoot. If I don't get my heart rate to lower, I'll surely faint on stage. That'll shatter my chill persona all in a matter of seconds. I force myself to think of something else, other than what is currently happening. All that comes to mind is how Brenden is not here, how I'm missing my own grad party, and the fact that whatever Sarah and I have is sure to end as soon as I tell her I'm leaving. Gosh, nothing is going as planned. Ironically, the highlight in the midst of all this crap was Disneyland.

The corner of my lips twitch. I accidentally chuckle. At the same time, my name is being called from the stage. I stand up. What an insane moment to have an epiphany. I allow myself to smile. My shoes feel like they are on clouds as I lightly ascend the stairs. Quickly, I check my pulse. It's at 100 BPM. A wash of relief comes over me. No fainting today. I approach the podium. Grabbing both sides of it, I look out at the audience, ready to give my speech with a new attitude. This is it.

"Ladies and gentlemen," I begin, taking out my notes. "Esteemed faculty, proud parents, and most importantly, the graduates of Thousand Oaks High." It takes me a minute to realize I'm reading it word for word, very monotone, so devoid of charm, very unlike me. I continue with my speech anyway.

"As we stand here today, on the brink of a new chapter in our lives, it's essential to reflect on the journey that has brought us to this moment. From the first day we stepped foot into this institution to this graduation ceremony, we've experienced countless highs and lows, victories and defeats. But if there's one lesson that truly stands out, it's that life is unpredictable." I stop reading again, sensing the secondhand embarrassment from the graduates. This person standing before them is not the chosen Class President they know and love. There's only one person who could help me through this right now.

My eyes search the crowd for Sarah. Her hair is so bright. I find her pretty easily. Our eyes meet. She beams up at me. I feel another sense of calm settle upon me. Inhaling, I think, "That's it. Forget this stupid speech." I crumble up the uncomfortably long, handwritten notes and toss them to the ground. The audience mumbles. Now, I've got their attention. They don't know what I'm going to do next.

Grinning, I joke, "Who wrote that speech?" breaking the tension coming from the students and faculty. "Let's try this again." I breathe in deep and let it go. My hands are finally steady. My voice is calm, collected. Yeah, I've got this. Although it's probably obvious I'm making it up as I go along, I hope some of my fellow graduates leave here today feeling inspired, especially Sarah.

"If you're like me, many of us have spent years meticulously planning our futures, mapping out every step of the way, only to realize that life has a funny way of ruining those plans when we least expect it, whether it's a sudden change in personal circumstance, an unexpected crisis, or a personal challenge that tests our resilience." My voice catches a bit on this sentence, but I clear my throat and continue. "We've learned that we can't always control the outcome, but amidst life's unpredictability, there's solace in finding our happy place – that sanctuary where we can retreat to in times of turmoil. For some, it's the satisfying feeling of being accepted to their college of choice, or maybe it's from being able to travel the world. For others, their happy place might just be in the magical kingdom known as Disneyland." I look at Sarah again. Her expression does not give away what she's thinking. I continue as I know she'll appreciate this next part.

"Yes, Disneyland – believe it or not, I used to loathe the place." Everyone laughs, as if I'm making a joke, but I mean every word. "I didn't think it was where dreams came true and worries seem to fade away. But recently I've learned, Disneyland can serve as a beacon of joy and optimism, reminding us to embrace the childlike wonder within us and to find joy in the simple pleasures of life." Sarah is now smiling. This gives me the encouragement I need to bring it home.

"So, graduates, as we embark on this next chapter of our lives, let's remember to cultivate our own happy places. Let's find comfort in the knowledge that no matter how unpredictable life may seem, we have the power to create moments of happiness and serenity amidst the chaos. Today marks not just the end of a journey but the beginning of a new adventure filled with infinite opportunities. As we face the vast future, let's pledge to face each day with unwavering determination and optimism." I pause and take off my cap. I keep my eyes on Sarah as I hold it up in the air. She stands up and so does the rest of the student body. "Everyone," I say into the mic. "Let's raise our caps high, with hearts full of hope and determination, to let the world know that we are ready to…carpe diem!" We throw our caps into the air in unison.

The end of my speech is met with a thunderous applause. Principal Hickman gives me the side eye, probably because he asked us not to throw our caps this year. Oh well. We make our own traditions here. I return to my seat, not shaking anymore, but rather energized. That wasn't so bad. It actually went by super fast. I can hardly believe it's over. Soon after I sit down, a wave of sadness hits me. The reality that I am leaving tomorrow stings. This will be the last time I see everyone. So, this is what it feels like to say goodbye to an age. I lower my head. Today truly marks the end of an era.

CHAPTER 18
The Yearbook Message

Sarah

At the end of the ceremony, my family swarms me. We take pictures together in front of the stage, where it says the name of my school accompanied by a lot of balloons. Teagan and Monica also join us. My face lights up, delighted because I love being surrounded by them all. Lowkey, it feels pretty great to be the center of attention, just for today. Oh gosh, is my Mom tearing up? I'm sure my face is starting to turn red.

"Mom," I whine, feeling very self conscious.

"I can't help it," she says, wiping her eyes. "My baby is all grown up."

Despite the embarrassment, I wrap my arms around her. "Love you, Mom." She squeezes me tight.

Of course, right when my face returns to a normal color, baby Zacky starts throwing a tantrum. My other kid siblings, Agnes and Rocco, start fighting about who gets to hold Mom's hand. Greg tries to calm them down, but it's no use. I think the heat is getting to them. Baby Zacky is not settling down. Amidst the frenzy, Mom kisses my cheek and tells me they are taking the kids to the car. A little AC and some juice boxes ought to calm them down.

"Does that mean I have to hurry up?" I really want to talk to Weston before we go home.

"No, no, take your time," Mom says. "We brought a few iPads for this very reason." She grins, holding Zacky close to her chest.

Greg picks up Rocco, separating him from Agnes. He sets him down, then gives me a thumbs up. He winks. "Proud of you, kiddo," he says, trying to fist bump me, but Rocco comes in between us and starts hanging off his dad's arm like a monkey. Crazy kid.

"Thanks." I return a thumbs up. "Rocco, you gonna give me a hug?"

He stares at me, still swinging off his dad's arm. "No." He wrinkles his nose at me.

Monica and Teagan have to cover their mouths to stifle their laughter. I roll my eyes. What a rascal. Greg tells Rocco it's time to go and starts pulling him away. At the same time, he tells Manny to congratulate me. The awkward eight year old tells me, "Good job," with a thumbs up. He sure is Greg's twin. I laugh, patting his head, telling him thanks as well. Agnes runs up to me, wraps herself around my legs, saying something I can't understand. I think she is saying congrats. She lets me go quickly, then rushes back over to Mom. She blows me a kiss before they retreat to the van. My heart swells. We are such a strange bunch, but I wouldn't have it any other way.

Monica, Teagan, and I sit on the grass, chatting about my party tomorrow to keep our minds off how they are both finishing senior year without me next year. That alone is putting us in a bad mood. So I don't even mention Bali. I brought it up to Monica a few weeks ago one time, and she freaked out. That reminds me, I still need to talk to Mom about that. Eh, I'll figure it out sometime next week. Besides, I'm not even sure I want to go anymore if Weston will be around this summer. I chuckle. We can't very well have a summer romance if I leave him by himself.

Monica groans, "What are you laughing about?"

"Nothing," I say, swallowing.

"Is it about Weston?" Monica raises a brow in a teasing manner.

I shake my head. "No," I lie.

"Ok, well, let's leave already." She stands up, along with Teagan. They do seem eager to go since we have plans to eat, but I can't leave without talking to Weston. I, at least, have to congratulate him.

"Ok, we will, just give me a minute," I say, digging out my yearbook from my tote bag. Maybe he'll sign mine, since I already signed his.

Teagan and Monica exchange glances. "You mean give you a minute to find the Senior Prom King?"

My face heats up. "No, not at all."

The girls laugh. "Don't lie," Teagan calls me out.

"Ok, fine, I just want to go congratulate him."

Monica rolls her eyes. "Go on."

They tell me to meet them at the van when I'm done chatting with my "lover boy" or so they decide to call him. I pull back my lips. Ah, I need to stop blushing. I can't go talk to him looking like a tomato.

The middle of the football field is where most of the students seem to be gathered. They are exchanging yearbooks again. I see Weston out of the corner of my eye. My heart flutters. He looks like he's in no rush to leave. Oh, I can't wait to talk to him. Last time we interacted at school was super weird, but I think this time it'll go a lot better. There's something about today that reminds me of when we were at Disneyland.

My lips spread into a wide smile, remembering how he added Disneyland to his speech. He looked at me. I know he did. A sigh escapes my mouth. It kind of sucks he didn't respond to my last few text messages, though. Maybe it had something to do with his grounding? Who knows. I mean, graduation week was also very chaotic. So I'm sure he was super busy. Still, I wish he would have sent like one message just to show he's not ignoring me. A girl can wish, right?

On my way to the center of the football field, I run into Marlee Keen and Lila Goulie. They were in my art class last semester. I am shocked they remember my name, let alone know who I am. We talk about our summer plans while switching yearbooks. My body freezes as Weston enters my peripherals. He doesn't know I'm actively willing him to come over here. Oh no. I grimace, hearing Gabe's annoying voice. I thought he was told to leave after that stunt he pulled. I turn around. Guess not. Ah man. His parents spot me.

"Sarah-Cakes, how are you?" Miriam greets me. I flush at the nickname his mother gave to me when I was ten.

Miriam tells Gabe and the rest of her family to say hi. Jaime gives a quick hello. His phone rings shortly after. He steps away to answer it. Gabe and his younger brother, Santiago, greet me cordially.

"Hey," Gabe says, not making eye contact.

At the same time Gabe's family greets me, Kaite Flemmings passes by us. She doesn't say a word, but anyone looking at her can tell she is mad.

Gabe turns to his mom, muttering, "I'll be right back."

Miriam huffs, "Gabriel Barthomeul, you get back here right now."

"Babe, wait," he yells, running after Kaite, who looks even more mad. I wonder why?

We watch as he grabs her arm and is met with a slap on the face. I cover my mouth, hiding a wide smile. Looks like she left a mark. Gabe's face is all red. Kaite keeps on walking, not giving him the time of day. What was that about? It was odd enough learning that Gabe and Kaite got together after the senior trip. It was even more weird to see them interact at school. I love that she slapped him, no matter how strange it is to see them together. I continue to hide my smile.

Gabe looks around, frowning. Part of me feels a little vindicated. I pull back my lips, careful not to break out in laughter in front of his mom. Miriam calls him back over to us, but he ignores her and proceeds to follow Kaite, who is now almost at the parking lot. Girl is a fast walker in heels. Those two are so toxic. They deserve each other.

Miriam groans, then composes herself while keeping a steady hold onto Santiago's hand. "Well, congratulations, honey." She brings herself to smile wide; it's so obvious it's fake. "See you at the party?"

"Thanks, and yes, of course," I reply with a smile just as fake as her, knowing full well I did not invite them. Mom gave me no choice. Good thing is, I doubt Gabe will show up, and if he does, I'm sure we'll avoid each other like normal.

"Great, see you then," she says, embracing me. "Let's go, honey," she tells Santiago. "I don't know where Jaime went."

"Oh, I think I saw him over there by the fences," I point. Sure enough, Gabe's dad is still talking on the phone. His Mercedes Benz dealership must be doing really well.

"Oh, perfect. Ok, bye, Sarah-cakes." She waves, walking away.

When they are far enough away, I breathe out, glad that unnatural interaction is over.

"Hey, can I sign your yearbook?"

Someone is behind me. I see their shadow toppling over mine. Goosebumps run up and down my arms. I know it's Weston. How in the world did he sneak up on me? I turn to face him. His cap is tilted to one side. It takes everything in me to not fall over, swooning over how cute he is. I swear, he is even more attractive today than in all four years of high school.

"S-sure," I stutter, handing him my book.

"Hold mine?" he asks, cocking his head to one side.

Blunderingly, I hold his yearbook under my arm. I can't believe he wants to write in my yearbook. I'm reeling right now. For a second, I just stare at him while he flips open the book and looks for an open spot to write. Once he finds one, he writes so fast. Wow, he must have had something in mind. I can't wait to read it. "Here you go," he says, handing it back to me. Oh, he's already done. That was short.

"Thanks."

We exchange books. I smile at him, rocking back and forth on my heels, racking my brain for something to say, anything. Like I should tell him that he did a good job on his speech, but the words are not coming out. He looks like he's struggling also. At least I'm not alone in this. I'm starting to think this whole interaction is going to be a complete waste of time.

"So," he says, clasping his hands together. "What did you think of my speech?"

"Oh, it was very good," I say, face lighting up, happy he brought it up. "I especially liked the part about Disneyland." I smirk. Hopefully, the conversation will flow now.

His cheeks turn a bit pink. "I thought you'd like that," he laughs.

We smile at each other as another wave of silence overcomes us. Why is talking to him so hard?

"Ahem," he clears his throat. "So, um, are you excited for your party?"

My head shakes. "Yes! Can't wait..." I suck in a breath. "Yous, I mean, you for yours?" My face is surely turning red. Why can I not speak today? He's got me all tongue tied.

Weston looks down. His jaw works. Why am I getting the

sense I struck a nerve? That's strange. He meets my eyes, seemingly very depressed. "I'm not going to mine," he admits.

My brows furrow. "What do you mean?" I breathe in and out. How could he not be going to his own party? I've already come to grips with him not coming to mine, but his own? It doesn't make any sense.

"I've been meaning to tell you this." He pauses. "I just didn't know how."

My whole body tenses. What is he going to say?

"I'm leaving tomorrow for Boston."

Ignoring the warming sensation in my chest, I tilt my head. "Oh," is all that comes out of my mouth. I grip my yearbook and fidget with the pages.

"Unfortunately, that means I won't be around this summer anymore," he sighs, frowning. "I'm sorry."

"Sorry?" I chuckle, taking a step backward. "Why would you be sorry?" Does he actually think I'm mad at him or something? I laugh like it's such a ridiculous notion, but a prick in my gut is telling me otherwise. Am I upset? No, I couldn't be.

"I know we were both looking forward to me staying." He steps forward, filling in the gap I made. "Even though I am leaving, I still want to get to know you," he says in a low voice.

"But how can you do that if you don't ever text me?" I blurt, not realizing how upset that had made me. My face continues to redden.

He closes his eyes. "I know. I'm really sorry about that," he admits, opening his eyes. "I have an excuse, though." I purse my lips. He adds, "There was a...family crisis, of sorts."

The small bothered part of me instantly disappears. "What? Is everything ok?" I ask, putting a hand on his arm. I quickly let go.

He grins half heartedly. "Yes, everything is fine. I don't want to get into it right now, but it's part of the reason why I can't stay."

I slowly nod at him, trying to understand. What does that mean, family crisis? If someone was hurt, surely he would have said something about that. Why can't he just tell me what made him change his mind? This actually is kind of frustrating. My heart sinks further and further. So much for having a summer romance. Feeling defeated, I think maybe this is for the best. Had he stayed and we really did get together officially, it would be so hard to say goodbye in the fall. I'd be heartbroken. So yeah, this is good. Yes, this is very good. I clutch my chest. The middle of it feels so heavy.

"Look," he says, inching closer to me. Ah, why is he so close? Does he know people can see us? "I wish I could stay, I really do." He reaches for my hand. My eyes peer into his, hope seeping into my throat as he stares back into mine. I'm such a sucker for him. So, I let him take it. Softly, he says, "You have to know, I regret not knowing you these last four years, but I'm so glad you went to Disneyland."

"I'm glad I went too." My heartbeat thumps with each second he keeps his wide chocolate eyes on me. Can he hear how loud it's beating? Oh gosh, I'm so embarrassed. His jaw tenses as his brows dip. He looks so sad.

"I don't want to leave," he admits.

"Then don't." Air fills my lungs. I hold my breath. If he doesn't want to leave, then he shouldn't have to. I wish he could read my mind. I'd tell him right now, "Please stay for me, Wes," but that would be ridiculous.

"I have to," he says. "For reasons I'll explain later, but understand it has nothing to do with you."

Letting go of my breath, I tell him, "I get it," nodding. "Just try to keep in touch?" I lift my eyebrows in a comical way.

His face lights up. "Oh, absolutely." His fingers twitch in mine. "Knowing I'll still get to talk to you is what's keeping me from," he exhales, "being sent into a deep depression." A tiny corner of his mouth curls upward. We keep our eyes on each other for a long second. It's not awkward this time. I can sense from the way he is looking at me that he is savoring this moment just as much as I am. He breaks the natural silence by asking, "Can I hug you?"

"Oh," I say, nervously. "Yeah, of course." I squeeze his hand.

He smiles, then wraps his arms around me so fast, essentially scooping me up. My feet are off the ground. This startles me, causing me to drop my yearbook. His, too, falls to the ground, but it doesn't phase him. He holds onto me tight. What I would give for someone to be filming us right now. I want to stamp this moment in my mind so I can always remember what it feels like to be wrapped in the arms of the Prom King.

I breathe him in, memorizing his fresh clean scent, so I can write this down in my journal later. It feels like he has me in his arms for one second. I know it was longer than that. Sadly, Weston lets me go, setting me back on the ground. We both laugh as we notice our yearbooks planted face down on the sod.

"Great, it's all dog eared now," I joke, bending down to pick up my book. It fell on the page where Weston wrote. I keep it open with my finger there.

He brushes off some grass from his book before closing it. Looking at me with puppy dog eyes, he groans, "I have to go."

"Text me later?" I bite my lip, hoping I don't sound too desperate.

He winks at me and promises, "I will."

Weston smiles at me one last time before turning to go. Once he's out of earshot, I have to catch my breath. If I had held it in any longer, I might have passed out. How ironic that would be. I smile, heart pounding, until he disappears from my view. I hope that's not the last time I see Weston Hill-Cho. No, it won't be. I'm sure of it.

My mind is still processing what just happened. In my head, our last interaction was supposed to go a lot differently. I will chalk it up to not being ready to say goodbye to him so soon. At least he signed this. I hold my yearbook against my chest. That was unexpected. It makes me think of his wonderful speech, and my heart leaps for joy. I still can't get over it. It does make me curious to know if I had something to do with it. Did he really have a change of heart? Does he still hate Disneyland? Looking down at my yearbook, I'm certain he does not. Alright, I'm probably exaggerating. He very well might still hate the park, and I doubt he'll ever consider it his happy place. Yet, maybe, just maybe when he thinks of Disney, he will forever think of me.

He really wasn't kidding when he said that life is unpredictable. Whatever family crisis he had to deal with, I'm sure he felt like it left him no choice but to leave this summer. I can't blame him. He's the type to plan things out, while I do the opposite and tend to live life one day at a time. It's exciting to me to not know what comes next. Knowing Weston won't be here is unexpected. However, it kind of frees up my summer again. There's so many things I can do with it. Bali is still calling my name, and I'm dying to see if it lives up to the hype. Gemma makes it sound like a dream. I think, maybe I will go. Who knows? I might change my mind about it tomorrow, and that's the beauty of the future. I can do whatever I want and still hope Weston remains a part of it.

Sighing, I lower my yearbook, desperate to see what he wrote. My finger is still holding the page there. I rip it open. Eyes widening, I read, "Meet me at the castle in 182 days. I looked it up. That's in six months."

Epilogue

Brenden

The Monday before Weston's graduation, I picked him up from school. I used to hate picking up my little brother, but that day was different. Things between us changed after he went back to Disneyland. I still don't know why he agreed to go, but something good came out of it. We've been surprisingly chill since then.

That Sunday, before his last week in high school, we spent the day playing video games, the old vintage ones, which reminded me of old times. Back before Ma figured out Weston was going places and I was headed for nowhere. It was before he would do anything she ordered. I used to resent that. I still kind of do. Whatever. That's not the point. The point is, we had a good time doing nothing productive for eight straight hours. That is unheard of for him. He never slacks off and I mean never. We didn't have to be playing video games all day, but I was just proud he was letting himself relax for once. Things were good between us, until I had to go and mess it up. Twice.

That day, he told me about staying for the summer. He was very excited and couldn't believe Ma agreed to that. Honestly, I couldn't either. It is so rare of her to let Weston make his own choices. So, it shocked me to my core when I found out. Plus, the boy never stands up to her. Ever. Period. I normally wouldn't suggest that he take a page from my book, but in that instance, I know it did him some good. He finally grew a pair.

After he told me he was staying for the summer, we made plans to go to the beach every Sunday to surf— it's my favorite pastime. It was going to be sick. He also told me about a girl he wanted to get to know. My memory is a little fuzzy on the details, but I think he met her at Disneyland. Weston has had many girlfriends, so I didn't think anything of it. I just remember looking forward to spending time with my brother. That is until I ruined it for the both of us. This was my first offense.

When I pulled into the driveway that day, the cops were waiting for me. I was arrested on the spot. I knew it was going to happen, I just didn't expect it to be so quick. They told my family I got mixed up in something illegal and needed to be taken to a holding facility. That gave Ma no choice to have pretentious Uncle Henry fly out earlier than she had planned. He is the only lawyer we know and could afford. I didn't want him as my lawyer, though, because we never got along. I would have rather had a court appointed one than him, and she knew that. In hindsight, it ended up being a good thing, but when it was happening, I had no idea what the heck an immigration lawyer was supposed to do for me, let alone him.

At first, I thought I'd be locked away for good. Ever since my small stint in juvie at 16, I found myself in increasingly illicit behavior. It didn't start off so serious in the beginning, but with each passing year, my skills seemed to level up and so did the items. There was money to be made in what I did. Despite this, I had wanted out. For a while, I actually thought it might be possible to turn my life around. I thought, maybe I really could be more like Weston and life could go in a different direction for me. I was very wrong, and because of that, I trusted the wrong person. How naive.

The authorities said it was a pretty straightforward case, and given my record, they processed me immediately. What I felt inside was like a raging fire ready to burn everyone in my path. I was furious. I wanted to blame everything on my stupid friend, Anton, whom I had been friends with since middle school. He is the definition of a bad seed. I made excuses for him, though, since he was all I had growing up. Together, we got into all sorts of trouble. It's one of the reasons why I ended up in juvie, although I don't blame him for that. Deep down, I know there has always been something wrong with me. I think I just came into the world broken, and that's where I'll stay.

After high school, we parted ways because I wanted to do my own thing. I knew if I continued hanging out with him, I'd end up in prison. I really, really wanted to avoid prison, much to everyone's disbelief, but I got restless. At that time, Anton weaseled his way into my life again. I knew what kind of stuff he'd been up to and didn't want to get involved, but he fed into my weaknesses until I ultimately gave in. I did, however, set conditions. Petty theft was one thing, but stealing cars was a whole other ball game. He knew I wanted out for good. However, Anton came to me, begging to leave a few cars at my house for his cousin, just temporarily. I didn't have to do anything. True to his word, I did not lay a finger on any of those luxury vehicles. They would simply show up on a random day, then be gone the next. He paid me decent enough. I knew they were stolen, though. I fricken took the cars, anyway, because I thought I was doing him a favor. Now, I understand he played me. That is what I get for helping a friend. Never again. I hate him. Regardless, I take full responsibility.

Uncle Henry arrived after I spent one night in the holding cell. Against my will, I told him everything. Ma stayed out of it.

To be fair, I didn't want her or Weston involved anyway. I've already put them through so much. They were both busy preparing for his graduation anyway. I'm glad for it. My mistake was the last thing they needed, given both of their history with anxiety attacks. God, we are all such a mess. It's a wonder my family even made it through the hearing.

In the cell, Uncle Henry gave me a piece of his mind, calling me an irresponsible, selfish screw up. He's not wrong. I tried to behave and not talk back, but once he started comparing me to Weston, it took every ounce of my self control not to punch him in the face. After I calmed down, I realized he wasn't wrong for that. I should be more like the golden boy. He is everything I am not and deserves so much more than what he's settling for. Truth is, at that point, I wanted what was coming to me.

The only good part about having my uncle as my lawyer is that he, despite thinking I'm a waste of space, was able to convince the judge to give me six months and a fine of 50,000 dollars. We counted that as a win, knowing I easily could have been sentenced to prison for three or more years. I don't have to wonder what I would have done had that happened.

Before I was taken away, they allowed my family to say goodbye. We were taken to a confined space behind the courtroom. Ma entered the room first. She didn't say anything to me. The silent treatment was most common growing up. So this didn't surprise me. What did, however, was her trembling, then touching my arm. Maybe it was her way of saying she cares? I have no idea, but her eyes did get glassy. At that moment, I had never felt that I disappointed her more. That sucked.

Uncle Henry went in after her. That's when he told me the truth of why he got my sentence reduced. It was all for my mother, not me. He threatened that if I ever did something stupid like this again, he'd ship me off to Korea to live with my grandfather, regardless of how old I'd become. It's such an empty threat. I've never met the guy because he disowned Ma after she married. Supposedly, he hasn't spoken to her since. Personally, I wouldn't mind meeting the cold hearted man. It would probably explain so much about why I am the way I am.

Finally, it was Weston's turn to go in. I remember our last conversation like it was yesterday. The officer at the door said to make it quick. He walked in to see me sitting on the floor, head in my hands, completely gutted. My eyes were red from a lack of sleep. He sat down beside me, like the way I sat next to him that night he got back from Disneyland. We didn't say anything to each other at first.

I broke the silence first by admitting to him, "I messed up."

He kept his lips pressed together for a long second, then said, "Yeah, you did."

"No, like, actually. I messed up big time." I laid a hand on the top of my head, then started to laugh in a way that wasn't humorous in the least.

"I know, but you'll get through this—You always do," he assured me. I bet he was referring to the time I went to juvie for joyriding, or perhaps it was the time I got caught stealing from the grocery store and I had to do 50 hours of community service. I don't know. There's been too many times to count. I'm relentless.

I shook my head and let my hand rest on one propped knee. "No, I won't." I grit my teeth. "You know why?" I asked. My whole body started to shake. I violently pointed a finger at myself as I stated, practically spitting, "It's because I'm a screw up, and I'll always be a screw up." I was beyond upset with myself.

"Bren, you're going to be fine," he said empathetically. "Look on the bright side," he began to say, even though it is not in his nature to do so. "You got six months when it easily could have been 5 years. Take the win, bro."

"No, Weston," I spat. "I'm just like him." He didn't have to guess I was referring to that lowlife we once called a father.

"There is no bright side to this. When I get out, I'll have to pay that fine. How exactly do you think I'm going to pay for that, Prom King?" He ignored the obvious dig at him, understanding I was in a very bad state of mind. He remained silent and allowed me to continue my angry rant. "I know how the system works. People with criminal records don't get jobs," I huffed. "And you think Ma or Uncle Henry are going to help me out? Heck, no. So, there's no bright side because we all know I'm going to end up back here anyway." I exhaled and leaned against the wall, looking utterly defeated. That's how I felt, completely hopeless, and I had no one to blame but myself.

Weston could clearly see just how low I had fallen. He seemed like he wanted to help, but it was out of his control. There was nothing he could do to fix the problem, or so I thought.

I sighed and added, "I'm just sorry; I messed everything up and won't be at your graduation. That fricken sucks." I looked over at him with the most apologetic expression I could bring myself to make. It broke me, and I think him, too, because the next words out of his mouth were, "I'm going to pay for your fine."

My brows furrowed. I remember thinking, did he just say what I think he said? No. That's not right. "What?"

He clasped his hands over his lap, looking sure of his decision, then said, "I'm going to pay the 50,000 dollar fine."

"Are you actually joking at a time like this?" I sounded angry but only because I really didn't believe him. I thought he was mocking me.

"I'm serious, Bren. I'll pay the fine."

Slowly, my face relaxed. The sharp pain in my chest began to fade. "How?"

He explained, "I'll use part of my tuition money and work for Uncle Henry over the summer to cover the rest."

I shook my head in protest. "No, absolutely not." I sounded

exactly like Ma. "You finally got what you wanted, Wes. I won't let you throw away your money or your summer."

The officer at the door knocked before opening it. He said it was time for me to go. However long I was in there was not long enough to say goodbye or to express gratitude towards my brother. Yet, regardless of how I felt, we had run out of time.

Once we were both standing, I put a hand on Weston's shoulder. "Look," I sighed, "I appreciate the offer, but I can't accept it." I attempted to smile, but it quickly turned into a frown. "I made this mess; I'll clean it up myself. Do yourself a favor and enjoy one last summer before you start school and… forget about me."

"You're an idiot," he tells me. I don't disagree with him. "I'm not asking for your permission."

I shake my head. "Ma wont let you."

"Or Ma's," he interjected. "I'm sick of both of you telling me what to do and telling me how to live my life. I'm done with that. Now, let me do my brotherly duty and pay for your freaking fine."

"I'm not trying to tell you what to do," I replied. "I just…." Something got caught in my throat. "I don't deserve-" My voice cracked. I was unable to finish that sentence.

Weston put a hand on my shoulder. "Yes, you do," he said with watery eyes. He is so emotional. After swallowing the lump in my throat, he brought me in for a hug. We don't touch each other in my family. It felt so foreign. I don't even think I remember the last time we hugged. It might have been before our biological father was out of the picture. Whatever. It was good we did.

After pulling away, I uttered in a low tone, "Gomawoyo, dongsaeng." Which means, "Thank you, little brother." With a hand on his shoulder, I said, "I promise you that I'll pay you back, down to the last cent." He ignored that sentiment like the stubborn boy he is.

The officer signaled after that our time was up. He put me in handcuffs, then escorted me from the room. Ma and Uncle Henry did not look at me as I was led past them. I'm sure they were too embarrassed to acknowledge my existence.

Almost halfway down the corridor, I turned my head around, just enough to get a glimpse of Weston. "I'll see you in six months!" I shouted.

That was seven and a half months ago. I've been out for over a month now. Weston meant what he said about paying my fine. 50,000 dollars is no easy feat. He slaved for my uncle over the summer and continued on, even after he started classes in the fall. When my brother puts his mind to something, he brings it to completion. That is why he is the chosen favorite. He had the fine paid in full before I got out.

He sacrificed his last summer of no responsibilities to afford it. For that alone, I owe him everything. Truly, I hate that he did that. Every chance I got, I tried to talk him out of it. When Ma found out, she was furious, of course, but even she did not possess the power to change his mind. The boy is so stubborn. Can't say it doesn't run in the family.

Ma started talking to me only after I got released. I had to beg her to come pick me up. She very graciously allowed me to come back home under the condition that I pay Weston back. I didn't want to move back in, but I had no other choice. It was either that or be homeless. I had to reassure her a thousand times that I was going to pay my brother back. She still doesn't believe me. That was before I realized how much worse life is now that prison is on my permanent record. It is almost impossible to get a decent paying job. Frick. I don't care. I'll work two or three jobs. However many it takes to pay him back with interest, even if it kills me. I only wish paying my brother back was the only issue.

Everyone, including myself, thinks I'm a screw up and will always be one. I wanted to prove them all wrong and still do, that is, until I messed up again. It was only a matter of time. Truly, I didn't see it coming. The bad part is Weston doesn't know yet, but in two days, he will find out. He is going to hate me. I still don't understand how it happened. The truth is that it was an accident— an idiotic mistake. I was reckless, and because of my recklessness, I will once again make one unhappy person even more unhappy, in fact, the unhappiest.

Acknowledgments

I want to start by expressing my deepest gratitude to my husband, Robert Gonzalez. You were the first person to read this story, and your unwavering support and insight have played an integral role in shaping it into what it is today. Thank you for always being there to brainstorm, problem-solve, and bring my ideas to life on the page. You are the best, and I couldn't have done this without you.

To my family—your love and encouragement mean everything to me. Thank you for always cheering me on, especially when it gets tough. Your belief in me is a constant source of strength. I love each and every one of you.

To my friends, who generously give their time and energy to help with edits and beta reading—you are irreplaceable. Your feedback and support truly make all the difference. I love you all. Thank you from the bottom of my heart.

Finally, to my readers—thank you for giving an independent author the opportunity to share my stories with you. Your enthusiasm and enjoyment are what keep me writing. I hope you liked this book, and I look forward to sharing the next one with you, as long as you're there to read it.

About the Author

Jade Gonzalez is a New York-based author known for her debut novel, *As The Sparrow Flies*. Specializing in young adult and coming-of-age stories, Jade brings over a decade of writing experience to her craft. With a college degree, she has honed her skills in crafting love stories that unfold just as imagined, as seen in her latest work *The Unhappiest Place On Earth*. When not immersed in a world of books, Jade enjoys spending time with her husband and two cats and listening to Taylor Swift records.

Visit her website
https://authorjadegonzalez.com/

instagram.com/color.of.jade
amazon.com/stores/author/B09CF1GCJ3
tiktok.com/color.of.jadegnz

Also by Jade Gonzalez

The Unhappy Series

The Unhappiest Place on Earth: Book 1

Book 2 coming soon!

More by Jade Gonzalez

As The Sparrow Flies…